"Will remind readers what chattering teeth sound like."
—*Kirkus Reviews*

"Voracious readers of horror will delightfully consume the contents of Bates's World's Scariest Places books."
—*Publishers Weekly*

"Creatively creepy and sure to scare." —*The Japan Times*

"Jeremy Bates writes like a deviant angel I'm glad doesn't live on my shoulder."
—Christian Galacar, author of GILCHRIST

"Thriller fans and readers of Stephen King, Joe Lansdale, and other masters of the art will find much to love."
—*Midwest Book Review*

"An ice-cold thriller full of mystery, suspense, fear."
—David Moody, author of HATER and AUTUMN

"A page-turner in the true sense of the word."
—*HorrorAddicts*

"Will make your skin crawl." —*Scream Magazine*

"Told with an authoritative voice full of heart and insight."
—Richard Thomas, Bram Stoker nominated author

"Grabs and doesn't let go until the end." —*Writer's Digest*

BY JEREMY BATES

Suicide Forest ♦ The Catacombs ♦ Helltown ♦
Island of the Dolls ♦ Mountain of the Dead
♦ Hotel Chelsea ♦ Mosquito Man ♦
The Sleep Experiment ♦ The Man from Taured
♦ White Lies ♦ The Taste of Fear ♦
Black Canyon ♦ Run ♦ Rewind
♦ Neighbors ♦ Six Bullets ♦ Box of Bones ♦
The Mailman ♦ Re-Roll ♦ New America: Utopia Calling
♦ Dark Hearts ♦ Bad People

Merfolk

World's Scariest Legends 4

Jeremy Bates

Ghillinnein Books

Merfolk

PROLOGUE

July, 2021

The Indian Ocean

With his stand-up fishing rod poking out of the holder at the aft of the boat, Karlo Winkler stared dully at the teasers and daisy chains splashing along the water outside the prop wash eight meters away. A light wind blew, causing a gentle swell over the ocean's surface, and the scorching noon sun beat down on the back of his neck. The small fishing boat he'd chartered had left the harbor before first light at four a.m. Eight hours later, and he'd yet to catch anything. Hell, he hadn't even gotten a nibble. In fact, he hadn't seen any hint of marine life. No dolphins, no whales, no sea turtles, nothing. It was as if the sea were dead.

Scowling at his bad luck, Karlo was about to head over to the ice box to grab another beer when his 120-pound braided line suddenly went heavy. A moment later the fishing pole bent wickedly. The reel spun and screamed.

"Missy!" Karlo exclaimed, grabbing the rod with both hands and raising the tip. "Missy, get your butt over here! I got something! I got something *big*."

NINETY MINUTES EARLIER

With her face shaded beneath a wide-brimmed straw hat and behind dark sunglasses, newlywed Missy Winkler stared out to the horizon where the vast blue sky met the deeper blue ocean. It hit home just how far they were from civilization. Not that Sri Lanka was a mecca of art and sophistication. What she'd seen of it on the drive yesterday from Bandaranaike International Airport to their 5-star boutique hotel was an impoverished island country.

Missy sighed, longing to be back in the air-conditioned suite in a bubbling Jacuzzi with a glass of chilled champagne. At least she had dinner to look forward to. She would prefer a French restaurant, or Italian; somewhere with class and taste and waitstaff who spoke English. Yet she knew Karlo would insist on something more "authentic," like last night, which involved sitting on cushions on the beach, eating local seafood, and watching fire performers.

Which, to Missy, was about as touristy as you could get.

She heard Karlo grumble something from where he was casting his fishing line from the port side of the boat, and she called lazily to him, "How's the fishing, pookums?" Lounging in a deckchair amidship, she faced starboard, still staring out at the forever-away horizon.

Karlo grunted something else that she couldn't make out above the rumbling diesel engine pushing them along at trolling speed. Missy didn't bother asking him to repeat himself. He'd been in a foul mood for most of the morning because he hadn't caught anything. Despite being sixty years old, he could be a real sook, his moody behavior almost childish. If anything, *she* should be the insufferable, irascible one. She'd wanted to go to Paris or Milan or Athens for their honeymoon, and instead here she was in some dumpy little boat, God-knows-where off the coast of a third-world country, where she had to have three showers a day because of the damn humidity, and where half the mosquito population likely carried dengue fever.

Why did I ever agree to come here? she wondered.

She knew why, of course. Because Karlo wanted to, and Karlo, who was nearly twice her age and worth many millions of dollars, called the shots in their nascent marriage.

Missy said, "Maybe you should try different bait, love button?"

"It's not the bloody bait. It's the location. I thought you said you knew where the bloody sharks were, Chan?" he snapped at the charter boat's skipper. "All the gamefish I could ask for, you told me. Blue and black marlin, sailfish, swordfish, yellowfin tuna, you told me." He huffed. "Well, where the hell are they, mate? On vacation?"

Missy raised her sunglasses and squinted in the bright sunlight. The brown-skinned skipper stood beneath the shade of the paint-blistered wheelhouse, picking at one of his fingernails with the blade of a large knife. He could have been in his early forties or his late fifties. She had no idea. The sun and sea and salt had not been kind to him, turning his skin into old leather, at least what she could see of it behind his scraggly, graying beard. His full given name was Chanidulala, or something ridiculous like that. "Chan" was much preferable.

"Patience, sir," Chan said simply. "They here. They come. We follow birds. Birds follow fish. Big fish follow small fish."

Standing on the aft deck, Karlo was dressed in a white linen shirt, Ralph Lauren khaki shorts, and leather boat shoes. Atop his mop of silver hair sat a cap embroidered with the logo of the Queensland Maroons, a State Rugby League team in Australia. Missy had met him in October of last year at the Brisbane International Film Festival. She had gone with three girlfriends, all single, all on the hunt for men with fame or wealth (or preferably both). Karlo didn't have much fame, but he had wealth, lots of it. He'd made his money in real estate and was now happily spending it producing Australian documentaries and short films. That evening, at an after-party on his sixty-foot yacht, Missy worked her magic on him, bedded him, and that was that.

Nine months later, she was Mrs. Missy Winkler.

"Maybe we should call it a day, pookums?" she suggested. "Try again tomorrow?"

"I'm not heading back without even getting a bloody bite," Karlo griped. Then, to Chan, "What the hell am I paying you for, mate? You said you knew where the fish were! Patience? We've been bobbing around out here like a message in a bottle since dawn!"

Chan set the knife aside and lit up a cigarette.

"Patience," he repeated around a waft of smoke.

"Not a single bloody bite," Karlo grumbled.

Missy sighed again. If they were going to be stuck out here for however much longer, she was going to make the most of the time and get a proper tan. She reached behind her back and unclipped her bikini top.

She shot the skipper a stern look. "No perving on me, Chan. Got that?"

Chan watched her remove her top, then averted his eyes.

Karlo left his fishing rod in the holder and joined her amidship. "What in God's name are you doing, love?" He frowned at her bare breasts.

"You know I hate tan lines," she said. "I've already been in the sun today for so long I'm going to look like a zebra tomorrow. And it's not like I can go topless at the hotel pool. There are kids around." She squeezed some sunscreen from the bottle next to her and lathered her breasts. The cool cream on her warm skin made her nipples hard.

"Just as long as you don't take off your bloody bottoms." He opened the big ice box and retrieved a green bottle of beer. He twisted off the cap and flicked it into the ocean.

Missy frowned. "I don't think you're allowed to do that, honey."

"Huh?" Karlo said, distracted. He looked at her, then at her tits.

"I think it's illegal to litter in the ocean."

He scowled. "What?"

"A turtle might try to eat the bottle cap. It could get stuck in the poor thing's throat."

"Fuck turtles! I haven't seen one all bloody morning. Besides, do you know how much trash humans dump in the ocean every year? How much plastic is down there?"

"That's the point, pookie. You shouldn't be adding to it."

"It's a bloody bottle cap!"

Karlo stomped back over to his fishing rod and slumped into the fighting chair. Missy watched him sulk in silence, wondering if this was what she'd signed up for the next forty years of her life.

More like twenty, she thought optimistically, given that Karlo, with all his drinking and cigar smoking, likely didn't have the greatest life expectancy. *Maybe I'll get lucky and he'll croak in ten. Wouldn't that be something? Ten years of domestic doldrums for a multi-million-dollar payout. Who wouldn't take that deal?*

A kilometer south of the boat, an island sporting an aquamarine reef rose out of the ocean. Featuring steep, jagged hills covered with emerald-green tropical vegetation, it reminded Missy of something out of *Jurassic Park*, a lost world home to giant lizards or other nightmarish creatures.

It gave her the creeps.

"What do you think about sleeping over there tonight?" Karlo asked out of the blue. He was also looking at the island.

Missy shook her head vehemently, even though Karlo couldn't see her. "No way, babe. No fucking way."

"Why not? It would save us the trip back to the mainland and

—"

"No fucking way," she repeated, thinking again about the chilled champagne and Jacuzzi and air-conditioned suite awaiting her at the hotel.

Tilting his head, Karlo finished his beer in one long gulp and didn't say anything more.

ΔΔΔ

Ten minutes later Karlo's line went heavy and the reel spun and screamed. Something had taken the pitch bait to the left of the teasers.

Karlo grabbed the rod with both hands and shouted excitedly, telling Missy to join him. She hurried over, stuffing her breasts back into her bikini top.

"What do you think it is?" she asked, pressing up against him.

"Give me some bloody room, will you?" he said, shoving her aside. "I have to reel in the bastard. Chan!"

"I'm here, sir," the skipper said, appearing next to him. "Loosen the drag and let it run."

"I knew you'd come through, mate! I knew it!"

ΔΔΔ

Whatever was on the other end of line, it was putting up one hell of a fight. After twenty minutes of hard hauling, Karlo had only managed to get half the line in.

"It's a record," he said, his ruddy face drenched with sweat. "Whatever it is, it's gotta be a record."

"I'm so proud of you, pookums," Missy said.

"I haven't bloody caught it yet! And my arms are about to fall off."

"Should I take over?" Chan asked.

"No bloody way! This bastard is mine."

Suddenly the rod bent so far Karlo feared it might snap in two.

"Stop winding," Chan instructed.

Karl stopped, and the fish stopped pulling. "What now?"

"We wait."

ΔΔΔ

A few minutes later the rod jerked and the line unspooled blisteringly fast as the fish took off.

"Bloody oath!" Karlo said, holding onto the rod with all his strength, fighting to keep the tip high in the air.

"Let it run again," Chan said.

When the fish was around a thousand meters from the boat, Karlo said, "I'm running out of line!"

"Tighten the drag."

Karlo tightened it. The rod bent again, but the reel was no longer spinning. Stalemate. This slogged on, one minute, then two, then five. Every so often Karlo tried jerking the rod to no avail. "It feels like the bloody thing's hooked to the bottom of the ocean," he complained. "Maybe it's dead down there?"

Chan frowned. "Maybe. I'll put the boat back in gear and try pulling it up—"

Yet even as he spoke, the tip of the nearly U-shaped fishing rod rose slowly.

"It's surfacing!"

"It's exhausted. Do you have slack?"

"Some."

"Then reel it in."

Despite Karlo's previous reluctance to share the catch with anyone, he thrust the rod at Chan. "You reel it in. I'm aching all over."

He gave his arms and back a stretch, then winked and grinned at Missy. "What do you reckon, love? Bloody exciting, huh?"

"It's wonderful," she said, though she didn't look excited. She looked how she had looked all morning: like she wanted to be anywhere else than on the boat.

He pinched one of her nipples through the bikini top.

"Ouch!" she cried, slapping his hand away.

Still grinning, Karlo went to the ice box and retrieved a cold beer. Returning to Chan and Missy, he finished half the bottle, set it on the fighting chair, and snatched the rod back from the skipper.

"Keep winding," Chan told him. "Not too fast."

Karlo began winding, thrilled by the massive weight on the other end of the line.

It's a monster. A bloody monster.

When he recovered about three quarters of the line, the rod once again bent suddenly, almost to the surface of the water.

"Hang on tight!" Chan told him.

"Don't lose it!" Missy cried.

Away went the line, peeling off the reel at a furious rate.

"Fuck's sake!" Karlo said. "You said it was exhausted!"

"Let it run!"

It wasn't long before the reel was almost out of line for the second time. Karlo locked the drag and held on with all his strength, praying the line didn't snap under the load.

"Shouldn't the bloody thing be jumping out of the water and tail-walking all over the place?" Karlo yelled, as he struggled to gain the line back inch by inch.

Chan shrugged. "If it's a billfish..."

"What the hell else could it be?"

Chan remained expressionless. "Keep winding."

ΔΔΔ

Nearly a full hour later Karlo spotted the kite, and a few minutes after that, the dropper.

"Take the rod!" he said, shoving it at Chan. He leaned over the hull, gripped the line, and walked it in until he made out a huge shadow beneath the surface of the water. "Jesus Christ..." he breathed softly.

Missy said, "Is that a shark?"

"It's a great white," Karlo said, awestruck, as the white-bellied beast rose dramatically to the surface. It floated on its side, one beady black eye staring up at him. The bait, a half-eaten mackerel, protruded from its smiling, tooth-lined mouth. Karlo's heart pounded. The bloody fish had the girth of a hippo and must have been at least four meters long from snout to tail. "Missy, get your phone! I need pictures—"

The shark thrashed and splashed. The abrupt movement caught Karlo off guard. He didn't have time to think or react, didn't let go of the line. The next moment he was flying through the air.

He crashed face-first into the ocean. The cold water shocked his body. He tasted salt in his mouth. Out of panic he kicked furiously. His head broke through the surface. He gasped and flailed his arms back and forth to stay afloat.

"Karlo!" Missy cried, staring down at him with terrified eyes. "Get out of that water right now! There's a shark in there with you!"

Not just any shark, he thought. *A great white that is probably very pissed off at me.*

Karlo swam madly toward the boat's stern. His hands gripped the uprights of the metal ladder; his feet found the underwater steps.

"Hurry!" Missy shrieked, bending over the ladder to help him. "It's right there!"

Right there! Right where?

Karlo scampered up the ladder, smashing his knees and elbows in his haste, Missy yanking him by his forearms, his wet shirt clinging to his body, his cap lost. In the back of his mind he knew he was doomed. Any second now the shark would strike. Missy would yank him up onto the deck and scream in horror when she realized he was just a head, arms, and upper torso. Everything below his waist would be gone. He would die moments later with no more dignity than the mackerel they'd used for bait...

It didn't happen.

Karlo lurched up onto the deck, clear of the water and the shark in it, coughing water from his lungs.

Whole.

Missy wrapped her arms around his neck and pressed her cheek to his, though this made it harder for him to catch his breath, so he shook her away. He rose unsteadily to his feet, his eyes going to the fishing rod holder attached to the port hull.

It was empty.

"Where's the dadgum rod?" he barked, eyeing the deck with wild eyes. "It's gone! It's bloody gone!"

"Who cares about that!" Missy said. "You're alive."

"To hell with being alive! Did you see the size of that great white? It was the catch of a lifetime and I never got a picture!" He whirled on Chan. "You. This is your fault."

"Me?" The skipper frowned. "I stuck the rod in the holder. The shark must have tugged it free."

"Why did you ever let go of it in the first place?"

"Because you fell into the water, sir! You needed help!"

"Take us back to land!" Karlo barked, stalking over to the ice box and grabbing a beer to help with his jittery nerves. "And don't think you're getting one penny of that bonus we talked about."

"But sir—"

"Don't 'but' me, mate. You promised me gamefish. Instead, you almost got me killed, and what do I have to show for it? Nothing! This has been a bloody fiasco."

"That's not fair, pookums—"

"And you!" he said, whirling on his wife. "You—you two-faced gold-digging bitch! You probably wanted that shark to get me, didn't you? That would have made your day. Yeah, I know. I know why you married me. I'm no bloody idiot." He twisted off the beer cap and launched it, discus-style, as far as he could into the ocean, losing his balance in the process.

"The turtles, pookie—"

"Fuck the turtles!" he bellowed, dropping flat on his ass.

PART 1
Colombo

"I started early, took my dog, And visited the sea; The mermaids in the basement Came out to look at me"
—Emily Dickinson

CHAPTER 1

ELSA

They call Sri Lanka "the land of eternal sunshine." This morning it was anything but. Cool, wet, gray. Summertime was the rainy season, the weather affected by the annual south-west monsoon that brought hard and heady showers until October. Even so, the rain tended to fall at nighttime, leaving the days bright and sunny, hence the country's moniker.

As the day rolled on, however, the weather would likely follow the usual pattern. The streets would dry, the sky would turn a clear blue, and the tropical humidity would reclaim the island's southern coast, a sticky and oppressive heat relieved only by the ocean breezes.

Dr. Elsa Montero didn't mind the year-round humidity and heat so much; she'd take it any day over the frigid, snowy winters of Hartford, Connecticut, where she'd been born and raised. She did miss the annual ski trips her family had enjoyed in Vermont and Maine...and of course a white Christmas. In fact, it had been all too long since she'd seen a sky drizzled with lazy snowflakes, front yards populated with crooked snowmen, and big two-story houses lit up with colorful Christmas lights. These memories sent a pang of sadness through her. Time was slipping away all too fast.

Elsa worked in a two-story white building on Mirissa Beach. It was flanked by a tour operator business on one side and a large hostel on the other. The hostel bustled year-round with foreign backpackers. Music could be heard pumping out of the three-story structure at all hours, and every now and then Elsa would catch a whiff of pungent marijuana floating on a warm breeze.

In her past life Elsa was an oceanographer and National Geographic explorer-in-residence, famed for her exploration of underwater cave systems throughout the Americas. Now, four years after her husband perished on a dive in Mexico, she worked as a shark scientist for the Sri Lankan Sharks Board Maritime Center (SBMC), an NGO that owned and maintained all of the shark safety gear and nets along the country's southern coastline. It was a small operation with only ten employees, and there was always something to keep her occupied. If you'd asked her ten years ago what she thought she'd be doing with her life at forty-two, would it have been this? No. Nevertheless, she enjoyed her work and was starting to find peace with herself, something that had long eluded her.

Pushing these thoughts aside, Elsa entered the SBMC building through the front door. "Good morning, Christine," she said to the young Sri Lankan girl seated at her desk on the other side of the rectangular-shaped room. Christine, twenty-one, was fresh out of university, bright-eyed, and pretty enough to turn most men's heads.

She pressed her palms together beneath her chin and said, "*Kohomada*, Doctor. Some storm last night! Almost blew the roof off my house."

Elsa wasn't sure whether the girl was speaking figuratively or literally, though she suspected it was the latter. Christine had yet to move out of her family home, a cinderblock structure with a corrugated iron roof in a shantytown overrun by wild fowl and stray dogs. She lived alongside three older brothers and a younger sister, which was most likely why she was always the first to the office building in the morning and one of the last to leave in the afternoon or early evening.

"I didn't even hear the storm," Elsa admitted. "I sleep like a baby, I guess."

"I never get that saying," Christine said. "Babies wake up at all hours of the night, don't they?"

"How about…like a log?"

"Do logs sleep?"

"Too early for this, Christine." Elsa dropped her handbag at her desk. "I haven't even had my coffee yet. Speaking of which, got you one too." She handed the girl one of the two coffees she'd picked up at the seaside town's only Starbucks.

Christine's big eyes lit up; on her salary, Starbucks was a rare luxury. "Oh! You didn't have to!" she said, accepting the paper cup, popping off the lid, and looking inside.

"It's a cinnamon latte."

"Yum!" She sipped, then said, "Mark caught a shark in one of the Matara nets about an hour ago. He's on his way back to shore right now."

Elsa's mouth twisted in concern. She was pleased the safety nets worked to protect swimmers from possible shark attacks. Yet at the same time, every dead shark weighed on her conscience. Far from being the monsters of the deep portrayed in Hollywood movies, they rarely attacked humans, and when they did, it was usually a case of mistaken identity, confusing humans for their regular prey. Most importantly, sharks were essential to the overall wellbeing of the ocean's ecosystem, and any dramatic change to their population would have a devastating effect all the way down the food chain.

"Was it another whitetip?" she asked. They'd caught two oceanic whitetip sharks in their nets over the last three weeks.

Christine shook her head. "Bigger."

"A thresher?" Elsa said, naming another common endemic species of shark that sometimes got entangled in their nets. Larger than the oceanic whitetip, threshers grew up to eighteen feet in length, though much of that was due to their unusually long caudal fin.

"No, not that either, Doctor. It's a *great white*."

Surprise crossed Elsa's face. Although great white sharks were largely coastal territorial predators, they had a knack of staying out of the shark nets that lined the beaches up and down the southern coast. In fact, in all of Elsa's time at SBMC, out of the dozens of sharks caught in the nets over that time, not one had been a great white. "Mark's sure of that?" she asked.

"He sent me a picture. Have a look for yourself." Christine tapped on her mobile phone's screen and brought up a picture of a huge shark floating on its back next to Mark's thirty-two-foot vessel. Sure enough, it was a great white, evidenced by the white underside, conical snout, and large jaws lined with deadly triangle-shaped teeth.

A *huge* great white, Elsa thought, a little starstruck.

"She must be close to twenty-five feet…"

"She, Doctor?" Christine said.

"Sexual dimorphism is present in great whites. Females grow larger than males, and I've never heard of a male reaching…well, this one has to be—"

Just then Christine's phone rang. She answered it in Sinhala. Elsa could hear Mark's voice on the other end of the line. Christine spoke easily and with a smile on her lips, causing Elsa to wonder, not for the first time, whether the girl and Mark were romantically involved.

When Christine hung up, she said in English, "He's transferring the shark to his trailer right now. Should be here in about fifteen minutes."

Elsa nodded. "I'll meet him in the shed."

ΔΔΔ

The shed was attached to the east side of SBMC's main building and accessed via an internal door. The large interior resembled a morgue, with a cement floor and cinderblock walls and shelves stacked with all sorts of miscellaneous items. An oversized stainless-steel necropsy table dominated much of the space. Elsa flicked on the bright overhead fluorescents, then pressed a button that raised the roller door facing the beach. A gust of briny, saltwater air blew into the shed, tousling her blonde, shoulder-length hair. The moody sky, she noted, was already breaking, revealing patches of bright blue. The aggressive surf foamed where it crashed and retreated against the beach.

Two hundred yards to the east, Mark's Toyota Hilux sped easily over the hard-packed sand close to the waterline, pulling a flatbed trailer burdened with its large cargo. He slowed as he angled toward the shed, the truck's tires chewing through the loose sand. When he stopped before her, Elsa couldn't take her eyes off the great white laying on its side on the flatbed. She estimated it to be at least fifteen feet from snout to forktail, its weight pushing one and a half tons. The crescent-shaped tail alone had to be at least six feet tall, the pectoral fins over three feet. The absence of clasper fins on the bottom of the body, which were used by males during mating, indicated it was indeed a female.

From the corner of its tooth-lined mouth protruded a black hook and two feet of trailing braided line. She lifted the line in her hands disapprovingly. The red marks around the shark's nose were likely caused by the steel line scraping across its skin as it thrashed.

"Snapped, not cut," Mark said, hopping out of the cab and coming to stand next to her. He was a fit young man in his mid-twenties, cleanshaven, with short, black hair parted neatly on the left, and a curl that had a habit of dangling across his forehead. His broad mouth was often spread in a confident, carefree smile, as it was now. Nothing ever seemed to get him down, making him pleasant to work with.

Elsa said, "I've never heard of anyone catching a great white on a line before."

Mark nodded. "It's not common, but it happens."

"You think whoever caught this one was fishing specifically for sharks?"

"We won't know until we look inside and see what kind of hook is in her belly."

Back inside the shed, Elsa climbed into the cramped cab of a mini-crane and drove it over to the flatbed so the short boom angled above the shark. Mark secured the cable around its caudal fin. When he gave her a thumbs up, she maneuvered the monster specimen to the stainless-steel table. They hosed it off, then collected parasitic copepods that liked to attach themselves to areas of low velocity on the body, particularly behind the pectoral fins and on the ventral side of the tail. They placed them in a dish (and would later send them to a laboratory for identification), then performed a morphometric assessment of the shark, which involved measuring nearly every inch of its torpedo-like body. Given that scientists rarely had the opportunity to examine great whites up close (in large part because the animals didn't float when they die and thus don't get washed up on shore), measurements were vital to gathering a better understanding of the growth and evolution of the species.

As she worked, Elsa lamented the slow progress of shark conservation in Sri Lanka. While efforts had been made to combat unregulated overexploitation, the country still lagged years behind the conservation efforts undertaken by neighboring countries such as the Maldives. The biggest impediment was the world's demand for shark fins, meat, and liver oil. Over the past ten years alone, Sri Lanka exported fifty-nine metric tons of shark fins annually. However, that was only the official report. There was also a flourishing black market, with many more tons of fins being exported as dried fish.

The cruelty, greed, and ignorance boiled Elsa's blood. She didn't want to put an end to the country's shark fishery altogether, yet it wasn't sustainable in its current form. This was the reason she joined SBMC in the first place. It was an opportunity, however small, to educate regulators and fishermen about the need for conservation while also promoting the ecotourism of sharks as an alternate revenue model to fishing for the local economy.

"Doctor, come have a look at this," Mark said, tugging her from her thoughts.

Elsa joined him where he was bent close to the shark's head, snapping a photograph of the milky white throat. "See that?" He pointed to what looked like a black puncture wound in the V-shaped scales. "Something's stuck in her."

"Let's find out what it is." She went to the steel shelves lining one wall and returned with a pair of needle-nose pliers. She pinched the lodged object between the tips of the tool and slowly extracted what turned out to be a four-inch-long bone with serrated edges. It was shaped like a pen, with one end tapering into a sharp point.

"A stingray barb," Elsa said, unsurprised. Sharks often preyed on stingrays.

Mark was nodding. "And look, another one."

She extracted the second barb, this one located farther down the throat, near the gills. It was roughly the same size as the first. "Want to wager what we'll find in her stomach?"

"I'm not a betting man, Doctor," Mark said. "But I will guess things didn't end very well for the stingray. I'll get the preparations underway for the necropsy."

△△△

Two and a half hours later Dr. Elsa Montero stood inside the brightly lit shed, looking out at the excited audience packed beneath the marquee that Mark and two other colleagues had erected on the beach. Elsa performed all her shark dissections in public, as it was one of the best ways to educate locals and tourists alike about the misunderstood creatures. Typically, a shark necropsy attracted a dozen or so curious spectators. Today, however, the great white had drawn a record crowd. She guessed there must be at least twenty people beneath the tent, as well as another twenty or so fifth graders from a prestigious international school. The students, all dressed in mauve shirts and navy shorts or skirts, had been on a field trip to the beach to participate in various sporting activities. Upon hearing there was a great white in the shed awaiting dissection, they had swarmed the roll-up door, shoving at one another and standing on tiptoes to steal a glimpse of the apex predator.

One brave girl with blonde pigtails poking out from the sides of her head ventured into the shed to stand right before the shark. She studied the fish's beady black eyes with apprehension, as though she thought it might somehow be watching her.

"If it's dead," she said without looking away from it, "why doesn't it close its eyes?"

"Because unlike you and I," Elsa replied, "great whites don't have eyelids. What's your name, little girl?"

"I'm not little. I'm ten, and my birthday's in July."

"My mistake, young lady. So what's your name?"

"Julie," the girl replied, finally glancing up at Elsa. "I'm not afraid of sharks."

"Have you ever touched one before?"

She shook her head. "Can I?"

"Be my guest."

The girl stepped forward and extended her hand. After a brief hesitation, she patted the great white's snout as though she were patting a dog. Giggling, she glanced back at her classmates, who were watching her with a combination of amazement, amusement, and alarm.

Elsa said, "Try moving your hand in the opposite direction."

The girl cried out, "It's sharp!"

Elsa nodded. "A little like sandpaper, isn't it? That's because the shark's skin is made up of thousands of tiny teeth, or what scientists like me call denticles. They're covered in a hard enamel and packed tightly together with their tips facing backward to reduce the water's drag on the shark's body as it swims through the ocean. From an evolutionary standpoint, these little teeth are the same as the big ones in its mouth."

The girl's eyes went to the great white's mouth, which hung partly open, exposing the many rows of thin, savage teeth. "Can I touch one?"

"If you're careful," Elsa said with a smile, pleased to see the child's curiosity outshine her fear. "They're very sharp."

The girl pressed her index finger to the plane of one triangular tooth. When it wobbled freely and unexpectedly, she snatched her hand back. "It moved!"

Elsa nodded again. "Sharks don't chew, so their teeth aren't attached to their jaws. This allows for forward and backward rotation and retraction, which is perfect for tearing off chunks of flesh from their prey that they can swallow whole—"

"Ow!" The girl had touched the tooth again, only this time she had run her finger over a serrated edge. She glanced up at Elsa accusingly. "It bit me!"

"It didn't bite—"

"Mrs. Jayawardene!" the girl wailed, jabbing her finger in the air. "It bit me! The shark bit me!"

The three teachers who had been conversing amongst themselves turned to face the shed. The short, scowling one—Mrs. Jayawardene, presumably—said, "What are you doing in there, Julie? Come out right now! In fact, everyone get in the shade of the tent and take a seat!" She clapped her hands loudly. "You heard me!"

Julie and the other students went obediently to the marquee and plopped down on the sand at the front of the standing-room-only audience. The teachers began straightening them into two lines.

Julie, Elsa noted, was excitedly showing her classmates the finger the great white had "bit."

When the students were settled, and it didn't appear as though any more spectators would be joining the gathering, Elsa nodded to Mark, who turned on his handheld video camera and pointed the lens at her. The feed was being sent wirelessly to a large flat-screen TV set up on the sand so everyone under the marquee would have a detailed view of the dissection.

Elsa switched on the lavalier microphone clipped to the collar of her blue SBMC polo shirt, stepped to the threshold of the shed in her rubber Wellingtons, and said, "Thank you all for joining us today. We have quite the show for you." She spoke with a professional cadence and authority, honed through the many scientific seminars and presentations she had given over the years. "I'll begin the necropsy of this great white shark in just a moment, but first I always like to ask my audience, what do you already know about sharks?"

"They eat people!" the blonde girl blurted out.

"Hand up!" Mrs. Jayawardene instructed.

Julie's hand shot up above her head and wiggled fiercely.

Elsa nodded at her. "Yes, young lady?"

"They eat people!"

Her classmates snickered nervously.

"No, that's not exactly true," Elsa corrected her. "The film *Jaws* convinced millions of people that great whites were cold-blooded monsters. But the truth is, they hardly ever attack human beings. In fact, you have a better chance of being killed by your kitchen toaster than a great white. Yes, they do occasionally attack swimmers or surfers, but marine biologists will tell you they don't like the taste of us. Most attacks are little more than 'test bites,' as they attempt to establish what we are. And because of our ability to get out of the water and get medical attention, most of these attacks aren't fatal. Those who do die, sadly, die from excessive bleeding. It's very, very rare for a great white to eat anybody alive."

"What do they eat then?" asked an Asian boy who was holding his backpack on his lap.

"Peter, hand!" Mrs. Jayawardene admonished, and Elsa realized the woman's scowl might just be a permanent fixture on her face.

The boy raised his hand.

"They have a varied diet," Elsa told him. "But their main prey are pinnipeds such as sea lions and seals, dolphins, porpoises, other sharks, and even turtles and sea birds."

"Dolphins?" Julie griped. "But I *like* dolphins."

"Julie, quiet!" Mrs. Jayawardene snapped.

"You might be surprised to learn," Elsa said, "that great whites are also eaten themselves. Orcas, otherwise known as killer whales, hunt even the largest great whites. They bite off the great white's tail from behind and finish it off when it can no longer swim. If the great white gets away unharmed, it won't return to that hunting ground for up to a year." She clasped her hands together behind her back. "What I want everybody to take away from today's dissection is that great whites—and sharks in general—aren't the fearsome creatures of the deep that they're often portrayed as. We shouldn't fear them or stigmatize them. They're simply a part of the circle of life, part of the food chain, doing what they have done for millions and millions of years, long before humans were around. In fact, many of them now need our help. Because of overfishing, some species are critically endangered and might one day go extinct, and nobody wants that, do they?" She smiled. "But enough talk. Is everyone ready for the dissection?"

This was greeted with cheers and a splattering of applause.

Elsa went to the stainless-steel necropsy table and picked up a large, thin filleting knife. Mark followed her with the video camera.

"You should all have a good view on the TV out there," she said, the microphone amplifying her voice with only the tiniest trace of feedback. "If anyone is squeamish seeing blood, you can look away or close your eyes. But remember, this is just a fish, a big one, but just like the fish you see on ice in the supermarket. One big piece of sushi. Now, I'm going to begin with the snout."

△△△

Elsa expertly sliced off the end of the great white's snout (to some gags from the crowd), revealing a cross-section of the complex system of tiny jelly-filled pores that processed olfactory information. She explained that sharks didn't use their noses for breathing—they used their gills for that—only for smelling. The pores picked up vibrations in the water and the weak electro-magnetic fields produced by the muscle contraction and move-ment of potential prey. They were so sensitive they could detect a half-billionth of a volt in electric fields, as well as traces of blood from as far as four or five miles away.

Next Elsa began removing the shark's jaws. Just as its teeth weren't fused to the jaws, the jaws weren't fused to the skull. This allowed it to spit out its gums, bludgeoning its prey and enlarging the size of its bite. While she made incision after incision, she kept up a steady commentary of facts and biology. She also added her usual jokes to keep the dissection light-hearted. "Why do sharks live in salt water? Because pepper makes them sneeze!" was one of her cringe-worthy favorites.

When she freed the jaws from the shark's head, Elsa and her colleague, Lasith—a local fisherman and marine biologist with a nicotine-stained moustache—lowered them to the cement floor carefully. A great white's jaws were worth $10,000 to $20,000. This, along with the substantial monetary value of their fins, and the prestige involved in catching such a notorious predator, was part of the reason they were currently listed as a threatened species on the IUCN Red List.

Crouching beside the gaping maw to show that she fit neatly inside it, Elsa explained that despite the massive size of the jaws, great whites didn't have a particularly powerful bite compared to other animals such as saltwater crocodiles, jaguars, or spotted hyenas. This was because, as she'd told Julie earlier, they didn't chew, and their razor-sharp teeth could slice through anything they came in contact with.

Standing up, she exchanged the filleting knife for a bone saw and performed the laborious task of decapitating the great white. She extracted the brain from the cartilage cranium and held it before her, allowing Mark to capture a combination of slow pans and tight close-ups that elicited a mixture of delight and repulsion from the audience. She then placed it in a white bucket with a wet thump. Later, she would take measurements and perform a detailed examination to compare its major regions to other, better understood, shark species.

The great white's heart was also in its head. Elsa removed the pink organ and again held it before her for Mark to film. Like the brain, it was relatively small in comparison to shark's body size, though the aorta still dwarfed a human finger.

"How's everyone faring so far?" Elsa asked the crowd as she

rinsed blood from her gloved hands in the shed's sink. "Nobody's fainted yet, I hope?"

"It's gross!" shouted Julie, and several of her classmates echoed this sentiment.

"Remember, the dissection is for science. Have you all learned something so far?"

There was a general chorus of agreement.

"Then it's been worthwhile," she stated. "And now it's time to take a look inside the great white's body." She returned to the necropsy table and made a long cut along the shark's abdomen. With Lasith's help, they lifted back the thick layer of skin and tissue to reveal the shark's enormous liver beneath. It was the size of a human and filled almost the entire gut cavity. Unlike other fish, sharks lacked gas-filled swim bladders that controlled buoyancy. Instead, they relied on giant, fatty livers packed with oil to keep them afloat, which was why they sank when they died and rarely washed up on shore.

As Mark filmed the oil oozing out of the organ, Elsa said, "You may be surprised to see there are no bones inside the great white, only cartilage. This is the case with all sharks. It allows them to be light and flexible in the water, while also enabling them to become the largest known extant fish species in the oceans. Whale sharks, for instance, can reach a length of sixty feet and a mass of twenty tons. That's about the weight of three elephants, thirty cattle, or a whopping two hundred and fifty people. Thankfully, they pose no threat to us as their diet consists mostly of plankton and small squid or fish."

Elsa, Lasith, and four other colleagues heaved the great white's liver from the gut cavity and plopped it down on a blue tarp stretched across the floor.

After catching her breath, Elsa said, "All right, ladies and gentlemen and boys and girls. I'm happy to announce that we've finally made it to the stomach! This is my favorite part of any dissection. Some of you older folks out there might recall that in *Jaws* Richard Dreyfuss found a crushed tin can and a license plate in the stomach of a tiger shark. Although that's just a movie, some strange stuff has indeed been found inside the stomachs of sharks over the years, including old boots, car tires, a bag of money, and even a full suit of armor! Any guesses as to what we'll find today?"

"A dolphin?" Julie called out.

"I hope not. But anything's possible. So let's get cracking, shall we?"

Elsa slit open the shark's stomach and nearly retched at the putrefying smell. Scrunching her nose in disgust, she sifted a gloved hand through the partially digested sludge inside the muscular sack.

"Much of this appears to be…half-digested whale blubber," she said, tasting the offending odor in her mouth. "Which means this great white had likely been scavenging on a floating whale carcass not long before it died…" Her fingers brushed something hard and heavy. She removed a piece of bone the shape and size of a small boat propeller. "Ah ha! I was right! This is a whale vertebra. By the size of it, I'd say it was part of a backbone at least twenty feet long. We'll send it off to a laboratory for proper identification." She handed it to Lasith, then stuck her hand back into the goop. A few moments later she cried out again when she discovered the rest of the fisherman's line that had trailed from the great white's mouth. She pulled it fist over fist until a nasty fishing hook emerged from the rotting whale blubber. She showed it to Lasith. "What do you think?"

He examined the hook closely. "Good news—the angler was not fishing for sharks," he said in his Sri Lankan English, colloquially known as Singlish. "This line and hook, it is for gamefish —sailfish or marlin. Bad news—the damage to the hook means the white tip put up a strong fight until the line broke. The escape would leave it exhausted."

"Exhausted enough to ride a current to shore and get tangled up in the Matara safety nets?"

"Yes, I think so. Struggling for oxygen the entire way. You will probably find high levels of stress hormones in the blood sample you took from the liver."

Elsa sighed, disappointed but not surprised. "Sharks," she explained to the audience, setting aside the hook and tugging off her yellow latex gloves, "need water moving over their gills to breathe. If they stop swimming, they drown. This great white, it seems, exhausted itself getting off the fisherman's line, which left it—"

"Doctor," Mark said, holding the video camera in one hand and his nose with the other as he peered into the shark's stomach. "I think I see a second bone…"

Elsa joined him at the necropsy table. "You're right," she said, snapping a glove back on. "Most likely another of the whale's vertebrae…" She plucked the bone free from the sludge—and frowned in momentary shock.

"Oh, no," Mark mumbled. He quickly recognized what she held in her hand and averted the video camera, but not before the human skull appeared on the outdoor television screen.

The crowd erupted in bedlam.

CHAPTER 2

MARTY

D r. Martin Murdock stood on the aft deck of the RV *Oannes*, the smoke from his corncob pipe drifting away from him into the briny air. He was staring out at the vast expanse of the Laccadive Sea to where it kissed the vermillion evening sky. Marty had purchased the twenty-two-meter ship from a local businessman who had been in the process of retiring his ragtag fishing fleet. At the time it had reeked of fish and showed its age in every grubby plank and window. Now, after a thorough retrofitting, it was a state-of-the-art research vessel featuring scientific equipment, high-tech electronics, and both a wet and dry laboratory.

The *Oannes* was also his permanent home.

It had never been Marty's intention to live aboard a boat, but his work often kept him there late into the evenings. When he found himself spending the night in the master stateroom more often than not, it became redundant renting a house in the city. And so he adopted the life of a sea nomad, waking each morning to the squawks of herons and spoonbills and seagulls, showering with spotty hot water, and bobbing around like a rubber duck in a bathtub during Sri Lanka's frequent tropical storms. It was an unusual lifestyle, but not an uncomfortable one.

"Wishful thinking never caught anyone a mermaid, *mon capitiane*."

Marty turned as his sprightly, short assistant, Pip Jobert, emerged from the companionway to the lower deck, where she had been working in the dry lab. Her typical outfit on any given day was a grungy tee-shirt, torn jeans, and an Australian slouch hat (one side of the brim pinned up with a rising sun badge) to keep the equatorial sun off her tanned face. Today she wore the slouch hat and torn jeans but with an oversized Metallica singlet that revealed her bra straps. A pair of Ray-Ban Aviators shielded her sea-green eyes. Her coffee-colored hair, which fell nearly to the small of her back, was braided into two individual ponytails. On her feet were a pair of sun-bleached flipflops so well-worn they had holes in the soles beneath each of her big toes.

Marty had never known what to make of Pip's Salvation Army fashion. Nevertheless, he didn't give it much thought anymore. The idiosyncratic clothing had come to embody her in the two and a half years they'd been acquainted—and in his mind she would be somehow diminished without it.

What mattered most to Marty, of course, was that Pip was a sonar technician bar none. The day she first showed up at the *Oannes*, unannounced, and told him she was replying to the help wanted ad he'd posted on a number of online job forums, he'd explained the spot was filled (this was not an excuse because she'd looked like she'd spent the night in a trash can; he had actually hired a Colombo University graduate student two weeks prior). Yet Pip persisted, bragging that she was the best sonar technician in the city, and she'd work the first week pro bono to prove it. Although being skeptical, Marty agreed to give her a trial run, as the grad student had taken off the week to study for an upcoming exam.

That week, Pip worked every day from dawn until dusk, chipping away at the massive amount of acoustic data he'd compiled during his research trips along the island-nation's west coast—and proved that her boast of being the best sonar technician around wasn't hyperbolic.

"Wishful thinking?" he said to her, removing the pipe from his mouth.

"That is right," she replied in French-accented English. "If you are not glued to a computer screen analyzing your sonar readouts, Marty, you are standing out here daydreaming about catching mermaids."

"In fact, I wasn't thinking about anything."

"I cannot believe that. People are always thinking of something, yes? You are not a rock."

"Thank you for pointing that out, Pip. Tell me then. What are you thinking about right at this moment?"

"I just told you. I am thinking that you are thinking about catching mermaids. But what I think you mean is, what was I thinking about *before* that? I will tell you. I was thinking about clownfish."

"Clownfish?" he said, amused.

"I watched a Disney movie last night, the one with the clownfish. It reminded me of a paper I wrote when I was a university student. My thesis questioned why some marine animals such as clownfish forgo their own reproduction to help others in their society reproduce. Very strange, yes?"

"Any ideas?"

"Of course. Do you think I wrote a paper without answering my thesis? I posited that the largest nonbreeder from an anemone inherited the territory when a dominant breeder died and left a breeding vacancy. Thus it assumes its own breeding role and contributes genetically to the next generation of clownfish."

"And what about the smaller nonbreeders from the anemone, or even nonbreeders from elsewhere? They simply cede this territory?"

"That is right."

Marty shook his head. "Sorry, Pip. You get a B for effort, but that's all. Ask any behavior ecologist and they'll tell you that nothing in the animal kingdom waits to inherit a breeding position. They contest it immediately. The guy gets the girl, the loser skulks off into the bush. It's why we have a little something called natural selection, not future selection."

"I am glad you were not my professor, Marty, because *he* liked my thesis. He gave me an A." She flicked a wave as she started down the gangway to the pier. "See you tomorrow."

"See you, Pip."

Clamping the stem of his pipe back between his teeth, Marty entered the ship's salon through a set of bi-folding doors. When he'd decided to call the *Oannes* his permanent home, he'd wanted a living area that felt homey, so he'd decorated the previously spartan salon—the main social cabin of a boat—with teak joinery and luxury textiles, plum velvet, button-tufted leather, Art Deco mahogany furniture, and objets d'art from around the world. He liked to believe the finished product was a Neo Baroque masterpiece reminiscent of gentlemen's yachts from the 1930s (though Pip always complained it felt like a room lifted from The Addams Family home).

The renovations had cost a small fortune, but money had never been an issue for him. His grandfather had been a successful treasure hunter known for discovering several famous shipwrecks. Old Alfred Murdoch hit the motherlode in 1981 when he located the wreckage of the RSS *Republic*, a steam-powered ocean liner that was lost off Nantucket in 1909. He successfully salvaged US gold Double Eagles and other valuables from the ship's rotting holds—appraised to be worth close to half a billion dollars at the time.

When Alfred died in 1983, the fortune was divided amongst his widow and three children, one of whom was Marty's father. As a child Marty was cosseted in luxury, splitting his time between a Georgian mansion in the heart of London and an even grander riverside estate in Oxfordshire. He attended one of the most prestigious private schools in the country, and the University of Cambridge after that, where he earned an undergraduate degree in marine biology and a doctorate in zoology. Thanks to a thirty-million trust fund he'd received on his twenty-fifth birthday, he was able to privately fund field research expeditions around the world, gaining a reputation as a foremost expert on ecology and conservation.

By his mid-thirties he became fascinated by a little-known hypothesis called the aquatic ape theory. First proposed by a marine biologist named Alister Hardy in 1960, the theory posited that about ten million years ago a branch of primitive ape-stock was forced by competition from the forests to the shallow waters off the coast of Africa to hunt for food, and these semi-aquatic apes became the ancestors of Homo sapiens. The idea stemmed from the fact that modern humans had several aquatic adaptations not found in other great apes. A lack of body hair. A layer of subcutaneous fat. The location of the trachea in the throat rather than the nasal cavity, as well as the overall regression of the olfactory organ. The propensity for front-facing copulation. Tears and eccrine sweating. Webbed fingers. The theory went so far as to argue that bipedalism evolved as an aid to wading through water, and that the use of tools evolved from using rocks to crack open shellfish and sea urchins.

Despite the aquatic ape theory being ignored or deprecated as a pseudoscience by academics and scientists, Marty took it seriously. He published a paper in a special issue of the *Journal of Human Evolution* in which he argued that the aquatic ape ancestors of modern humans were, in fact, not extinct but had evolved into fully aquatic mammals.

The scientific community's response was swift and harsh. Biologists, anthropologists, evolutionary theorists, paleoanthropologists, and other experts pounced on the hypothesis, many calling it "crank anthropology" akin to alien-human interbreeding and Bigfoot.

Nevertheless, all publicity is good publicity, as they say, and Marty began packing lecture halls in the UK and US as a guest lecturer, while also conducting interviews on radio stations and podcasts and major television stations.

Within a year, he had become an international name and the face of a newly coined scientific discipline, sirentology—the study of mermaids and mermen, collectively known as merfolk.

In 2017, at the height of Marty's popularity, a well-respected filmmaker contacted him, claiming to possess video evidence that supported his merfolk theory. Marty was initially skeptical. Despite the filmmaker's credentials and reputation, the timing of the video evidence (surfacing just as the idea of merfolk was capturing the public's imagination) seemed too coincidental. Even so, Marty agreed to meet the filmmaker, and when he saw the footage with his own eyes, his skepticism vanished.

The video had been taken just after dawn by an American man walking his dog along a remote stretch of beach in southern California. It began with the man spotting three beached whales (the US Navy had been testing sonar blasts two kilometers off the coast at the time, which were believed to have killed the whales). The man filming the footage was speaking to someone on his phone. His voice rose in excitement as he spotted something farther down the beach. He hurried toward it before slowing to a walk and steadying the camera on a beached bottlenose dolphin.

Partly obscured by its smooth, gray body was some sort of large fish.

The man was about ten meters away from the dolphin and the fish...only the second animal was now clearly no fish, as it had two very distinct arms protruding from its sides. As the man drew closer, the camera revealed more of the bizarre creature. It lay on its chest, facedown. Its head was covered with scraggly black hair. Its tightly muscled upper body resembled a human's (especially the arms, ending in huge, webbed hands). The skin was a light shade of blue. From the waist down the legs fused into a powerful tail that terminated in a forked fin. This was covered in horny skinfolds like those found on armadillos.

The man closed the final few feet to the creature very slowly. He nudged its shoulder with a toe. It didn't move. He crouched, panning the camera up and down the thing's body. He reached a hand under its shoulder. Grunting, he rolled it over onto its back. The face was humanoid...yet horribly different too. There were no eyebrows or facial hair, and the forehead seemed broader than a human's, the jaw slimmer. The ears and nose were almost non-existent, and the mouth was a lipless slit. The large, wide-spaced eyes, black and pupilless, stared blankly at the camera.

Then it hissed.

The man fell backward. Gasping, he scrambled away, gained

his footing, and ran a short distance before swinging around. He focused the camera on the creature. It was twenty or so meters away, flopping across the sand toward the ocean in the awkward, clumsy way of a seal on land. It reached the foaming surf and splashed through the shallow water. A wave crest crashed over it. When the water flattened in the subsequent trough, the creature was gone.

A thousand thoughts had run through Marty's mind while he'd watched the astounding footage, and for the next hour he bombarded the filmmaker with questions. When the man pitched Marty a Netflix documentary based on the footage, and asked if Marty would be interested in narrating it, he agreed without hesitation.

That decision turned out to be the biggest mistake of his life.

"Dumb bastard," he muttered to himself, catching his reflection in an ornate mirror. The middle-aged man looking back had skin the color of copper, craggy yet cultured features inherited more from his grandfather than either of his parents, and dark stubble. There was a tiredness in his blue eyes these days, a weariness borne from a dwindling lack of purpose and the recognition that his best days were behind him. He still believed wholeheartedly that merfolk existed in the planet's oceans and seas; he simply no longer believed he would be the one to ultimately uncover the evidence. Years of fruitless searching could erode even the most determined man's optimism, and despite being only forty-five, he felt as though time were running out. The world was turning without him, moving inevitably forward, while he remained trapped in a bubble, longing for the past and a life that no longer existed.

Setting aside his pipe to burn out, Marty withdrew a bottle of Scotch from the liquor cabinet below the mirror and allowed himself a generous pour. He went to the baby grand piano in the corner of the salon, sat on the padded bench, and stared at the sheet music propped on the rack before him without seeing the notes.

He set the glass on the piano's glossy top board and tapped a white key. The solitary, mournful note carried eerily in the darkening twilight.

△△△

An hour and four drinks later Marty's spirit was buoyed, and his fingers danced over the piano keys as he played Dire Strait's "Walk of Life," singing along in a nobody-is-listening, gruff baritone.

He didn't realize his phone was ringing until it had gone silent. He looked around the salon, waiting for it to begin ringing again. It didn't.

He got to his feet—and almost fell flat on his face as he lost his balance while lifting a leg over the piano bench. He found his phone atop a stack of *National Geographic* magazines piled haphazardly on an Edwardian writing desk. He was surprised to see the missed call was from Jacqueline DeSilva, a reporter for the *Daily Mirror*.

Marty had met Jacky at a scientific ichthyology conference not long after he'd arrived in Sri Lanka. After the final panel of the afternoon concluded, he was making a quiet exit from the hotel's packed conference room when she approached him. He was surprised and alarmed when she called him by his name. He hadn't told anyone from his old life that he had moved to Sri Lanka. Even so, he kept his cool, making polite chitchat. When she excused herself to use the restroom, he ducked outside and had been in the process of flagging down a taxi in the helter-skelter traffic when she found him again and convinced him to join her for a drink at a nearby bar. They ended up having a good time, and he invited her back to the *Oannes*, where they had an even better time. Marty was looking forward to their next date—until Jacky sent him a link to a feature article she'd written about him in the *Daily Mirror*. It was generous and well-researched... and made him tremble with rage. To be fair, he'd never told her not to write anything about him, yet he thought he'd made it clear he'd come to the country seeking anonymity.

As he expected and feared, the story was picked up by major newspapers around the world, including London's *The Telegraph* and *The Guardian*, with one headline blaring "THE MERDOC FOUND WASHED UP IN SRI LANKA" and the other "DISGRACED MERDOC LOOKING FOR MERMAIDS IN INDIAN OCEAN." ("Merdoc" was a pejorative play on his name that the media had gleefully applied to him after the Netflix documentary was exposed as a fraud...and one they had apparently not tired of.)

Marty cut off all communication with Jacky, ignoring her calls and texts until she stopped trying to get in touch with him altogether.

And that had been that.

Nothing for nearly three years.

He'd all but forgotten about her.

So why is she calling me now?

ΔΔΔ

Marty was considering ringing Jacky back when his phone rang first. It wasn't Jacky though; it was Radhika Fernandez, the woman Marty was currently pseudo seeing. He'd met her about a year after the Jacky fiasco. He'd been at his preferred local pub, an unpretentious place popular with all rungs of society, including a good number of expats. He'd been minding his own business in a corner booth when Radhika slid into it across from him and began complimenting him on one thing or another. She was clearly drunk. He was too, which was probably why he couldn't remember what they talked about. But it must have been interesting because they remained at the pub until closing. After that night, they began getting together every week or two. She didn't recognize him as The Merdoc, and he didn't tell her anything about himself that might give away his identity. However, the more time they spent together, the more aggressive her inquiries became, until he bluntly explained that his past was off limits.

She wasn't happy with this declaration, but she accepted it.

Marty held the phone to his ear. "Hello, Rad," he said.

"Feeling lonely, mister?" she said playfully.

In fact, he was. With the piano muted, the salon seemed suddenly lifeless and uninviting. "Want to come by for dinner?"

"I've been playing tennis at the club. You don't mind if I'm in my whites?"

"No dress code here. You've seen my assistant."

"I'll be there shortly."

Marty hung up and went to the dinette off the starboard side of the salon. It was appointed with stainless-steel appliances, a stone bench, and a butler's pantry. The fridge was stocked with freshly caught seafood, and he went about prepping deviled crabs, hot butter cuttlefish, and jasmine rice. Everything was almost ready when Rad arrived. He mixed her a vodka soda with a slice of lemon and joined her out on the foredeck, sitting in a steamer chair facing the sea. It was dark now, a wash of stars glittering overhead as far as the eye could see. Vintage brass lanterns lit the deck in warm hues.

"You got here quickly," he said, handing her the vodka. Her white top clung tightly to her breasts and thin waist, while the matching miniskirt showed off her toned legs. She had a pale, aristocratic face. Her hair, parted Cher-like in the middle of her head, fell straight down over each shoulder like black water. Designer sunglasses were pushed up on her forehead, and fancy silver earrings dangled from her earlobes.

"The nice thing about having a driver," she said, her brown eyes twinkling, "is that they're always waiting at the curb, waiting to take you somewhere."

Marty frowned at Rad. Her voice was raspy, like she had woken up with a hangover. He hadn't detected it on the phone, though it hadn't been the best connection. "You okay?" he asked her.

"What do you mean?" she said, staring out at the sea.

"Let me see."

"See what?"

"Your throat."

Sighing dramatically, she tugged loose the scarf she had wrapped around her neck. Ugly purple and brown bruises marred her throat.

"Jesus, Rad," he said, shaking his head.

Marty knew what the bruises were from, of course. Rad was into erotic asphyxiation. He'd learned this on their fourth date, when she'd asked him to choke her during a session of spirited lovemaking. He couldn't bring himself to do it, and they continued on as if she'd never asked. Only she *had* asked. And the request had made him uncomfortable. He spent much of the following days thinking about it. He couldn't get his head around why anybody in their right mind would want to be choked during sex. Everybody had their quirks, and he wasn't afraid of trying new things, but choking pushed the bounds of acceptability in his mind.

Despite his apprehension at Rad channeling *Fifty Shades of Grey*, he continued to see her. She didn't bring up the choking stuff during their next few dates, and he was thinking it had been a one-off request, when during another spirited session of lovemaking she'd blurted in a throaty, frantic voice, "Hurt me!" He asked her to clarify what she meant, which killed the mood. When she told him to choke her, he once again refused, which *really* killed the mood. She began calling him out, saying, "Don't be a wimp, Marty!" and "Be a man, Marty!" Finally out of frustration and anger and a sense of emasculation, he wrapped his hands around her neck and squeezed. Immediately her taunts stopped. Her eyes rolled back in her head with pleasure. Her body language—her sensuality and her passion—shot to a new level. It was easily the best sex they'd ever had. Probably the best sex he'd ever had.

The next day, after some research on the internet, Marty decided Rad was getting turned on by the thrill of looking over the edge, and of forcing him to look over the edge alongside her. Indeed, she was an adrenaline junkie by nature. She had more adventure-filled stories than anyone else he knew, and in each one she was always pushing the limits of what was safe and responsible and sane, from cage-diving with saltwater crocodiles to walking along the wing of an airborne plane.

Understanding what drove Rad's desire for erotic asphyxiation, and understanding that the deviant sexual activity was a lot more common than he'd previously believed, Marty felt a little better about his complicit participation. Yet choking was not his "thing" and never would be. Sex should be sensual and romantic, he thought, not violent. What they were doing could not be called lovemaking. They were fucking, plain and simple.

Which, for the time being, was fine with Marty—and fine, apparently, with Rad too.

"Who did that to you?" he asked her, surprised to find it bothered him that she had been with another man, despite the two of them acknowledging their open relationship.

"What does it matter, Marty?" she said. "You don't know him."

"Your tennis partner?"

"You're cute when you're jealous."

"I'm worried for you, Rad."

"You do the same thing to me!"

"I've never left bruises."

"Would you prefer if I had him pull a plastic bag over my head?"

"I'd prefer if you gave up the damn fetish altogether." He saw that his words had surprised and stung her, and he added, "Sorry. I guess I should check on the food."

He went to the dinette, turned off the stove burners, and slid the food into the oven to keep warm. When he returned to the foredeck, Rad was plucking a small silver case from her clutch. She lit up a cigarette, blowing the smoke over her shoulder. "How was whatever you do here all day?" she asked him.

What little he'd told Rad about himself was this: he was a university professor on an indeterminate leave from teaching while he searched the seas for new species of marine life. This wasn't far from the truth—he was simply leaving out the fact that the new species of marine life was merfolk. "Pip discovered a pod of whales that came by this way last year, only now they were two members short."

"A regular Einstein, that girl."

"She's an excellent sonar technician."

"Do you like her?"

"Excuse me?"

"You work together all day, just the two of you. Isolated out here…"

"Enough, Rad."

"Why don't you want to talk about her?"

"What you're implying is nonsense."

"What do you talk about with her other than sonar?"

Marty filled the bowl of his pipe with tobacco and lit up. "Clownfish," he said around a mouthful of pungent smoke. "We discussed their breeding behavior today."

"Breeding behavior, huh? Do clownfish have any particular fetishes?"

"No, but they have some peculiar fishishes."

Rad stared at him, her eyes disapproving.

"It was a joke. Fetishes, fishishes—"

"I got it, Marty. I just didn't find it funny."

"Look, Rad, I'm sorry I mentioned—"

"Forget it." She stubbed out her cigarette in an ashtray on the table between them. "Is the food ready—?"

Marty's mobile phone rang. He took it from his pocket and checked the number.

It was Jacky.

"I should probably take this," he said, standing.

△△△

"Martin speaking," he said, entering the salon.

"Professor Murdoch. It's Jacqueline DeSilva—we met a couple of years ago."

"I remember. Long time."

"A very long time. How are you, Martin? Marty?"

"Marty's fine, and I'm good. It's nice to hear from you."

"Is it?"

He glanced through the window to the foredeck. Rad was facing away from him, watching the sea, which was now indistinguishable from the black sky.

"Marty?"

"I'm here. And, yes, it is nice to hear from you."

"Where are you?"

"At home."

"On that boat of yours?"

"That's right."

"I know this is out of the blue, but I need to talk to you."

Marty wondered what she was up to. "I have a few minutes right now."

Dead air on the line for a moment. Then, "No, in person."

Marty's curiosity got the better of him, and he said, "I'm free tomorrow morning—"

She said, "I'd rather we talk tonight. I have a flight tomorrow morning."

"I can't tonight. I'm with someone right now."

"It's important, Marty. *Really* important."

Marty's heart stopped. *Was he a father?* No. Impossible. What a ridiculous thought. They'd only had that one night together on the *Oannes*, and they'd used protection... Besides, if he'd gotten Jacky pregnant, the kid would be more than two years old already. Why would she wait so long to tell him such news? "I'm sure it can wait until—"

"Who are you with?"

"A friend."

"A woman?"

"Yes." He glanced through the window again. Rad was fiddling with her phone. "And I should get back to her."

"Marty—"

"I have to go, Jacky. If this is as important as you say, call me tomorrow."

"Marty—"

"Talk then." He hung up and returned outside.

Rad set her phone aside as he took a seat.

"Business or pleasure?" she asked, lighting a fresh cigarette.

"Someone I knew once. She wanted to talk."

"About what?"

"She wouldn't say."

"Did you tell her you're on a date?"

"Is this a date?"

"I didn't know you were seeing anybody, Marty."

"I'm not seeing her, Rad. We went on a single date three years ago. I haven't spoken to her since."

"Then what does she want to talk about?"

"I don't have a clue."

△△△

After eating and washing up, Marty and Radhika retired to the salon. He'd been teaching her how to play the piano, and now they attempted to play Sonny and Cher's "I Got You Babe." When Rad hit a B-sharp instead of B-flat, she laughed and said, "Enough for me, Marty. Night cap?"

"Sure," he said, locking his fingers together and cracking his knuckles.

Rad went to the liquor cabinet and poured two sherries.

She handed him one and said, "What's her name?"

"Who?"

"Who do you think?"

He chuckled. "You're still going on about her?"

"What's her name?"

"Why?"

"Maybe I know her."

"Why would you know her?"

"You know how cliquey Colombo can be among certain circles."

"You don't know her," he assured her.

"So tell me her name," she insisted.

"Jacqueline DeSilva. She's a reporter for the *Daily Mirror*."

Rad was immediately on her phone.

"What are you doing?"

"Googling her."

"You're cute when you're jealous," he said, throwing her words back at her.

"I'm curious, that's all. Is this her?" She showed Marty the photo she'd found. It was the one Jacky used in her bylines.

He nodded.

"She's pretty. Did she break up with you?"

"It's complicated."

"Entertain me."

"We were incompatible, that's it."

"That's not complicated. What aren't you telling me?"

"Do you want to go out somewhere?"

"You're changing the topic?"

"How about Beach Wadiya?"

"My Lord, you mean you're serious about actually setting foot off this ship? You're not going to burst into flames when you touch land, are you?"

"I go to Wadiya once a week. It's where we met, if you've forgotten."

"I haven't forgotten. Fine, let's go—"

"Hello?" someone called.

△△△

Marty and Rad went to the gangway. The silhouette of a woman was visible down on the pier. She waved, saying, "Ahoy, mateys!"

"Bloody Christ," Marty muttered. He couldn't see Jacky's face, but he recognized her voice. "Wait here," he told Rad, and stalked down the gangway. At the bottom, he unclasped the *"PRIVATE:*

NO BOARDING" sign hanging on a chain and stopped in front of Jacky. She had always reminded him of a bird of prey, her nose beakish, her eyes quick and sharp.

"Good evening, Dr. Murdoch," she said, a smile lifting the ends of her lips and dimpling her cheeks.

"What are you doing here, Jacky?" he demanded. "I told you we could talk tomorrow morning."

She peered past him. "Do I know her...?"

"No, you bloody don't."

"She looks familiar. Why don't you invite her down?"

"We're heading out."

"Stop being so damn stubborn, Marty!"

"*I'm* being stubborn, Jacky? You're stalking me!"

"Why don't you want to hear what I have to tell you?"

"We haven't spoken in three years. I'm sure whatever you have to tell me can wait another day."

"It really can't."

"Do we have a child?"

Jacky stared at him before bursting into laughter.

"Right," he said, turning away from her.

"I'm missing all the fun, it seems," Rad said, coming down the gangway and blocking his way up it.

"Let's go," Marty told her.

She stopped next to them. "Aren't you going to tell me what's so amusing?"

Jacky said, "Marty believes I'm here to tell him he's the father of my child."

Rad chuffed. "Being the prolific lover that Marty is, I'm sure it's hard for him to keep track of just how many children he has fathered."

Jacky extended her hand. "I'm Jacqueline DeSilva."

"Marty mentioned that," she said, shaking hands. "I'm Radhika Fernandez."

"I *do* know you. You have a show on ITN...? I knew I recognized you!"

The Independent Television Network was a Sri Lankan state-governed network that broadcast content in Sinhala, Tamil, and English. Rad was a longtime host of an English travel show that chronicled her travels throughout South Asia.

"Mad Rad, that's me," said Rad. "Would you care to join us for a drink?"

"Sure—"

"I don't think so—"

"Don't be so rude, Marty." To Jacky, "Have you ever been to Beach Wadiya?"

△△△

Beach Wadiya was less than two blocks away from the pier, located along a stretch of Galle Face that overlooked virgin beach. It was a Thursday night and the pub was crowded. The hostess showed them to a table that was being cleared of dishes and wiped down. A waitress promptly came by, and Rad and Jacky ordered the same cocktail.

"Marty?" Rad said.

"Nothing for me."

She said to the waitress, "A Scotch on the rocks for Mr. Grumpy Pants here."

"No, thank you," Marty told the girl.

"Yes, please," insisted Rad. "In fact, make it a double." Then she sat down at the table with Jacky, and the two of them began chatting like old friends. The waitress blended back into the milling crowd. Reluctantly Marty sat as well. For the next several minutes he listened silently to Jacky and Radhika's animated conversation. Jacky was asking about an episode of Rad's show filmed in the mountain range that ran parallel to the west coast of India. Rad and her crew had been exploring a cave when they came across a twelve-inch-long centipede hanging from the rocky ceiling by some of its feet and feeding on a dead bat. It had devoured most if its meal in about three hours (which Rad's production team had time-lapsed down to a handful of seconds).

"It makes my skin crawl thinking about that little horror," Jacky said, shivering. "And you pitched your tents right outside the cave! Weren't you afraid that the centipede might crawl into your sleeping bag at night?"

"I made sure my tent was zipped up. Besides, centipedes, no matter how large, don't attack humans unless in self-defense. They prefer more manageable prey like frogs, mice, birds, small snakes."

"I think you're incredibly brave. You'd never catch me in half the places you've visited."

The waitress returned with the drinks. Marty immediately took a burning sip of his Scotch, while Jacky and Radhika clinked their blue cocktails in a toast.

"Lovely meeting you, Rad," Jacky said.

"Likewise, Jacky," said Rad.

"Did you two want to get a private room?" Marty quipped.

"Ooh, a threesome," said Rad. "I'm up for that! I've been trying to get Marty to be a little more adventurous in bed for some time now!"

He scowled. "That's not what I meant—"

"How long have you two been together?" Jacky asked.

"We're not together," Marty said promptly.

"No, we're not," Radhika said. "More like friends with benefits."

"I see," Jacky said.

"Can we change the topic?" Marty said.

Rad frowned at him. "Why are you being such a sour puss?"

"You know I've slept with both of you, right?"

"That's a conversation starter," said Jacky.

"My point is, you should feel uncomfortable around each other. You shouldn't be acting like best friends."

"Would you prefer for us to fight over you instead?" Rad asked playfully. "Pulling hair and ripping clothes and rolling around on the sand?"

Marty took another, longer sip of the Scotch, leaving little more than ice cubes in the tumbler. "Why don't we skip the small talk and get to the point of why you're here, Jacky."

"Absolutely." She folded her hands together on the table. "I take it you haven't watched the news today, or you'd know why I'm here."

Marty rarely watched the news. CNN and the BBC were the only two English-speaking channels that his TV received. Sometimes he put them on as background noise, or when he wanted the simple pleasure of hearing people (other than Pip) speaking English. But that was about the extent of his interest in the wider world. "I had CNN on today for a while," he said, "but I wasn't paying much attention to it."

"I'm talking about the local news."

"I never watch the local news."

"You should, Marty. You're living in Sri Lanka. You should watch Sri Lankan news."

"It's in Tamil, which I don't speak."

"You should learn! You're living in—"

"What's the big news?" he asked impatiently.

"I recorded the segment. It's better if you watch it."

Jacky brought up a video on her phone and handed the device to him. The paused frame showed a woman standing in front of a weather map. "Did you come all this way to tell me there's a tropical storm on the horizon?" he said sardonically. "Should I be back at the *Oannes* battening down the hatches?"

"Press Play."

Rad leaned close to see the screen. Marty tapped Play. The weather segment ended, replaced by a reporter standing in a shed with a microphone held up to her bright red lips. He didn't understand a word of what she was saying.

"I told you I don't speak—"

"Just watch."

Soon the camera panned to a decapitated great white shark lying on a steel necropsy table. The shot cut to a bleached-white skull on a blue tarp and next to a wooden ruler. The lower jaw was missing, as were all of the teeth. Yet this specimen was clearly human, as demonstrated by the globular cranium, the zygomatic arches below the eye sockets, the triangular nasal cavity, the maxillary bones, and the hard palate in the front of the mouth.

Except, he thought, his brow furrowing, *the frontal bone that formed the forehead protruded far too much to be...*

The shot cut back to the reporter.

Marty jabbed the screen, pausing the video. He dragged the buffer bar back several seconds. When the skull appeared again, he zoomed in on it.

Without looking up, he said, "Did this skull come from inside the shark?"

"Indeed it did."

Rad said, "What's wrong with its forehead?"

Jacky said, "Ask Marty what he thinks."

Rad looked at him. "Marty?"

He finally pulled his eyes away from the small screen. He blinked, stunned.

Can this be what I think it is?

"Was there a body too?" he demanded.

Jacky shook her head. "Only that skull."

"Who dissected the shark?"

"An American oceanographer. I spoke with her earlier today."

Rad grimaced. "What's gotten you all worked up, Marty? You haven't dumped any enemies into the ocean recently, have you?"

Marty didn't reply. He was finding it hard to think straight. His thoughts were moving too fast, contemplating too many possibilities at once.

"Seriously, Marty," said Rad, touching his forearm. "What's gotten into you? You look like you've seen a ghost."

"I don't think that's a human skull," he told her flatly.

CHAPTER 3

MARTY

"The forehead might be a bit wonky," said Rad. "But the rest of it certainly looks human to me."

"It's humanoid but I don't think it's human," Marty clarified.

"Humanoid but not human?" Rad's expression filled with amusement. "Please don't tell me you think this is the skull of The Great Gazoo or some other little green man from outer space?"

"No, it's terrestrial," he said, trying to read Jacky's expression.

"Okay, what's going on?" Rad asked, shooting them both suspicious looks. "What do you guys know that you're not telling me?"

Marty took a moment to quiet his riotous thoughts and said, "Are you familiar with the sound a dolphin makes?"

"Of course." She impersonated Flipper, clucking her tongue in rapid succession.

"Do you know why they make that sound?"

"To communicate with other dolphins, I imagine."

"No. Dolphins communicate with whistles and groans and sighs and squeals and other noises. The high-frequency pulses allow a dolphin to build an image of its environment. When the pulses, or clicks, encounter an object, they bounce back to the dolphin, which can then calculate the object's size, shape, speed, distance, and direction, allowing it to 'see,' so to speak."

Rad shrugged. "Echolocation. So what?"

"The clicks are produced in small air sacs in a dolphin's melon, which acts as a kind of acoustic lens, focusing and modulating the clicks in whichever direction the dolphin is facing."

"Melon?"

"A swollen mass of extra soft tissue located between a dolphin's snout and the blowhole." He added pointedly, "What you might call its forehead."

Rad's eyes flashed in surprise. "What are you saying, Marty? That skull is human, not dolphin, and as far as I'm aware, humans don't have a melon."

"But *is* it human?" he asked her.

"What else could it be?"

"What do you know about mermaids, Rad?"

△△△

Marty spent the next few minutes outlining his aquatic ape theory, and one of his central hypotheses that if humanity's ancestors had evolved into fully aquatic marine mammals over the course of millions of years, human eyesight, even greatly enhanced, would not suffice in a dangerous underwater environment. For merfolk to successfully navigate the murky ocean depths and track prey and evade larger threats, they would have evolved a physiological process for locating distant or unseen objects.

The most obvious candidate was echolocation.

Rad listened to him without uttering a word. By the dismissive look on her face as he wrapped up, he knew she wasn't buying any of it. She dug a cigarette from the silver case in her clutch and lit it with a quick, flustered motion. "Is this why you never told me what you do on your boat every day, Marty? Because you're hunting *mermaids*?"

"I told you I'm a marine biologist and a zoologist, and I'm mapping the ocean with sonar, all of which is true. But yes, I believe mermaids and mermen exist—the non-binary preferred plural form is 'merfolk'—and yes, they're the object of my search."

"Umm, now *I'm* not following," said Jacky. "Rad, you don't know who Marty is?"

"Who he is? You're talking like he's famous or something... You're *not* famous, are you, Marty?"

"I was on a TV documentary," he said uncomfortably. "But I don't think we need to get into that right now—"

Jacky said, "He's The Merdoc, for crying out loud!"

"The *Merdoc*?" Rad looked like she'd been slapped. "You mean...from that Netflix show?"

"You know of it?" Marty said, surprised. "I figured since you never recognized me, you never watched the documentary."

"I didn't watch it, but of course I know *of* it. Who doesn't? It was huge. Especially after... Oh, Marty." Sympathy, or perhaps pity, filled her eyes.

Marty knew what she had been about to say: *Especially after it was discovered to be a gigantic hoax.*

Rad now had her phone out, her thumbs tapping rapidly. "Dr. Martin Murdoch. *Murdoch.* That's why you never told me your last name. You knew I'd learn who you were." She stared at Marty. "What the hell? What the *hell*, Marty? Why didn't you ever tell me any of this? What was the big secret?"

"I haven't told *anybody* this, Rad. Not since coming to Sri Lanka. The documentary's not something I'm proud of."

Rad said, "*You* knew, Jacky. You knew Marty was The Merdoc?"

Jacky nodded. "However, Marty never told me. I recognized him at a science conference. My gig at the *Daily Mirror* is general news and current affairs. I covered the Netflix documentary's fallout. I could have picked Marty out of a hundred-person lineup."

"Well, this is...a trip, isn't it? I think I want to slap you, Marty. But..." She stared at him again with that disconcerting who-are-you look. "Whatever. I don't care. You're The Merdoc, okay. Jesus Christ, okay. And you think that skull in that video belongs to a mermaid?"

The mention of the skull got Marty's blood racing. He felt as though he were a child, and it was six a.m. on Christmas morning. Even so, he did his best to temper this excitement. He wasn't going to be taken for a sucker again. The skull could be a fake, part of another hoax, or someone's sick joke. He said, "I'm not going on the record saying anything until—"

"You're not on the record, Marty! It's just us, okay? I'm not going to call up TMZ, okay?"

"I'm excited, Rad. I won't deny that." To Jacky, "You told me you're flying tomorrow morning. I take it you're going to see the American oceanographer who discovered the skull?"

Jacky nodded. "That's right. She works for an NGO in Mirissa. I've already arranged to interview her."

"And you came to see me tonight because you want me to join you?"

"Right again."

"Why?"

"*Why?*" She issued a short laugh. "Because you're the world's foremost expert on merfolk!"

"I mean, what do you want from me? I assume you're planning on writing an article about the skull?"

"Yes, of course. Imagine—merfolk exist, and I'm the one to break the story! What do I want from you? That's quite obvious, isn't it? I want you to verify the skull's authenticity."

Now Marty laughed. "Don't give me too much credit, Jacky. I can run genetic and histological analyses and other tests on the skull in the *Oannes'* lab. That can rule out it belonging to any known species of ape or human. But it wouldn't confirm that the skull is merfolk. It would simply confirm it's from an anthropoidal species unknown in the fossil record."

"Right. A species unknown in the fossil record with a humanoid head that lives in the ocean? Come on, Marty! How many candidates fit that description?"

He held up his hands. "Hey, you don't have to convince me. I'm just saying, if you write a story claiming that skull is proof that merfolk exist, you're going to get pilloried in the media. And having my name attached to a sensational claim like that won't be good for either of us."

"This isn't the damn Netflix documentary, Marty! This isn't someone in a suit brought to life by a Hollywood special effects team! This skull is the real deal! It was discovered in the belly of a shark that randomly washed up in a beach net. That can't be faked."

Marty knew she was right. If his tests revealed that the skull was indeed unknown in the fossil record, that alone would be groundbreaking. At the very least he would be credited with discovering a new species of primate. At best his aquatic ape theory would once more be the center of serious scientific debate and analysis. He might remain The Merdoc to the pundits in the media, but he would no longer be defined as a quack host of a debunked mockumentary. He would be doing serious science, which would go a long way to repairing his reputation as a credible marine biologist and zoologist.

In either case he would be in the world spotlight again—for the right reasons this time.

"Stop keeping me in suspense, Marty," said Jacky. "What do you say? Are you coming with me tomorrow or what?

Marty finally allowed a grin to touch his lips. "I say the next round of drinks is on me."

CHAPTER 4

RAD

Radhika Fernandez was battling conflicting emotions. Anger and betrayal that Marty had not told her the full truth of who he was. Excitement and wonder that he was a world-famous personality. Embarrassment that she had been so clueless all these months. More wonder that the skull of a mermaid might have just washed up to shore in the belly of a great white—wonder and a great dose of skepticism, that was. Because it seemed…too good to be true, she supposed. Why wash up here? Why Sri Lanka? Why just down the coast from where the foremost mermaid hunter had decided to relocate?

The world, of course, was full of coincidences that seemed too good to be true, but that didn't mean they weren't real. Was this one of them?

Then again, people made their own realities. Charles Darwin would never have found the Galapagos Islands had he stayed home in England. He found them because he went looking for them—or a place like them.

Rad eyed Marty, who was organizing travel plans with Jacky. Marty…who lived on a multi-million-dollar state-of-the-art research vessel…who went on week-long sojourns to map the ocean floor and record the sounds of what lurked beneath the waves…who spent nearly every waking hour of every day analyzing that data.

You've been such a fool, she thought. *A blind fool.*

She made a short, strident sound that might have been laughter.

Marty stopped midsentence and glanced at her curiously. His eyes were bright, alive, the bluest she had ever seen them. He seemed ten years younger than he had an hour ago back on the *Oannes*.

"What time's the flight tomorrow morning?" she asked him.

"Seven o'clock," Jacky said.

"I'll book my ticket now," said Marty, and began tapping on his phone.

"You don't think the skull is real, do you?" Jacky said to Rad.

"Real? Yes, I think it's real. I mean, I don't have any reason to believe it's not real. I just…I suppose I don't know…what to make of it."

"That's what I meant. You don't think it's a mermaid skull?"

Rad considered her response. "I believe I have a pretty open mind. I've traveled all over Asia for my TV show, often to remote locations. I've seen the entire spectrum of primates, mammals, amphibians, reptiles, birds, and fish up close and personal. I know—better than most—how diverse and wonderful and weird life on this planet is. And I'm not naïve enough to believe we've seen all that Mother Nature has to offer. I know there's so much out there yet to be discovered—especially in the unexplored depths of the oceans."

Marty looked up from his phone to listen to her.

Rad continued, "Look, I'm not trying to be profound or anything. I'm just saying that…well, I *should* be open to the existence of mermaids. I *want* to be. I want to be as excited as both of you obviously are about the skull. But I'm just…not. How about I leave it at that?"

"I think it's a perfectly reasonable answer," Jacky said.

"You're safely on the side of ninety-five percent of the scientific community," Marty said.

"That's sort of what I mean," Rad went on. "You would think if mermaids existed, they would be known to science by now."

Jacky said, "Like you mentioned, the world's a big, unexplored place, especially the oceans."

Marty said, "Not to mention, we *have* identified them. They've been referenced ever since ancient Mesopotamia and classical Greece, from almost every corner of the world. Once you start keeping track, it's astounding how ubiquitous merfolk sightings have been throughout the ages. There've been dozens of eyewitness accounts of merfolk by local Sri Lankan fishermen in the last twenty years alone. It's why I began my search here."

"I've never heard about them."

"The mainstream media doesn't cover them, not here, not anywhere. Ever since P.T. Barnum's Fiji mermaid in 1842—which was the head and torso of a juvenile monkey sewn onto the back half of a fish—merfolk have fallen back into the realm of myths and legends. Nobody wants anything to do with them."

"Was Aquaman a merfolk?" she asked, apropos of nothing.

"Aquaman had legs, Rad," Marty told her lightly.

"How do you know merfolk don't have legs if you've never seen one?"

"I don't know that conclusively. It's what the science suggests. Legs are meant for walking, not swimming."

"Turtles have legs."

"Well, they walk around on land sometimes, don't they?"

"But you believe merfolk have arms?"

Marty nodded. "Arms—and hands, with opposable thumbs—helped primates develop better defense systems, such as throwing rocks and wielding sticks. They allowed primitive humans to use and to create tools. If merfolk have a powerful piscine tail to propel them through the water, which I believe they do, there would have been no reason to surrender their arms and hands for fins."

"I can almost picture a merfolk king sitting on a golden throne with a crown and scepter."

Marty smiled at her. He knew her too well, and he wasn't going to be dragged into a farcical discussion. He went back to booking his plane ticket.

The silence that followed was protracted and awkward.

"Well!" Jacky said abruptly, getting to her feet, "it's late, and

Marty and I have an early flight tomorrow. I think I'm going to call it a night."

"Likewise," said Rad, standing. "I'll walk you to the street."

"You're not coming back to the *Oannes*?" Marty asked.

"The *Oannes*," she said, saying the word as if for the first time. "Why do I have the feeling your secret identity has been staring me in the face this entire time?"

"In Babylonian mythology," he told her, "a water god was depicted as having the upper body of a man and the lower body of a fish—the first recorded reference of a merman. The Greeks called him Oannes."

"Of course," she said dryly. She held her elbow out for Jacky. "Shall we?"

CHAPTER 5

MARTY

When Marty returned to the *Oannes*, he found he was too wired to sleep. In the salon he took the bottle of Johnny Walker he'd been drinking earlier from the liquor cabinet, changed his mind, and exchanged it for a bottle of Glenfiddich. He dumped too much whiskey into a tumbler and went to the foredeck, where he lit his pipe and paced beneath the gibbous moon. He was thinking about the video of the skull Jacky had shown him.

And tomorrow I'll be holding it in my hands, seeing it with my eyes.

He dialed Pip's number.

"Marty?" she answered sleepily. "Is everything okay?"

"Yes, and sorry for calling so late. Something extraordinary has come to my attention."

He explained.

"*Mon dieu!*" Pip exclaimed when he finished. "This is amazing, Marty! Will we sail to Mirissa tomorrow then?"

"I'm going to fly with the reporter to get there as soon as possible. I don't want anything to happen to that skull. I was hoping you'd be okay piloting the *Oannes* on your own?"

"Why—yes, of course. I pilot her myself on all our research expeditions, *mon capitaine*. Do you not have confidence in me?"

"One hundred percent confidence, Pip. I just wanted to make sure you'd be comfortable piloting her on your own."

"I am comfortable, do not worry. If I set sail at first light,

I should reach Mirissa by midafternoon. We will rendezvous then."

$$\triangle\triangle\triangle$$

Marty returned to the salon, poured himself more whiskey, then sat in the chair in front of his computer. After a cursory glance at his emails (all junk mail), he found himself on You-Tube, typing his name into the search bar. The top result was Part 1 of the Netflix documentary, which the streaming giant had uploaded themselves, and which had more than fifty-million clicks. Below it were spinoff documentaries and commentaries from the likes of National Geographic, Harvard University, the BBC, and Discovery Channel. He'd watched all of them, and none were flattering.

Now, as he often did against his better judgement when he'd had a few too many drinks, he clicked on the first clip of the documentary and sat back with a clenched jaw.

Yet for the first time since the show's merfolk was discovered to be a phony, he didn't experience bitterness and resentment at seeing himself advocating it on camera.

In fact, he felt wonderfully invigorated, if not vindicated.

He would show all those assholes in the media and academia that they had laughed at the wrong guy.

CHAPTER 6

Merfolk: From the Deep. The making-of the original Netflix documentary.

M arty sat on a stool in a soundproofed film studio in Central London. The small room featured a lighting grid attached to the ceiling and a green screen behind him. The air-conditioning was cranked full blast. He wore a worsted wool suit and blue-and-white striped tie. A twenty-something hipster named Gus stood behind a digital television camera on a pneumatic pedestal. A similarly aged girl named Jamie, dressed all in black, was adjusting a large white reflector to his right. The acclaimed Welsh director Fat Mike stood in one corner, talking animatedly on his phone. Fitting his sobriquet, he was an obese man with a moon face and a beard formed from manicured stubble that covered only the first of his two chins. He wore baggy jeans, a sports jersey, and a Dodgers baseball cap, the brim pulled snugly down his brow so it pooled his eyes in shadows.

Abruptly he hung up the phone and came over to stand next to the camera pedestal. "How's everything goin'?" he asked in a high-pitched, squeaky voice that belied his size. "We ready to shoot?"

"Ready," Gus said.

"Ready," Jamie said.

"All righty then. How you doin', Double M?"

"Freezing," he said.

Mike belched laughter. "Yeah, well, you don't want all these lights to melt you, do ya? So this is gonna be pretty straightforward. You tell us everything you know about merfolk. We'll do the editing and cutting, mix what you have to say with our footage and some filler, and Bob's your uncle."

"Sounds easy enough. What do you want me to start with?"

"Like I said, it doesn't really matter when we take it to the cuttin' floor. But…I don't know, somethin' pretty straight forward. How about the legends? Legends come from somewhere, don't they? So we're all ready?"

The girl joined the hipster behind the camera. They both gave a thumbs up.

"All righty then," Fat Mike said, sinking his bulk into a foldable wood-framed director's chair with FAT MAN emblazoned on the canvas back. "In five, four, three, two…roll camera."

"Rolling," the hipster said.

"Marker."

Jamie held the slate in front of the camera which stated the scene and take number. She clapped the sticks together.

"Action!"

Marty looked into the camera lens. "Merfolk," he began, "have been around since the beginning of recorded history. The first known reference appeared painted on cave walls in the Stone Age roughly 30,000 years ago." He thought he sounded professional and authoritative, just as he'd practiced at home in front of the mirror. "The earliest written mention of a merman," he went on, "dates back over 5,000 years to the ancient Babylonian deity, Oannes, who's described as having the upper body of a human and the tailed lower body of a fish. The earliest mention of a mermaid dates back at least 3,000 years to Atargadis, an ancient Syrian goddess who is similarly described. In Greek mythology, you have the son of Poseidon and Amphitrite, Triton, the messenger of the sea, often depicted as a merman blowing into a conch shell. Coincidentally, you might also recognize him as the father of Ariel in the Disney movie."

Nobody cracked a smile.

"The Romans and Chinese," Marty continued, "made numerous references to merfolk in their histories, as did the Arabians and Persians in their famous folklore, *Arabian Nights*. In Ireland, we find the Merrow; in Scotland, the Ceasg; and in Japan, the Ningyo, all variants of half-human/half-fish creatures. Mainland Europe has the Melusine, a fresh-water mermaid sometimes depicted as having two tails, like the mermaid in the Starbucks logo. Several modern religions such as Hinduism worship merfolk-like deities to this day."

"And that's a cut!" Fat Mike said halfheartedly, shifting his bulk as if uncomfortable in the chair. "This is good stuff, Double M, but maybe tone down the pop culture references, yeah? Now what about actual sightings? Eyewitness accounts and all that? Can you go there?"

"I thought the Disney and Starbucks references would appeal to—"

"No, they were shite, Marty. Gotta be brutally honest. Absolute shite. We don't want to trivialize any of this, yeah?"

"I suppose…"

"Just keep doin' what you're doin'. You look good. Knowledgeable. That's what we want, what matters. So eyewitnesses?"

"Sure."

Fat Mike nodded. "Still rollin'?"

"Still rolling," the hipster replied.

Fat Mike pointed a finger gun at Marty and pulled the trigger. "Action."

Marty collected himself and said, "Beyond the myth and lore regarding merfolk, there have also been countless eyewitness reports of fish-tailed humanoids in our oceans and seas. In fact, there have been more high-publicized sightings of merfolk over the centuries than any other creature unknown to science. In 1493, Christopher Columbus chronicled in his ship's logbook that he and his crew encountered three mermaids with distinctive human facial features off the coast of what's now the Dominican Republic. In 1560, a group of Jesuits caught seven merfolk in their fishing nets off the coast of Ceylon, present-day Sri Lanka. The Viceroy of India, a learned physician, dissected the bodies himself before numerous witnesses. In 1603, several farmers of good reputation observed a mermaid off the coast of Wales for more than three hours. A few years later, in 1608, Henry Hudson encountered a mermaid that he described as having flowing black hair, white skin, and the fully developed breasts of a woman. In 1723, a Danish Royal Commission tasked with proving that merfolk didn't exist ended up discovering a merman near the Faroe Isles. In 1739, newspapers reported that sailors of the English ship *Halifax*, recently returned from the East Indies, confessed to eating mermaid flesh. In 1830, a group of locals cutting seaweed on the island of Benbecula, off the west coast of Scotland, witnessed what appeared to be a 'woman in miniature' swimming with impossible ease and grace in the churning sea. A few days later the creature washed ashore at Culle Bay, where it was witnessed by the entire town and described as having dark hair, tender white flesh, the breasts of a woman, and a lower body like that of a salmon's, lacking the scales. Three years later, in the Shetland Isles, which consist of about a hundred islands just north of Scotland, an esteemed natural history professor captured a merman, which he described as short-haired and monkey-faced. And in 1890, in the nearby Orkney Isles, hundreds of eyewitnesses reported sightings of a black-headed, white-bodied creature that became known as the Deerness Mermaid. Reports of similar sightings continued throughout the 19th and early 20th centuries, though they were increasingly ignored by the major newspapers of the times. The age of science—including the biological sciences—had dawned, and people began to dispute or dismiss what they couldn't comprehend."

Marty paused, thinking that was a good place to break. Fat Mike, however, nodded at him encouragingly.

Marty continued: "So what should we make of all these eyewitness reports? Truth? Fiction? Group hysteria? Mistaken identity? Skeptics tend to believe they're the product of the latter. Identifying animals in water, they argue, is inherently problematic, given that eyewitnesses typically only see a small part of the creature that is not submerged. When you add poor and distant viewing conditions, positively identifying even a known creature such as a human-sized manatee or dugong can prove difficult. A glimpse of a head or flipper or tail just before it dives under the waves—and voila, you have a merfolk."

He paused again, but this time for dramatic emphasis.

"If you ask me, I've always thought this argument to be bollocks. After all, we're not talking about a single eyewitness report. We're talking about thousands, from isolated geographical regions around the world, and over the course of five millennia. Can all these scholars and scientists and explorers and entire townships be wrong? All making the same misidentification? All confusing mythology with reality? Which, it's important to point out, are not always diametrically at odds with one another.

"In other words, just because something is considered a myth or legend doesn't mean it's not based in science. Eyewitness accounts of giant squid, for instance, have been common among mariners since ancient times. They're the basis for the Kraken and the Lusca and the Scylla, in Scandinavian, Caribbean, and Greek folklore respectively. Mythologies based on realities. And speaking of giant squid—despite being the largest invertebrate on Earth, it was only in 2004 that researchers in Japan snapped the first images of one. You'd think such a large animal would be hard to miss, wouldn't you? But we must remember that most of our planet is covered with water—and only about five percent of that has been explored. Indeed, most of what we know about giant squid comes from dead carcasses that have floated to the surface and were found by fishermen. Now, imagine if giant squid were not solitary animals but social ones. Social animals like us that perform death rituals such as burying their dead. Intelligent animals like us that learn and adapt. Intelligent animals that have learned and adapted to keep far away from fishing nets—and encounters of any kind with humans.

"So if you ask me, yes, the universal misidentification of merfolk is hogwash. Merfolk do exist. Their mythology arose from the reality of their existence. Live specimens have been recorded in the past, and it was just a matter of time before they were re-corded with modern technology. And that time is now."

"And that's a cut!" Fat Mike bellowed, heaving himself to his feet. "I knew you were the man for this doco, Double M! I just knew it! You're going to be a smash hit, mate. People around the world are going to love you."

△△△

Marty woke at a little past midnight in the chair in front of his computer desk. A video he didn't recognize was playing on You-Tube. He remembered sitting down to watch the Netflix documentary, though he didn't think he got through more than ten minutes before he passed out.

He slapped the laptop lid closed, shuffled below deck to the master stateroom, and flopped down on the antique four-poster bed. Despite being bone-weary and still drunk, he found it difficult to fall back asleep.

In the end, he tossed and turned into the early morning before waking at five a.m. to his radio alarm blasting AC/DC's latest single. He cranked the volume and began packing a small carry-on.

PART 2
Mirissa

"The difference between a Miracle and a Fact is exactly the difference between a mermaid and a seal."
—*Mark Twain*

CHAPTER 7

MARTY

Airports are the great equalizer. Every country, wealthy or otherwise, has one. You can be in Frankfurt Airport or Kuwait Airport, New York's JFK or Peru's Jorge Chávez, Paris' Charles de Gaulle or Moscow's Domodedovo, and they're all the same: clean, organized, modern.

Bandaranaike International Airport was no different. The Uber ride through the beat up, sometimes slummy streets of Colombo spoke to the country's poverty. But you wouldn't know that inside Bandaranaike. Stepping through the automatic glass doors, Marty could have been anywhere in the world.

He made his way to the Cinnamon Air ticket counters where he'd agreed to meet Jacky. Dressed in khaki shorts, a green blouse, and stacked sandals, she stood with her suitcase at the entrance to the check-in queue.

She saw him approach and smiled. "Good morning, Marty."

"We're almost twins," he said, glancing down at his khaki pants and lime-green golf shirt.

"Except my clothes aren't from The Gap."

"Actually, they're from a Nike store."

"Nike sells khakis?"

"They're golf pants—"

Jacky's eyes widened. "Rad!"

Marty turned to see Radhika clad in a wide-brimmed straw hat and sunglasses. She was hurrying toward them, all smiles and waves. "Surprise, fans!" she greeted, throwing her arms wide and hugging Jacky. She tapped her cheek with a finger, and Marty planted an obligatory kiss there.

He immediately asked, "What the hell are you doing here, Rad?"

"I'm coming with you! I wasn't planning to. But I was up early, had nothing to do—I'm not filming again until next month—and decided this could be quite the adventure, after all. So I bought a ticket online and here I am!"

"I'm happy you're here," Jacky said.

"Marty doesn't look happy. Marty—can't you at least *pretend* you're happy to see me?"

"I don't like surprises. And what's with the shirt?"

She was wearing a fitted pink tee-shirt emblazoned with the black silhouette of Bigfoot.

"I wanted to get into the spirit of things, but I didn't have anything mermaidish, so I figured this would do. You don't like it?"

"It's not condescending at all."

"It's *fun*, Marty. Live a little." The head of a tiny Pomeranian emerged from a rattan beach bag that was slung over her shoulder. It yapped happily.

"You brought a *dog*?"

"Yes, I did," she said in baby-talk while kissing the Pomeranian between its fluffy ears. It licked her cheek affectionately. "My baby goes everywhere with me. Don't you, Marty? Yes, you do."

Marty frowned. "Who are you talking to?"

"My dog."

"His name's Marty?"

"So?"

"You named your dog after *me*?"

Rad laughed. "You and your ego! I've had Marty since he was a pup, long before I met you. Don't you remember? When we met, and you introduced yourself, I told you that my dog's name is Marty too. I named him after Martin Sheen. *The Subject Was Roses* is one of my all-time favorite movies."

"All right, people," Jacky said, glancing at her gold wristwatch, "why don't we move this fascinating conversation to the queue.

The flight's boarding in half an hour, and we want to be on it."

△△△

A bus drove the dozen or so passengers across the runway to a small single-engine turboprop with a purple and white livery. The sun was now high in the sky, brightening the morning. Marty followed Jacky and Rad up a small set of aluminum stairs into the hatch of the aircraft. A smiling flight attendant checked their boarding passes and waved them down the cramped fuselage.

"I'm right here," Rad said, stopping in the aisle. "2B."

"I'm 2A," Marty said, slightly stooped to avoid brushing his head on the ceiling.

"I'm 8D," said Jacky.

"Why wouldn't they put us all together? We checked in together, and the flight's not full."

"It's Sri Lanka, Marty. Your British standards are set too high."

A mustachioed man behind Marty cleared his throat impatiently.

"I guess we'll see you when we land," Marty said, shuffling sideways to his window seat.

Rad settled into the seat next to him, resting her beach bag on her lap. The toy dog—Marty couldn't bring himself to think of it as his namesake—was looking at him with its beady black eyes, its tongue lolling out of the side of its mouth.

"Has it flown before?" he asked.

She nodded. "He flies with me all the time."

"He doesn't bark?"

"Marty never barks."

"Do you have to call him that?"

"It's his name."

"I know, but... Can't you call him M or something, at least for today?"

"How about I call *you* Em? How would you like that? It's a girl's name, for heaven's sake."

"And that dog oozes masculinity," he mumbled, lifting his butt to retrieve the ends of his seatbelt. He fastened the buckles, leaned back in the seat, and closed his eyes.

"What are you doing?" Rad asked him.

"Wake me when we land," he said.

"I thought you'd be too excited to sleep. This skull is like the holy grail for you."

"I didn't get much sleep last night."

"I didn't either, but I'm not taking a nap."

"Why didn't you get much sleep?"

"I stayed up watching your documentary. It's on YouTube these days. Did you know that?"

Marty scowled. "Why the hell did you watch that?"

"I'm still trying to get my head around you being The Merdoc. I wanted to see what all the hype was about."

"Please stop calling me The Merdoc. It's pejorative."

"I think it's a good nickname. Reminds me of The Horse Whisperer, and The Merdoc is way better than The Mermaid Whisperer. By the way, it's really good. The documentary. *You're* really good. I don't know why you're so embarrassed by it."

He opened his eyes. "Because it was a lie, Rad, all of it!"

"No, it wasn't, Marty. The video of the..." She lowered her voice. "The mermaid might have been a fake. But what you talked about, all that stuff about historical sightings of merfolk and their physiologies and social structures, that was based on research and honest speculation. You should be proud."

He turned slightly in his seat to look behind him. A teenager wearing a large set of headphones sat directly behind him. An elderly woman reading the snack list was behind Rad. Neither were paying them any attention.

He faced forward again and said, "I propagated a worldwide hoax."

She said, "So what? The documentary was entertaining, and it made you famous. Doesn't sound too bad to me." She was silent a moment before adding, "You never said they had wonky foreheads. You never once mentioned echolocation."

"Because their mermaid in the video didn't have a melon. Their special effects guys either never thought about giving it one or, more likely, they wanted to keep it a stereotypical mermaid: beautiful, exotic, seductive. Anyway, I'm done talking about this, Rad."

"Done! I've known you for two years, Marty, and I hardly know anything about you! I think you owe it to me to talk about whatever I want to know."

"Not the documentary."

"Come on! So it was a hoax. So you got punked. So what. Can't you let it go?"

"Let it go?" he said angrily. "*It ruined my life*, Rad. How do you let something like that go?"

"I mean, you're here now, in Sri Lanka. You have a *new* life. You're on the verge of the greatest discovery of your career. Live in the moment."

"I'm trying to."

"If you want my opinion, to do that you need to be at peace with yourself. And for that, you need to talk about what's eating you up. You know what they say about repressing negative emotions—"

"I'm not repressing anything. Jesus, I'm simply trying to leave the past behind and move on with my life. Why don't you get that? If my family died in a house fire, you wouldn't be prodding me to talk about them, would you?"

"If their memories were eating you up inside, I would."

Shaking his head again, he closed his eyes again.

The Pomeranian yapped twice. Radhika murmured to it, using Marty's name over and over, which made her impossible to tune out.

△△△

"Marty?"

He didn't know if Rad was talking to him or the dog. He cracked open one eye and looked sideways at her.

"Were you sleeping?"

He'd been dozing in the netherworld between sleep and non-sleep. "Was," he said emphatically. "What is it?"

"I've been thinking about something you mentioned in the documentary."

He closed his eye.

She elbowed him sharply.

"Ow!" he said, glaring at her. "Give it a rest, Rad."

"You know when you were talking about whales?" she went on, unperturbed. "You mentioned how they used to live on land, evolving from small animals into the biggest fish in the ocean."

"Mammals," he corrected her. "The biggest mammals in the ocean."

The general theory regarding the evolution of whales was that around fifty million years ago there were several different groups of amphibious hoofed mammals that favored hunting along the rivers and estuaries and salt marshes of prehistoric Asia, as the bodies of water allowed a convenient escape from predators. Some of the mammals were deer-like and racoon-sized, while others were more crocodile-like with large jaws, or otter-like with powerful tails. Over time, their descendants spent more and more time in their aquatic environments, and their bodies adapted for swimming. Their forelimbs became flippers and their tails' flukes, their hind legs disappeared, and blubber replaced their fur coats to keep them warm and stream-lined. The now fully aquatic mammals began to expand their ranges and diversify, eventually giving rise to the two groups of whales alive today: baleen filter feeders that lost their teeth (such as blue and humpback whales), and those that kept their teeth (such as dolphins, porpoises, orcas, and sperm whales).

"Mammals, fish, whatever," said Rad. "My point is, those tiny land animals became the biggest things in the ocean."

"It's the best-documented example of macroevolution in the fossil record." Marty stifled a yawn. "The buoyancy of water prevents growth restrictions, and the bigger you are, the easier it is to stay warm."

"And whales need to stay warm because they're warm-blooded?"

"That's right."

"Merfolk are mammals too…"

He sighed. "What are you getting at, Rad?"

"Well, merfolk are warm-blooded and need to keep warm too. You mentioned in the documentary they've been spotted all over the world, not just in tropical waters. So…maybe merfolk are gigantic, like whales? Or at least a lot bigger than us?"

"You saw the skull. It was the same size as yours or mine."

"It could have belonged to an infant."

Marty rubbed his forehead, sensing a headache looming. "I doubt that very much."

"Why?"

"I just do."

"Come on, Marty! Humor me. I think I'm onto something. This is a totally feasible—"

"It's not," he told her curtly. "Look, whales as you think of them started inhabiting the oceans forty to thirty million years ago, okay? They were solitary animals, and there were some damn big predators in the oceans then. Being large helps an animal keep warm, but it's also a good deterrent against getting eaten. That's perhaps the most important reason why whales grew so large. Merfolk, on the other hand, are presumably intelligent and social, like us. A more fitting aquatic equivalent would be dolphins, which are intelligent and live in pods with strong social bonds. They work together to hunt and deter threats. They don't need to be the size of a house to get by."

The flight attendant parked the service trolley in the aisle next to them. Rad ordered a coffee with sugar and cream, while Marty demurred.

"Yes, he'd like a coffee too, please," Rad insisted.

"No, I would not, thank you," he said.

"Okay, two for me then."

The flight attendant poured two coffees, set them on Rad's fold-down tray, and moved on to the next row of passengers.

"I told you I don't want one," Marty told her.

"Ow! Too hot!" she said, sipping one of the coffees and setting it back down on her tray. "I ordered you one because I know you too well, Marty. You're going to see me enjoying mine, and you're going to ask for a sip. I'd rather you just have your own."

"I'm not going to ask for a sip."

"You always take food off my plate when we're out for dinner."

"That's different."

"You also finish my alcohol if I don't want it."

The looming headache began to throb, and it wasn't solely from being tired and hungover. Rad could be maddening sometimes. Still, he probably should have asked the flight attendant for a glass of water.

"Are you my fan, Marty?"

"What?"

"Are you my fan?"

"Of your show?" He shrugged. "I watch it…sometimes."

"So you're my fan?"

"Sure, Rad. I guess. I'm your fan."

"Well, I take care of my fans." She nodded to the second coffee.

He eyed it apprehensively, at the same time realizing he was parched.

"Take it," she pressed. "I got it for you."

"What the hell," he said, and took the coffee.

CHAPTER 8

MARTY

T hey landed thirty minutes later at Koggala Airport, an Air Force base that served both military and domestic flights. The runway was a thin strip of tarmac in a large field. They followed a path to a World War II-era terminal, where Rad and Jacky popped into the restroom and Marty purchased a bottle of water from a vending machine. When they regrouped in front of the building, they hailed a small yellow taxi, Marty getting in the front with the driver, the girls in the back. Thankfully the car was air-conditioned, and the planned roughly thirty-minute drive to Mirissa Beach was pleasant—until the driver was forced to pull over due to a flat tire. He didn't have a spare and walked with them along the oceanside, two-lane highway for nearly a kilometer until they reached a strip of residences and stores with cracked and crumbling walls and corrugated iron roofs (or in some cases, no roofs at all). A few people were sitting in front of their shops doing not much of anything, while wild fowl scratched around in the dirt and stray dogs stretched lazily on their sides in the shade. The only available transportation for hire, it turned out, was a red auto rickshaw that incongruously flew an American flag. Like all the trishaws (as they were colloquially referred to), it featured three wheels and three seats, one in the front and two in the back. Jacky and Rad climbed into the passenger cabin. Marty insisted he could fit on the bench seat with them, but they said he was too sweaty from the long walk.

Which left him no other choice than to stand on the trishaw's back bumper and hold onto the metal luggage bars that spanned the canvas roof.

The driver pushed the two-stroke engine up to sixty kilometers an hour on the two-lane road. The wind blasted Marty's ears and tore at his clothes as he hung on for his life, alternating between curses and prayers. When they came upon a herd of cattle blocking the road, the driver slowed to navigate through the oblivious beasts.

Marty leapt off the sheet-metal contraption, grateful to have his feet on solid ground once again.

The trishaw continued onward without him.

"You bloody idiot!" he shouted. "Stop!"

It pulled over on the dirt shoulder. Jacky and Rad tugged back the curtains and stuck their heads out the windows.

"What are you doing, Marty?" Rad called.

"Did you fall off?" asked Jacky.

He was too angry to reply and trudged silently to the vehicle. When he reached it, he said, "Move over, Rad."

"No way, Marty. You're even sweatier than before!"

"Maybe that's because for the last ten minutes I've been trying not to die."

"Were we going too fast?" Jacky asked.

"Yes, you were going too bloody fast!" He glared at the maniac driver, a young man with a peach fuzz mustache. "What the bloody hell were you doing? You must have been going sixty kilometers an hour!"

He stared blankly, and Marty knew from his attempt to negotiate the fare earlier (which Jacky eventually settled in Tamil) that the kid barely spoke two words of English.

"Rad, *move over*," he said again.

"Sheesh," she said, but both she and Jacky scooted to the left. He squeezed in, so his thigh and shoulder pressed tightly against Rad. Her dog yapped in protest from the beach bag.

"I feel like a sardine in a tin," Jacky said.

"Comfy, Marty?" said Rad. "Because we're certainly not."

"Get moving," he grunted at the driver.

The kid stared, uncomprehending.

"Go!" Marty barked, pointing straight ahead. "Drive!"

ΔΔΔ

The sleepy roads of Mirissa were lined with bars, restaurants, surf rentals shops, pharmacies, a couple of tattoo parlors, hostels and guest houses, and a variety of residences, some of which were rather grand in size and structure (though just as dilapidated as everything else). The main street ran parallel to the beach and was livelier than the others, populated with loitering locals and tourists strolling at the leisurely pace of people with nothing better to do.

"I like the laid-back vibe here," Jacky said. "It's romantic. Has Marty ever taken you here, Rad?"

"I wish. He hasn't taken me anywhere."

"But you've been dating for two years."

"I told you last night, Jacky," Marty said, "Rad and I are not dating. We see each other every now and then."

"I don't know about you, Marty," she replied. "But if I eat a sandwich every now and then, I'm still eating."

The driver swerved across the road and stopped on a patch of gravel before a two-story white building. Marty couldn't read the teal sign, as the white letters were written in Sri Lankan, but Jacky confirmed this was the Sharks Board Maritime Center, the NGO where the American oceanographer worked.

They exited the trishaw, and Marty's excitement bloomed.

We're here. The skull's right inside that building.

He dug some money out of his pocket and paid the driver what they'd agreed upon, including a little-deserved tip.

He knocked on the building's glass door. A short, pretty girl in her early twenties opened it. He supposed she was relegated to door duty because she was the youngest female in the office. Misogyny and patriarchy were still entrenched in Sri Lankan society.

Then again, he thought, peering past her into the office and seeing a lot of young women, *maybe her desk is simply closest to the door.*

The girl placed her palms together and bowed. "*Ahyubowan,*" she said, a customary greeting that meant *Long life.* "Can I help you?"

"I'm Jacqueline DeSilva," Jacky said. "I spoke to Dr. Montero yesterday. She's agreed to sit for an interview with me. Is she here?"

"Welcome, ma'am. Dr. Montero is working in the shed. Follow me, please."

The girl led them through the office to a heavy wood door, and they stepped into a morgue-like room. The roller door that faced the beach was open, letting in bright sunlight and fresh air.

The American stood at a stainless-steel necropsy table with plastic vials, a tin bucket, and a large three-ring binder. Marty was surprised by her stature. He was six-foot-one, and she was only an inch or two shorter. Blonde-haired and blue-eyed, she wore a mustard-colored blouse rolled up at the sleeves, baggy denim shorts, and a pair of white Reeboks.

"Dr. Elsa Montero," Jacky said, crossing the room and extending her hand. "Thank you so much for agreeing to see me."

"I must say," she replied, plucking off a blue latex glove and shaking her hand. "I didn't know you'd be bringing an entourage." She gave Marty and Rad a brief smile.

"This is Dr. Martin Murdoch and Radhika Fernandez. I'm sorry, I should have let you know others would be accompanying me."

"Miss Fernandez, I believe I've seen you on the television?"

"Mad Rad, that's me," she said, bobbing a curtsy.

Marty was scanning the room for the skull but didn't see it anywhere. He stepped toward the necropsy table and peeked into a large tin bucket. It was filled with what looked and smelled like feces. Wrinkling his nose, he backed away.

"That's excrement from a blue whale," Dr. Montero told him. "Not very easy to come by, let me say."

"You never thought of collecting old coins or stamps instead?"

"I don't collect it. I study it."

Rad said, "You analyze *whale feces*?"

Dr. Montero nodded. "To understand better how iron passes through the ocean's food chain, yes. A blue whale's favorite meal is krill. It will eat millions of them a day, up to three tons. Its iron- and nutrient-rich excrement feeds algae, which feeds more krill, which feeds other blue whales. It's an amazing cycle, isn't it? Hopefully, the more we learn about krill stock, the better we can manage and conserve it. Which in turn will help whale numbers begin to recover."

"Which is what we all want," Marty said.

Dr. Montero gave him a curious look. "Do I know you, Dr. Murdoch? You also seem familiar…"

"He's The Merdoc," Rad offered happily.

Marty shot her a look.

"The Merdoc?" Dr. Montero said, frowning. Then understanding lit her eyes. She seemed about to slap her forehead before stopping herself. "Of course! Dr. *Martin Murdoch*. I watched your documentary a few years back." The understanding turned analytical. She glanced at Jacky. "What kind of story are you writing exactly, Miss DeSilva?"

"Just Jacky. And the story…well, that depends on what Dr. Murdoch has to say about the skull."

"You believe it belonged to a mermaid?" she stated flatly to Marty.

"Given I've only seen a brief video clip of it, I'm not in a position to make a judgement. You're still in possession of it, I hope?" The question came across as more fraught than he would have liked.

"It's lucky that Miss DeSilva called me when she did—"

"Jacky, please."

"Then you can call me Elsa. And had you called an hour later yesterday, Jacky, I would already have turned the skull over to the authorities. However, I was able to talk them into letting me hold onto it for the time being. So to answer your question, Dr. Murdoch, yes, it's still in my possession." She went to the steel shelves lining one of the room's walls and returned with a cardboard box. She set it on the necropsy table, peeled back the top flaps, and lifted out the bleached-white skull.

Marty didn't take his eyes off it. "May I?" he asked, holding out his hands.

Dr. Montero passed him the skull. As he turned it this way and that in his hands, he experienced the same unfiltered wonder that he did when first viewing Fat Mike's merfolk video. Yet that had taken him time to digest and to ultimately conclude that he believed what he was seeing. This was different. The skull was in his hands. It was tangible. There was no digital magic between him and it. There was no convincing himself this time, no wishful thinking.

The skull was authentic. It was merfolk. He felt it with every fiber in his being.

To nobody in particular, he said, "It's so very much human, isn't it? The bulbous cranium, the flat face. But it's different too. Look here." He drew a finger along the top of the skull. "A sagittal crest, which is only found in some early hominins. And here, the brow ridge is quite pronounced, one of the last traits lost on the path to modern humans. But, my God, look at that frontal bone! It's not receding as it is in apes, and it's not vertical as it is in humans. It's *protuberant*. Look at it!" He glanced from one face to the next—they ran the gamut from delighted (Jacky) to skeptical (Rad) to plain unreadable (Dr. Montero)—and added, "To be clear, these are only my initial, visual observations... Dr. Montero, I've seen the look on your face far too many times from the orthodoxy to not know it well. You think I'm an out-and-out crank peddling cryptid pseudoscience."

"I've followed your work for many years, Dr. Murdoch," she said. "I find your aquatic ape theory fascinating. However, to be perfectly frank, I have yet to see any evidence to convince me of the reality of mermaids and mermen, and this skull has not changed my position on that." She saw that he was about to interrupt and held up a hand. "The enlarged forehead struck me as quite unusual, certainly. Indeed, it compelled me to do some armchair research last night, and my conclusion is the skull is that of a person who suffered from cloverleaf deformity."

Rad said, "Cloverfield deformity?"

Marty said, "Clover*leaf*. It's a genetic disorder in which mutated genes cause the sutures on a skull to fuse together prematurely. The results are facial deformities such as abnormally formed eye sockets, flat nasal bridges, a small upper or lower jaw —and a misshapen head, often bulging at the front. However," he added, "it's usually noticeable at birth and corrected with surgery."

"Perhaps in a developed country it is," Dr. Montero said. "But I should remind you, we're not in a developed country."

"No, we're not," he agreed. "Yet while cloverleaf deformity may account for the protuberant forehead, it does not and cannot explain the other abnormalities I noted."

"I'm not familiar enough with the anatomy of the human skull to agree or disagree with you. I'm an oceanographer, not a forensic anthropologist—as are you, Dr. Murdoch."

Marty smiled tightly. Scientists could be some of the most obstinate people on the planet. They understood that disciplined methodology—the rational interpretation of observational evidence—was the only way integrity could be maintained during the scientific process; the only buffer between science and snake oil, so to speak. Yet when faced with observational evidence that was at odds with their worldviews, critical thinking and healthy skepticism all too often devolved into bias and stubbornness.

He had hoped better from Dr. Montero.

"I would be happy to hear the opinion of a forensic anthropologist," he told her, finally setting the skull back in the cardboard box. "If you know of any in town, please invite them over. In the meantime my assistant is piloting my research vessel from Colombo to Mirissa as we speak. She should be here by noon. I have a DNA lab aboard that could settle the matter more definitely than the opinion of any medical examiner. That is, if you don't object to a genetic test being performed on the skull, Dr. Montero?"

"No objections at all. In fact, I would be very interested in your findings." She turned to Jacky. "Now, Miss DeSilva—Jacky— about the interview. I'm still happy to sit down with you, but I want you to know beforehand that I won't be speculating about anything outside of my field of expertise. Which is to say, I'll answer any questions you have about the great white necropsy, but I won't opine about the skull."

"That's fair enough," Jacky said.

"Come inside the office with me then. It's air-conditioned, and there's a machine that brews passable coffee. Dr. Murdoch, Miss Fernandez, a colleague of mine filmed the necropsy. Perhaps you'd be interested in viewing it in the meantime?"

ΔΔΔ

The necropsy was over thirty minutes long, and when Marty and Rad came to the dissection of the shark's stomach near the end of it, they were fascinated as Dr. Montero removed the skull from what appeared to be a soup of putrefied whale blubber. Marty replayed this section of the video several times.

He slumped back in his chair and said, "I think we can safely say that wasn't a hoax."

Rad said, "Unless they force-fed the skull to the shark while it was alive, or shoved the skull down its throat when it was dead."

"You really believe that?"

"Nope."

"Which leaves us with one of two scenarios. The skull either belonged to the unfortunate victim of cloverleaf deformity, or a fantastical creature that has populated the myths and legends of nearly every human culture since the dawn of civilization. Which do you think?"

"Does it matter?"

"No. But I'm curious."

Rad scowled. "You're such a dick sometimes, Marty."

He blinked in surprise. "What? Why? I mean, your opinion

matters to *me*. It just doesn't matter in the big picture, does it? Neither does mine, for that matter. Science alone will inform us if it's human or not."

"Smooth recovery, Merdoc."

Now Marty scowled. "All right. How about we address this Merdoc business once and for all? I'm sorry, Rad. All right? I'm sorry I wasn't transparent with you about who I am. It wasn't personal. I hate being known as The Merdoc. I hate it. I want nothing to do with that fool. I guess I didn't tell you everything because I was afraid you'd act like everybody else."

"And how's that?"

"You'd ridicule me. You'd call me The Merdoc. You'd do exactly what you've been doing since yesterday."

"I'm only pushing your buttons because you lied to me. If you told me the truth from the beginning—"

"What truth, Rad?" he snapped. "What lies, for that matter? I simply didn't tell you I was on a television show. If you never told me you had a television show because you didn't want to for whatever reason, I don't think I'd be all up in arms about it."

"That's not the same, Marty, and you know it. You were one of the most famous people on the planet for a while, or one of the most talked about at least. That's probably something you should tell the person you're fucking."

"Yes, you're right, Rad," he said, lowering his voice. "*Fucking*. And that's all it is, isn't it? What we're doing? Fucking. You've made it pretty bloody clear you don't want anything more than that, so I don't know where you get off—"

"*I've* made it clear?" she snapped back. "You call me maybe once a week, or once every two weeks. That's on you, not me."

"Why's it on me? You can call me—"

"You're the man, Marty! You call me, you chase me. That's how it works, nature's rules, from the lowliest insects all the way up to us. Courtship, ever hear of it? And besides, I *do* call you. I called you last night, didn't I?"

"What are you getting at, Rad? You want us to start dating? Get serious, get married, have kids? Is that what you want?"

She glowered at him. "Jesus, you really are a dick." She shot to her feet and stormed out of the shed.

"Rad!"

She disappeared from sight.

ΔΔΔ

When Dr. Montero and Jacky returned to the shed, Jacky said, "Where's Rad?"

"Beats me," Marty said. He was back at the necropsy table, examining the skull.

"She didn't just vanish into thin air, did she?"

He shrugged. "She went for a walk. I don't know where."

"You two had a fight, didn't you? You did. And let me tell you, Marty. I don't blame her for being pissed off with you. I'd be pissed off if the man I was dating turned out to be Dr. Jekyll and Mr. Hyde. I'd better go look for her. Which way did she go?"

"To the right," he said dismissively.

After Jacky left, Dr. Montero said, "You certainly have a way with women, Dr. Murdoch."

Marty let that slide and said, "Would you mind emailing me a link to that video when you have a chance?"

"That shouldn't be a problem," she told him. "What did you think of it?"

"You conducted the necropsy commendably, and the discovery of the skull was believable."

"Believable?" She appeared amused. "Of course it was believable. *It was a real necropsy.*"

"What I mean is, I've fallen for an elaborate mermaid hoax before..."

"And now you're seeing mermaid hoaxes everywhere? Let me be perfectly clear then, Dr. Murdoch. My colleagues and I didn't plant that skull. We're not chasing our fifteen minutes. I didn't solicit Miss DeSilva to come to Mirissa; she contacted me. Really, to think I orchestrated some sort of elaborate plan to lure you down here to lend credence to a publicity hoax is simply preposterous. Not to mention insulting."

"You're putting words in my mouth. I don't think any of that at all. I've been perfectly clear that I believe the skull to be authentic."

"You know...I envy you, Dr. Murdoch." She picked up the skull, studying it for a few silent moments. When she spoke, she seemed to be addressing it rather than him. "When I was a child, there were about a hundred beat-up National Geographic magazines in my family's basement. I used to pore over them for hours and hours on end. I always imagined I was one of the adventurer-scientists in the pictures, traveling the world over and seeing things that no one else would ever see firsthand. In high school I became fascinated with the seas and oceans and the secrets they held, and becoming an oceanographer was a no-brainer. It combined everything I loved: travel, discovery, mystery." She returned the skull to the table. "My point, Dr. Murdoch, is this. That was a long time ago. I'm forty-three years old now, and that magical sense of adventure I once held dear, that magical belief there were mysteries to be uncovered around every corner and beneath every wave, that's become a relic of the past. I don't know where it's gone, but it's gone." She smiled faintly at him. "But that's not the case with you, is it? The world is still mysterious and wondrous in your eyes. It must be..."

"Because I believe in merfolk?"

"Because you believe in something...so fantastic...yes."

Marty considered that—not sure whether it was a compliment or veiled insult—and said, "As you well know, Dr. Montero, marine biology is a mathematical and topographical map, or model, of our oceans and everything inside them. A scientist's personal beliefs relating to that model are irrelevant. All that matters is that he or she helps to create a more accurate model by uncovering more of its attributes, and thus knowledge and truth. And that is exactly what I am committed to discovering: knowledge and truth. I am not some self-delusional Pollyanna.

I don't believe in merfolk because I *want* to believe in them, because of some boyish wonder. I believe in them because my research has built a very strong case for their existence, and I would be derelict in my duty as a marine biologist and scientist to not pursue that case, whether it is ultimately proved to be true or not."

"Yes, all scientists seek knowledge and truth. All scientists are curious. What I'm saying is that not all of them are passionate. I used to be passionate. Now…not so much. I suppose that is what I meant when I said I envy you. I envy your passion."

"Thank you, Dr. Montero. That is kind of you, and I appreciate your candor."

"Let's quit being so stuffy. Elsa is fine."

"As is Marty."

"Did we just agree on something?"

"Indeed we did," he said. Then, "Now that we're on more cordial terms, I'd like to ask you a few questions about the necropsy video, if I may? You discovered a whale vertebra in the shark's stomach."

"Two, in fact," she said, going to the steel shelves and retrieving another cardboard box. "Though the second one was post-video, after all the ruckus over the skull died down." She set the box on the necropsy table and opened the flaps.

Marty lifted out one of the irregular-shaped bones. It was large and unremarkable and clearly belonged to a whale. He returned it to the box. "Did you find any other bones post-video?"

"Those were it, I'm afraid. If it matters, during the morphometric assessment my colleague and I retrieved three stingray barbs from the great white's throat."

Marty raised an eyebrow. "Three?"

"That's not unusual. Great whites have a particular gastronomic preference for rays."

"But this particular great white also had a gastronomic preference for merfolk, which makes the three stingray barbs in its throat very interesting indeed."

"I'm afraid you've lost me."

"May I take a look at the barbs, Elsa?"

Elsa retrieved yet another box from the shelves, this one more closely resembling a shoebox. She set it before him and removed the lid.

The three stingray barbs rested on an old rag to prevent them from rolling around. He examined each one carefully and said, "Did you notice that they're all nearly identical in width and length?"

"You find that significant because…?"

"May I use that for a moment?" He indicated the microscope on the desk where he had watched the necropsy video.

She went to the desk, moved the laptop aside, and set the high-powered trinocular microscope in its place. Marty flicked it on and placed the stingray barb on the stage, arranging it so the base was beneath the objective lens. He pressed his eyes to the binocular eyepiece, twisted one knob, then another, bringing the specimen into focus. He magnified it with a higher objective and adjusted the diaphragm below the stage, reducing the light.

He sucked back a short, sharp breath.

CHAPTER 9

ELSA

Elsa watched Dr. Martin Murdoch as he studied each sting-ray barb under the microscope with growing excitement. When he glanced up at her, he was grinning like he'd won the lottery.

"You've got me curious," she admitted.

"Have a look for yourself."

He stood and gestured for Elsa to take the vacated seat. She sat and pressed her eyes to the microscope's eyepiece. After several long seconds she said, "What am I looking for?"

"Extraneous biological matter."

"You mean the green-pigmented structures?"

"Yes."

"Membrane-bound organelles. Richly colored chloroplasts. Chain-like compartments." She paused a beat, confused. "It's green algae, Marty. So what?"

"Keep looking."

"There are some brown-pigmented foreign body structures as well. Thick-walled, elongated cells, axially orientated." She looked up at him. "Wood cells?"

"Indeed."

She frowned in confusion. "I suppose I could understand a bit of algae growing on the stingray's barb. But what's wood tissue doing there?"

"It's not just on that barb, Elsa. *It's on the base of all three.*"

"Again, Marty—so what?"

"You told me you've followed my work," he said, pacing eagerly. "You should know then that I hypothesized that merfolk are a tool-wielding species, likely on par with early hominins."

Elsa now understood what had gotten him so animated. "You believe that these barbs were lashed onto sticks with some sort of aquatic plant? That they were the tips of...crude spears?"

"Spears or harpoons, yes. Is there any other explanation?"

Elsa kept her poker-face dutifully in place as she wondered how to proceed, how to make him see reason...and realizing in the process that such an effort would be futile. He was going to believe what he wanted to believe, what he had long ago programmed himself to believe.

She said, "There are countless other explanations, Marty."

"Name one."

"A lot of wood sinks to the ocean floor. It creates ecosystems for all kinds of fauna—including stingrays."

"Since when do stingrays attack wood? And the wood tissue was on the base of the barbs, Elsa, not the tips. Both the wood and algae tissue, on the base. Why would that be? Why only on the base, which would have been sheathed in the ray's tail before the barb broke off?"

"Marty..."

"Wood tissue on *all three barbs*, Elsa."

"You're making assumptions and leaping prematurely to conclusions."

"I know, I know." He ran a hand through his hair, fidgety, distracted. "I need to study the diagnostic anatomical characters of the wood and algae tissue to make exact identifications. I need to recreate a spear or harpoon with the identified material, test it under laboratory conditions, confirm it could be used as a viable weapon..."

"Marty..."

"Open your eyes, dammit!"

"My eyes are open!" she shot back. "As is my mind! But this is just"—a number of derisive adjectives crossed her mind before she blurted—"ridiculous."

He fumed. "Ridiculous? Really?" He shook his head. "No, why do I bother? What does it matter to me what you believe? I couldn't care less."

"I'm glad I'm not alone in the Marty-doesn't-care-what-you-think category."

Elsa turned to see Jacqueline DeSilva and Radhika Fernandez standing at the rollup door. It was the TV host who'd spoken. She held a green smoothie in one hand. Her dog was poking its head out of her beach bag, panting in the heat.

Marty wasted no time explaining to them the discovery of the extraneous biological matter on the stingray barbs.

Radhika said, "Spears? Merfolk use *spears*?"

Jacqueline said, "My God, this story is going to be huge!"

"All right, I've heard enough," said Elsa, holding up her hands, wanting out of the discussion before it became even more farcical. "I'm glad you're all excited about Marty's discovery. I wish I could be too. But it's time I get back to work. Marty, you can keep the skull until tomorrow. That should be long enough for you to perform whatever tests you wish—"

A deep, bovine blast of a foghorn sounded from outside.

"That must be Pip," Marty said, glancing at his wristwatch. "The girl has impeccable timing, doesn't she?"

CHAPTER 10

MARTY

Marty spent the next several hours in the dry lab on the *Oannes*. Amongst the other world-class diagnostic and research equipment were molecular capabilities for genetic experiments, including DNA and RNA extraction and analysis.

Legally, Marty likely needed permission from the police to extract a bone sample from the skull. If he were home in England, he would have sought such permission. But this was Sri Lanka, and he didn't think anybody would notice or care, and if someone did, a bribe would go a long way to soothe any hurt feelings.

After he had sterilized his equipment and suited up in protective gear, he drilled into the skull's foramen magnum, extracting a small piece of bone and crushing it into powder.

The mitochondrial DNA he was after was within the eukaryotic cells, in the fluid surrounding the nucleus. He broke open the wall of one eukaryotic cell using a special enzyme, spilling out its contents. The process was kind of like cracking open an egg into a bowl, except it occurred on the microscopic level. He isolated the mitochondria from the other organelles using centrifugation.

Then he got down to sequencing the genome.

CHAPTER 11

ELSA

E lsa spent the afternoon studying the whale feces and recording her findings. As was often the case, she worked into the evening and was the last one to leave the office. She locked up and was about to walk home when she changed her mind.

It was seven thirty p.m. Dr. Murdoch had had plenty of time to perform the DNA analysis of the skull, which meant he had more than likely already been confronted with the reality that it was human, after all. Elsa would not feel vindicated by this inevitable outcome. She felt sorry for Dr. Murdoch. To believe he had discovered evidence to support his life's work, and then to discover he was wrong…that would be devastating. Of course, he would have nobody to blame for that but himself.

Scientists are wrong all the time. Indeed, science can be defined as a system of self-correction that, through trial and error, eventually yields a closer understanding of how nature works. Therefore, an essential part of science is that scientists not only try to falsify their hypotheses to prove that they are true, but that they do so with an open mind. To become emotionally attached or obsessed with a particular theory is to set oneself up for almost certain disappointment.

Elsa went down the path between the SBMC building and the hostel, emerging on the beach. Dr. Murdoch's research vessel was moored at the end of the beach's pier, a large silhouette illuminated from within. She had seen it during the day, and it was an impressive ship, one that would cost more money than she would ever have in her lifetime.

Must be nice to be a trust fund kid, she thought with a dash of asperity. *But at least he's spending his inheritance on the pursuit of science, even if it is questionable science.*

Breathing in the brackish ocean air, she crossed the hard-packed sand and followed the pier to the boat. She could hear music, somebody playing a piano.

"Hello?" she called.

Nobody answered.

She ascended the gangway. To her right a pair of teak doors led to the ship's salon. Through adjacent windows she saw that the room was filled with opulent furniture and luxury textiles that could have been transplanted from a Baroque mansion. Dr. Murdoch sat before a glossy black piano, his back to her, halfway through a Billy Joel song. She went to the doors and eased one open, knocking on it at the same time to announce her presence.

The music stopped. Dr. Murdoch swiveled around on his little bench, surprise on his craggy, tanned face. Then he grinned.

"Elsa! What a surprise!" He got to his feet.

"Good evening, Marty. I'm sorry to disturb you. I thought Miss Fernandez and Miss DeSilva would be here with you."

"They're staying the night, yes. They went to the hot tub a little while ago."

"You have a hot tub on this ship?"

"I live on this floating bucket, and for the sake of my sanity, I believe I should be afforded a few luxuries, don't you agree? Now, I assume you're here about the genetic testing of the skull? Come with me. It's better you see for yourself."

ΔΔΔ

Dr. Murdoch led Elsa below deck to a sprawling state-of-the-art dry lab featuring all sorts of electronic equipment. Numerous computers streaming data ringed the room. Along one wall were cabinets, incubators, a safety hood for handling hazardous substances, and a large refrigerated unit. A petite woman sat in a chair at one workstation, studying information on an extra-wide monitor.

"Pip, this is the good Dr. Montero. Elsa, this is my assistant, Pip. She's from France, but her mother is Chinese, which is why she looks like that."

"Looks like *what*, Marty?" the woman said in French-accented English.

He shrugged. "Like you do."

"So you are a racist now?"

"You clearly have Asian and Caucasian features. I simply commented on that."

"You know some people are clumsy with their feet?" Pip said to Elsa. "Marty is clumsy with his mouth."

"Let me take back my words then," he said. "Elsa, this is my assistant, Pip. She's from France, but her mother is Chinese, which is why she's so stunning."

"Yes, that is better, *mon capitaine*." To Elsa, "You are here to see the result of the genetic test, yes?"

"That's right."

"Don't keep the good doctor waiting, my dear."

Pip rolled her eyes. "My dear? He only says that when he is in a really good mood. Me, I prefer the grumpy old Marty better." She manipulated the mouse. Several windows on the monitor disappeared before others appeared. "Here it is," she said, opening a final window.

Elsa bent closer and read the words on the screen:

DNA testing result:
Mitochondrial DNA with mutations unknown in any human, primate, or known animal.

Elsa reread the second sentence several times. Her immediate thought was that there had been a mistake, or the DNA sample was contaminated, something along those lines.

Because if what you're seeing is true…

Dr. Murdoch was grinning at her, his eyes alight.

"It's incredible, Marty," she said hesitantly.

"It's more than bloody incredible, Elsa. This is not the discovery of a new species of frog. It's a clearly human-like creature that is neither human nor ape! A human-like creature that, given its dramatic mutations, is very distant from Homo sapiens, Neanderthals, and Denisovans."

"How distant?"

"I've always believed the closest known ancestor to merfolk to be Australopithecus. AL 288-1, commonly known as Lucy, is the best-known specimen from the genus. Do you know much about her?"

"Only that she lived in Ethiopia about three million years ago, and she was named after a Beatles' song. Sorry, paleontology isn't my specialty."

"She was a hirsute chimp-like primate with a skull, jaws, and teeth more ape-like than human. Her arms were long and strong with curved fingers, her legs were short, and her shoulders were narrow, all of which were adapted for climbing and foraging in tree branches. But what makes her special is that she's the oldest known bipedal hominin. Her pelvis and knees and ankles all reflect a fully upright gait."

"Our oldest ancestor," Pip said, blowing a bubble with pink chewing gum.

"That we don't know for certain," Marty said. "The evolutionary process that gave rise to us wasn't linear. Numerous hominins lived side by side. There were variations amongst species, interbreeding, evolutionary experimentations, extinctions. When Lucy was discovered, about seven early hominins were known. Now there are at least twenty on record and the number keeps growing. However, Lucy's species is certainly a good candidate for Homo sapiens' direct ancestor—and an equally good candidate for merfolk's as well."

Elsa frowned. "Because it was bipedal? What am I missing, Marty? Last I heard, merfolk had fish tails for swimming, not legs for walking."

Pip's bubble popped. "I am going to the kitchen to make a sandwich," she said, taking the gum from her mouth and sticking it to the top of an empty Pepsi can. "I will leave Marty to eat your ear off, Dr. Montero. He has eaten mine off all day."

"It's *talk* your ear off, Pip. And forgive me for being excited about the biggest scientific discovery of the century."

Grinning, she sprang off her chair and left the dry lab.

"She makes idiomatic mistakes all the time," Marty said, "and the thing is, I think she does it on purpose. What was I saying?"

"You were making the case that Lucy's species was a good candidate as an ancestor to merfolk…because they were bipedal?"

"First a little context," he said. "During the Pliocene Epoch some 5 to 2.5 million years ago, the climate in East Africa was changing, becoming drier and cooler, reducing forested areas. For tree-dwelling species like Lucy's, this meant less food. For them to survive, they had to adapt. Bipedalism may have evolved in the trees as a method to walk along branches that would otherwise be too difficult to traverse on all fours. Yet as you know, it proved to have many benefits on the ground as well. It allowed australopithicines to see over tall grass for predators, and it allowed energy efficient locomotion in open places such as the expanding savanna. The latter was especially important because it let them roam farther and farther in search of food. All the way—"

"All the way to the ocean," Elsa finished.

Marty nodded. "You understand now. However, bipedalism not only got australopithicines *to* the ocean, it allowed them to thrive there. Walking erect let them keep their heads above the water as they waded in the shallows for food. Refined motor control in their hands let them use stone artifacts for cracking open shellfish."

"And according to your aquatic ape theory, they developed more and more aquatic adaptations over time, with one group returning to land and passing on their adaptations through their descendants all the way down the line to us, and another group remaining in the ocean and evolving into fully aquatic mammals."

"Exactomundo, my dear."

"Why did the one group return to land? If there was ample food in the ocean and less competition, why return to land where they would ultimately be driven to extinction?"

"The main factor was likely changing environmental conditions. Another would be the control and use of fire. Warmth, light, protection from predators, a way to create more advanced hunting tools, a method for cooking food. In other words, fire made life on land suddenly a lot more attractive."

"Only it wasn't Australopithicus but Homo erectus that mastered fire."

"Not true. Recent evidence suggests early hominins tamed fire as early as two million years ago. Australopithicus went extinct 1.9 million years ago. Which means the aquatic australopithicines that returned to land could have been using fire for quite some time before being out-competed by the genus Homo."

Elsa stopped playing the devil's advocate for a moment so she could process everything that Dr. Murdoch was telling her. In the ensuing silence, her first thought was: *It all makes sense. It all fits. It's just…crazy.*

Marty was watching her closely. Clearly he didn't think any of this was crazy, and he was waiting for her decree.

She pressed her hands against the sides of her face, her fingertips on her temples. "I'm trying to believe all of this Marty…"

"You don't have to *try*, Elsa. This is the scientific method at work, from hypothesis to testing and analysis. The DNA result is right there!" He jabbed a finger at the computer monitor.

"*Your* result, Marty. Your result is right there. You need replication, external review—"

"Yes, yes, of course. Which is why I'm having Pip send samples to three labs in London tomorrow morning. When they confirm —"

"There will still be skeptics," she interrupted. "Scientists, academics, they'll call it another Piltdown Man. Especially given—"

She stopped herself.

"Especially given, what, Elsa?" His eyes darkened. "Especially given my involvement with the Netflix documentary? Well, double fuck that! This is different. If they can't see that, fuck them too! All of them."

Elsa took a step backward, surprised and a little frightened by his vitriol.

Marty softened immediately. "I'm sorry. Forgive me. I just feel —" He shook his head. "I just feel... Well, you're right. There will always be skeptics. No matter what I publish, no matter my evidence, there will always be skeptics. I'll always be the god-damned Merdoc, won't I?"

Suddenly he seemed older, tired, a beat-down scientist who had been kicked one too many times.

"Will you be sailing back to Colombo?" she asked, to change the topic.

He blinked. "Sailing back to Colombo? Good Lord, no! My work here is just beginning. Tomorrow I'm going to attempt to hunt down the skipper that piloted the boat that hooked the great white."

Elsa frowned. "Whatever for?"

"Like us, merfolk are social creatures, or so I presume. Where there is one, there are likely many. Ergo, where the shark ate one seems like an ideal place to start looking for a live specimen."

"You're planning to look for a live merfolk?" She couldn't hide her surprise.

"Naturally. What do you think I built this boat for in the first place? Pip and I have been searching for a live specimen out here for nearly three years. Up until now, rather blindly, I admit. But if we can narrow in on where the shark ate the merfolk..."

"It's a good spot to start looking," she agreed. "*If* the great white hung around the same location after eating the merfolk. Because it could have eaten it half an ocean away from where it was eventually hooked on the fishing line."

"It could have, but I don't think it did. Ask yourself why there was only a skull in its gut? Why not a body? Where did that go...?"

Elsa did ask herself this—and the answer came immediately. A great white's stomach lining is peppered with secretory cells, some of which produce hydrochloric acid, so it's capable of breaking down bone. But animals that have a high bone-and-muscle to fat ratio, such as humans, are simply too much work to metabolize for too little caloric benefit. That's why almost all great white attacks on humans are exploratory bites: the sharks realize right away that humans are not worth eating. If it is assumed that merfolk are physiologically similar to humans, then the great white likely voided the merfolk from its stomach within twenty-four hours of swallowing it.

"The great white threw it up," she said. "And it was still in the process of throwing up the skull when it was caught."

"And given that the complete voiding of undigested matter in a great white's stomach can take up to three days, but usually no longer, I believe it's fair to assume the great white attacked the merfolk within seventy-two hours of getting hooked on the fishing line."

"That's an impressive deduction, Marty. Yet three days is still a heck of a long time. And great whites are fast swimmers."

"Indeed they are. But as you most certainly know, they have particular and predictable swimming habits. They will often spend months in one hunting ground before traveling hundreds if not thousands of kilometers through open ocean to reach another. Did you happen to measure the lipid stores in the great white's liver during the necropsy?"

She nodded. "They were nearly full."

"Well, there you go!" he said triumphantly. "Lipids fuel a great white's migratory swim, which mean it wasn't migrating when it was hooked but rather foraging in a hunting ground somewhere off the coast. Consequently, it wouldn't have traveled very far at all during the seventy-two hours in question. How many fishing charter operators do you think there are along the coast here?"

"Hundreds, most likely," she told him. "There are at least a dozen in Mirissa alone. However, I think I can save you a lot of time." She paused a beat. "I know where the shark was hooked."

CHAPTER 12

MARTY

"It was tagged!" Marty exclaimed, repeating what Elsa had just told him. It was the second-best news he'd received that day, and he couldn't believe his luck. Over the last two years, he'd become accustomed to disappointment and setbacks in his search for merfolk. That the stars were finally aligning for him seemed too good to be true.

Elsa said, "My colleagues at SBMC tagged it. We routinely tag several species of sharks to identify their migratory patterns, seasonal feeding movements, and daily habits."

"Was it an acoustic or SPOT tag?" he asked eagerly. Acoustic tags employ a basic transmitter-receiver technology, so a tagged shark has to come within range of an underwater receiver for its ID code to be recorded. SPOT tags, however, are the latest in tagging technology. They employ a much more powerful transmitter that communicates with a network of satellites each time the wet/dry sensor on the tag senses that the shark's fin has broken the surface of the water, allowing the shark to be tracked actively, and much more precisely, over broad geographical areas.

Elsa said, "Since 2018 we've used SPOT tags exclusively."

"Excellent!" Marty's mind raced. "Your data—how would I go about viewing it? If it's not too late, or too much trouble, I would happily come to your office…"

She was shaking her head. "Not necessary. It's all uploaded on the web. May I use this computer?"

"Absolutely."

Elsa sat in the seat Pip had vacated. As her hands darted across the keyboard, she said, "The young girl who showed you to the SBMC shed earlier has a PhD in information technology from Colombo University. She's now overhauling the digital side of our tracking program. She's also working on a very nifty app that will allow everyday people to upload photos of shark sightings along our beaches. The goal is to crowdsource critical data points to help facilitate the peaceful coexistence between humans and sharks."

With a few clicks of the mouse, she summoned a map using satellite imagery of Sri Lanka and its territorial waters. Hundreds of blue dots congregated along the island country's coastlines while others, isolated at wide intervals, were located farther offshore.

"Each of those blue markers," she explained, "represents the last known location of a shark that we've tagged. The great white that you're interested in is...that one right there." She clicked on a dot in one of the clusters along the southern coast. An information window sprang up on the right side of the screen, displaying a photograph of a huge great white shark thrashing alongside the hull of a boat. Below this was a name, as well as the shark's sex, weight, and length.

"Mary Jane?" Marty said, reading the name.

"We name all the sharks we tag. We also put them up for adoption. Would you be interested in adopting one, Marty? The money goes toward the purchase of new SPOT tags."

"I'm afraid I simply don't have the space for a shark on this boat."

Elsa glanced up at him.

"It was a joke, Elsa. And sure, I'll adopt one. But first things first." He pointed to a button on the screen that read: MARY JANE'S TRAVEL LOG. "Can we have a look at that?"

She clicked the button. A new window popped up:

Mary Jane

Date tagged: Feb 26, 2019
Location tagged: Indian Ocean
103 days
7701 km
Filter track by: All activity / Week / Month /
Year / 2 Years / Specific dates

Marty said, "Filter by all activity."

She clicked again.

A yellow line appeared on the satellite map, tracing a meandering route along Sri Lanka's southern coast. Elsa hovered the mouse cursor over the westernmost part of the line. A date and time appeared. "This is where Mary Jane was originally caught and tagged," she said. "You can see that since then she took up temporary residency at hunting sites here, here, and here." At the locations she indicated, the yellow line zigzagged chaotically. "Each are in relatively shallow shelf water, typically between five meters and one hundred meters deep."

Marty pointed to the easternmost end of the line where it turned abruptly south and crossed the shelf break into the deep ocean. "What do you make of that? There wouldn't be much food that far offshore, and it doesn't look as though Mary Jane was striking out on any migratory route. She's simply swimming back west, parallel to the coast."

Elsa shrugged. "SPOT tracking is a relatively new technology, Marty, and we're still trying to make sense of what we're learning about the world of white sharks. If you want my best guess? Mary Jane was spooked from the last hunting ground. Believe it or not, great whites aren't the ocean's apex predator."

"Of course they're not. We are."

"Yes, but humans aside, killer whales are king. Documented accounts of orcas targeting great whites date back decades, although the rising frequency of the attacks is a new development. Shark populations have been increasing due to restrictions on fishing, while global warming is expanding the geographical areas in which they can live. Another best guess? Sharks and orcas may simply be bumping into each other more often than they used to."

"Or perhaps due to overfishing, orcas are running out of their usual food source, forcing them to search for other prey such as great whites?"

"Perhaps. But whatever the reason, orcas are bigger and smarter than great whites, and a definite threat to them. So, yes, it's possible an orca, or several orcas coordinating their hunting in a pack, spooked Mary Jane into deeper, uncharted water."

Elsa hovered over the yellow line where it terminated next to the shoreline a little east of Mirissa. "July 8, 2021, 8:44 a.m. This is the last ping received, where my colleague retrieved Mary Jane from the shark net."

"Which means this would be where she spent the last few weeks of her life." He pointed to a preceding section of the line where it circled around on itself multiple times. "Can you zoom in there?"

The section of map magnified, revealing an island in the center of the circling line.

"Ah ha!" Marty said, the exclamation steeled with affirmation. His research was coming to life right before his eyes; one of his main hypotheses about the probable habitat of merfolk was that they lived in the shelf waters around islands.

Elsa zoomed in further until the names of political and physical features appeared.

"Peytivu…" he said, reading the name above the island.

"'Island of Demons,'" she said.

CHAPTER 13

MARTY

"Island of Demons?"

"That's what Peytivu means in Tamil. Or perhaps Demon Island—"

"Here you guys are!"

Marty and Elsa turned to find Rad and Jacky standing at the doorway to the dry lab, their hair wet and falling in tangles over their bare shoulders all the way to the white towels wrapped around their torsos. Their cheeks were flushed, either from the champagne in the flutes they each held, or the steaming water from the hot tub. They almost looked like twins.

"Pip told us you were down here," Rad said. "Isn't she a peach? So cute I want to squeeze her cheeks. Hi, Dr. Montero."

"Hello, Miss Gonzalez."

"What?" Jacky said. "Are we back being all stiff and proper already? I *hate* stiff and proper."

"Me too," Rad said. In a snooty voice she drawled, "You *must* come to our country house this spring, darling. It's absolutely divine."

Giggling, Jacky gripped Rad's forearm and drawled back, "Oh, you poor thing. Just *one* country house? We have *two*, and we've already downsized."

Marty was bemused. "How much have you two clowns had to drink?" he asked them.

"We're celebrating!" Jacky said. "Elsa, I take it Marty told you the good news?"

"He did indeed. The DNA result is quite remarkable."

"And Elsa has given *me* some good news as well," Marty told them. "The great white shark was tagged with an electronic tracking device, which means we know the approximate location of where it ate the merfolk, which means Pip and I have a place to start looking for other merfolk right away."

"Right away?" said Rad. "Like when?"

"Tomorrow morning."

"Tomorrow morning! What about Jacks and me?"

"Jacks? What, are you two BFFs now?"

"Don't change the topic, Marty. You can't just kick us to the curb."

"We'll only be at sea for a few days, long enough to set up a hydrophone array and perform some preliminary sonar mapping of the sea floor. The real work is decoding the data, which we'll start when we return to shore."

"Why don't we go with you?" said Jacky. "I can't think of a better place to get started on my story. Rad, you're not filming again until the beginning of next month. Interested in coming along?"

"A few days relaxing at sea *does* sound rather enticing…"

Marty shrugged. "If you two want to come, so be it. There's plenty of room. What about you, Elsa? Care to join the party? The more the merrier."

"No, no, not me," she said. "But thank you for the offer." She glanced at her wristwatch. "My, it's late. I should be getting home. It's been a wild day, and I think I need a good night's rest to…get my head around everything."

"Understandable," he said, producing his corncob pipe from his pocket and clamping the stem between his teeth. "Let me show you to the gangway, and we'll see you when we return in a few days' time."

PART 3
Demon Island

"There is, one knows not what sweet mystery
about this sea, whose gently awful stirrings seem
to speak of some hidden soul beneath..."
—Herman Melville

CHAPTER 14

Merfolk: From the Deep. The making-of the original Netflix documentary.

"I know it's been a long day, Double M," Fat Mike said, reclining in the director's chair and sipping a can of Diet Coke from a fluorescent orange straw. "So how about we do one more scene? You good with that?"

Marty had just returned from the bathroom and was settling onto the stool in front of the green screen. "Sure," he said. "Got something in mind?"

"What they look like. Their physical appearance."

"Isn't that redundant? You'll be showing video footage of a merfolk."

"Your exposition will lead right into that. Maybe you can explain why they look like they do. Why they have tails and all that shite."

"They have tails so they can swim, Mike."

Fat Mike slapped a knee. "Funny, mate! Make sure you mention that on camera. Just as deadpan as you did now. You ready?"

"Sure."

"Roll camera!"

"Camera rolling," Gus said.

"Marker!"

Jamie clapped the slate's sticks together.

"Action!" Fat Mike bellowed.

"In 1758," Marty said, "the Swedish scientist Carolus Linnaeus developed the two-name system—Genus and Species—for identifying and classifying all living things. Under class Mammalia, he placed Homo sapiens at the top of air-breathing vertebrate animals. He also acknowledged the existence of Siren, noting the species exhibited paradoxical biological traits. It was clearly an aquatic mammal since its hind terminated in a fish-like tail, but it lacked the blubber and thick skin of other marine mammals. Other physical traits antithetical to those same marine mammals included a neck, external ears, and forelimbs with opposable thumbs.

"The resulting question that everybody always wants to know the answer to: Does this species, which has since become known as merfolk, look at all like humans? What I can tell you from the literature I have studied is that it certainly resembles us, sharing characteristics such as large foreheads, binocular vision, protruding noses, and out-turned lips. It has long been my belief that the large foreheads are not only indicative of a well-developed cerebrum, but necessary to conduct the physiological process for locating distant or invisible objects in the oceans. This is called echolocation, which can be found in most species of dolphins and toothed whales—"

"Cut! Cut! Cut!" Fat Mike said, lifting off his baseball cap and scratching his head with sausage-like fingers. "Echolocation, Double M? What the hell are you talkin' about?"

"Merfolk are presumably a social species like us, and thus echolocation would be necessary for social communication underwater. This would require a bulbous forehead to house the mass of adipose tissue known as the melon—"

"The *melon?*" Fat Mike shook his head. "No, doc, sorry. Can't have you talkin' about fuckin' melons. You saw the video footage. That thing that washed up on the beach didn't have a fuckin' melon in its fuckin' forehead. Its forehead looked just like yours or mine."

"We don't know that for sure, Mike. The shot of the merfolk's face was not particularly clear, and its hair obscured much of its forehead."

"Yeah, yeah, but I just don't know how well shite like echolocation and melons are gonna go over with the audience."

"We have authentic footage, Mike. We don't need to sell the public on anything."

"I hear ya, mate. I do. And although we have authentic footage, there are still gonna be the doubters. So I don't want to get too carried away here. Tell you what, let's sit on the echolocation talk for now. Can you explain the blue skin?"

Marty shrugged. "Could be a form of camouflage. Makes it more difficult for predators to see them from below when they're swimming near the surface?"

"Fuck yeah! See, that's what you should be talkin' about. Easily digestible stuff. Stuff people don't have to think too hard about. What about their eyes? Why do they have yellow eyes?"

"I don't know why they have yellow eyes, Mike."

"What about their hair then? That merfolk had a mane on it to rival a bloody lion's."

"I don't know why they have hair either. I always hypothesized that they were bald-pated."

"Well, fuck, Double M!" Fat Mike exclaimed. "This is the kind of stuff you need to have answers for. It's what the audience is gonna want to know. It's what's gonna make them *believe*. Make shite up if you have to. Just don't go overboard. No echolocation, no telekinesis, none of that sci-fi shtick. Stick to the basics, keep it real, keep it sexy, and she'll be apples." He glanced at his diamond-encrusted Rolex. "Okay, gotta call it a wrap for today. Have another watch of the footage tonight, mate. Have a good think about explanations for things people want to know. The color of its eyes, its hair—even how it takes a fuckin' crap. And I'll see everyone back here bright-eyed and bushy-tailed first thing tomorrow mornin'."

△△△

Marty snapped awake, bathed in sweat, his pulse fast and his embarrassment acute.

I'm going to show all you assholes, all you doubters, I'm going to show you...

CHAPTER 15

ELSA

Elsa lay in bed, in the dark, staring at the shadow-veiled ceiling. She glanced at the glowing digital clock on the bedside table once again. 1:14 a.m. Thirty minutes since she'd last checked. Usually when she couldn't sleep, she thought about food. Cooking was a hobby of hers, and most nights she would prepare herself small yet satisfying meals. Yesterday had been stacked eggplant parmesan. The day before that, bourbon shrimp, and the day before that...either lemon garlic salmon or beef and mushroom stroganoff. She couldn't remember. The days tended to blur together the older she got.

She began planning out the meals she would make in the coming week, but she barely got through the second one when she found herself thinking about Dr. Murdoch and his expedition tomorrow. She couldn't possibly accompany him and his friends, could she? No, she had already declined. Besides, they were nutty, all three of them. Dr. Murdoch was brilliant but delusional, and the two women were... Elsa didn't know. Were they delusional as well? Did they truly believe in merfolk? Or were they going along with Dr. Murdoch's theory with a grin and a wink.

Jacqueline's motive was clear: she wanted to write a sensational story. And she could write it with impunity. She was a journalist, not a scientist. She was simply reporting the news; she wasn't creating it or advocating it. Regardless of the blowback the story would most certainly receive, she had nothing to lose and everything to gain.

And Radhika? What would be her motive for enabling Dr. Murdoch's ludicrous claims? She was in a relationship with him. Loyalty then? Obligation? Dr. Murdoch was worth many millions of dollars. Perhaps there was a financial motive involved?

But what did any of that matter to Elsa? It didn't...only it did. Because she felt an attraction to Dr. Murdoch's theory. Yes, she thought it was ludicrous. Or at least the rational, sensible part of her did. But there was another part of her she wasn't so well acquainted with, a youthful, wondrous part that wanted to believe that there was more to the world than meets the eye, that there were miraculous mysteries left to be discovered that defied the restrictions of reason and sensibility.

So what was she to do? Stay behind and analyze whale feces while Dr. Murdoch and company set sail on an adventure that, while doomed to failure, might actually be...*fun*? Or get off her ideological high horse, let her hair down for the first time in recent memory, and join them?

It should have been an easy decision. Elsa's three years in Sri Lanka had been anything but interesting. She'd met no new friends. She'd had no romantic encounters. Her work, while important, was unremarkable and lacking the critical acclaim she'd garnered in the US.

Of course, asceticism and anonymity were precisely what she'd wanted and why she'd come to the country in the first place. She'd wanted an uninspired life because she didn't believe she deserved to have a better one.

She'd lost that privilege when she killed her husband.

Elsa had been scuba diving in the oceans for most of her adult life, she felt at home in them, so it was only a matter of time before she was drawn to the thrill and challenge of cave diving in untouched underwater environments. Since 2010, she had participated in numerous cave survey and exploration projects across the Americas, with her work benefiting a wide range of government institutions, universities, museums, and geographic societies. In 2015 she became involved in an ambitious international diving expedition to map unexplored parts of the Huautla Cave System in Mexico, which had recently been labelled the deepest cave in the western hemisphere.

Her husband, Ron, was a fellow marine biologist and first-rate scuba diver, yet he never showed any interest following in her footsteps. He once told her, "When scuba diving in open water, you always know that by swimming up you will reach the surface. When cave diving, even if you know which way is up—it doesn't matter. So thanks but no thanks, darling." Nevertheless, the Mexico expedition was going to be a multi-week undertaking, Elsa had wanted Ron by her side, so she pressed him relentlessly to join the expedition until he finally relented. It had been a selfish act on her part. Cave diving was demanding and dangerous in the easiest of environments, and Huautla was anything but, as it would involve decompression dives at some of the most remote places inside the earth.

On her team's third day underground, Elsa and Ron began what would be Ron's fatal dive by descending seventy-five feet through a five-foot-wide shaft. At the bottom Elsa led the way along a horizontal tunnel that required her to army crawl on her elbows and knees until the tunnel opened into a huge room filled with columns and stalactites in every direction. It was only then, when she turned in the pitch-black water to share the awe-inspiring moment with Ron, that she realized he was no longer behind her. She returned through the horizontal tunnel and found him stuck in the narrowest section, entangled in the guideline that connected them both. While she was trying to free him, he began breathing quickly, which overloaded his rebreather with carbon dioxide. Switching mouthpieces at depth was extremely risky, but Elsa saw no other option and gave him a cylinder of gas to reduce the amount of carbon dioxide being absorbed in his bloodstream. During the switch, Ron's panic got the better of him, he swallowed too much water, and died within seconds before her eyes. There was no question in her mind that his death was her fault, and she had been living with that guilt —and the ghastly image of his frightened eyes in the final moments of his life—ever since.

"Oh, Ron..." she murmured to the lonely, empty room. She glanced at the clock again. 1:37 a.m.

She closed her eyes and began planning another meal in her head.

CHAPTER 16

MARTY

Pip went to the Mirissa post office to mail bone samples to different labs in the UK, and Marty, Rad, and Jacky visited a few shops, purchasing food and other necessities for the excursion on the *Oannes*. At 10 a.m. they were about to set sail when Marty spotted Elsa hurrying down the pier.

"Hello!" he called from the deck, waving to her. "Have you come to see us off?"

She stopped at the bottom of the gangway. "Good morning, Dr. Murdoch," she said, slightly out of breath. "Actually, I've reconsidered your offer. I've decided to accompany you on your voyage, if the invitation is still open?"

"Of course it is!" he said, pleased that she had changed her mind. He noticed she was wearing a medium-sized backpack. "I see you've packed light?"

"I'm a simple person."

"Well, come on aboard then. I'll show you to your cabin."

△△△

Marty spent some time on the bridge with Pip, charting their course, before settling in front of his computer in the salon. Demon Island, he learned, was one of Sri Lanka's eighteen national parks. Unlike the others, however, it was designated a wildlife sanctuary in 1964 and visitors were not permitted.

Moreover, little scientific research had been undertaken on the island over the last two decades due to the civil war that had consumed the country. All of which meant there was little information—at least in English—about the place. Nevertheless, Marty did come across one curious story which, if true, might explain the island's nefarious moniker. It occurred in 1703, while Sri Lanka was under Dutch colonial rule. At the time the island had been named Wormerveer, after the town in North Holland. A Dutch soldier named Jeronimus Pelgrom, stationed on the mainland, was convicted of sodomy and sentenced to spend the rest of his living days marooned on Demon Island. He was provided a tent, water, seeds, tobacco, clothing, a Bible, and writing materials. He wasn't expected to survive six months. When soldiers returned to collect his corpse, they found him gaunt but alive, having survived by eating sea turtles and seabirds and drinking rainwater. He was also raving drunk. As a former distiller, he had learned to brew a potent spirit from the roots of a native plant. He claimed the island was cursed by God and haunted by evil spirits, and he begged the soldiers to take him back to the mainland. They did not, and the castaway Jeronimus Pelgrom was never seen alive or dead again.

When Marty checked the time, he was surprised to find that almost three hours had passed. He stood and stretched and went to the aft deck. The sun was a blistering gold disc in the blue, cloudless sky. The calm ocean appeared to stretch to infinity with not a speck of land in sight. Jacky sat at a table beneath a large straw sunhat she had purchased in a surf shop, earbuds in her ears, working on her laptop. She gave him a quick wave before resuming her work. Rad lay stretched out on a deck chair in a red bikini she'd bought at the same surf shop. She'd slathered herself in sunscreen and was reading a Clive Cussler hardcover novel from the bookcase in the salon. The Pomeranian was curled in a ball on the deck next to her, apparently sleeping.

She looked up at him and said, "Hi, Marty. This is a great book so far. You remind me of the guy."

He was flattered. "Dirk Pitt?"

"Of course not. He's a tall, dark, and handsome adventurer with opaline green eyes. I mean *this* guy." She showed him the back of the dust jacket, which was plastered with a photograph of the gray-haired author.

"Thanks, Rad."

"It's a compliment."

"Thanks."

"Don't tell me you're grumpy already? It's not even noon."

"I'm not grumpy at all. In fact, I'm in a fantastic mood." Which was true. He couldn't remember the last time he had felt so buoyed and alive and optimistic about the future. "How are you feeling?"

"Me? Why do you ask?"

"You had a lot of champagne last night."

"You know me better than that. I can handle anything you pour down my throat...what?"

She'd caught him looking at her throat. She wasn't wearing a scarf today, likely because the bruises were no longer visible.

She said, "I feel like a zoo animal when you look at me like that, Marty."

"I'm not looking at you like anything. I just noticed you weren't wearing a scarf today."

"You're never going to be comfortable choking me, are you?"

Alarmed by her candor, he shot Jacky a look. She appeared oblivious to the conversation.

He said, "We're not talking about this right now."

"No, we never talk about it, do we? Can you take a couple of steps that way?" She waved her hand to the right.

"Am I in your sun?" he asked, moving.

"Thanks." She flipped onto her stomach, reached behind her back, and unclipped her bikini top. "Would you be a doll and rub some sunscreen on my back?"

He retrieved a bottle of Coppertone from the deck, sat on the edge of the reclined chair, and squeezed some lotion onto his hands. He rubbed them together and began massaging the lotion on Rad's back.

"Mmmmm…" she said. "How much longer until we get to this island?"

"Shouldn't be too long now."

"The plan?" she murmured into the cushion beneath her face.

"Pip and I will map the ocean floor around the island so we know where best to deploy the hydrophones."

"What are hydrophones? Underwater microphones?"

"Essentially, yes. Light doesn't travel very far underwater, which makes cameras rather useless. Sound is a much more efficient form of underwater information transfer. The hydrophones we deploy will convert whatever they detect into audio signals that get transferred back to the ship. Special software will display them as graphs and other images that Pip and I can study in detail."

"So you're…listening for merfolk?"

"That's right."

"Ah, there! Can you feel it?"

Marty worked on a knot in her shoulder.

She sighed, and they were quiet for a little bit. Then she said, "How do you know what to listen for if you've never heard a merfolk before?"

"The acoustic characteristics of marine mammals differ considerably between species. Short-pulsed echolocation clicks of dolphins are distinct from those of porpoises, and they're nothing like the long-frequency modulated songs of whales. Not to mention the vocalizations of seals, sea lions, manatees, and other large aquatic creatures. Merfolk vocalizations, it stands to reason, would be equally unique."

"Mmmmm…" she said, and he wondered if she was even listening to him.

"Do you want me to choke you?"

"Mmmmm…"

He moved on to another knot. She sighed again and said, "If you hear one, how are you going to go about catching it?"

"We moor the hydrophones in an array on the seafloor. This allows us to determine the direction any sound is coming from and follow it to its source."

"Yes, but how are you going to *catch* one? Throw on a pair of goggles and flippers and jump overboard?"

"I'm glad you take my work so seriously, Rad. Even now, after the recent discoveries, you're still making jokes—"

She rolled onto her side. "I'm sorry, Marty. I don't mean to sound snarky. I guess I'm still a little jaded about your big lie. Don't worry, I'll be back to my charming, irresistible self soon. Okay?"

"Sure."

"So tell me—I'm genuinely curious—if you find a merfolk, how are you planning to catch it?"

"Dynamite."

"Marty!"

"The underwater shockwave should stun a merfolk long enough for us to collect its body."

"If it doesn't kill it!"

"There's a chance the blast would rupture its lungs, yes, and that would be unfortunate. Yet while a live specimen would be ideal, a dead specimen is better than no specimen."

Rad sat straight, covering her breasts with an arm. Her expression was incredulous. "Seriously, Marty? If you make first contact with a creature from myths and legends, a creature that potentially has human lineage, your plan is to *blow it up with dynamite?*"

"It would be for the greater good, Rad. Morality is determined by the end result. In this case the capture of a merfolk, dead or alive, would change everything we know about human evolution, about our seas and oceans, about our history. It would be the greatest boon to biological science since Darwin's theory of natural selection. Surely that outweighs the life of one creature, which would expire eventually."

"That's a heartless argument, Marty."

"If the death of a single slave during the antebellum era would end slavery and prevent the Civil War, wouldn't it be justified?"

"That's not even close to the same thing, and you know it."

"Would you kill the slave?"

"Give it a break, Marty."

"Would you, Rad?"

"No, I wouldn't."

"What about you, dog?" he asked the Pomeranian, which was looking up at them sleepily. "Would you do it?"

The dog yapped loudly, what sounded to him like an affirmation.

"Good, Marty," he said, and got up and left.

△△△

He went to the pilothouse to check on Pip, who was standing in the dimly lit room before the ship's wheel, throttles, and control board.

"*Bonjour, mon capitaine.*" She pointed to the GPS screen. "We are only a few nautical miles from the island now. Is something…wrong?"

"Rad doesn't think our plan to blast-fish a merfolk out of the water is ethical."

"Ethical? What is ethical?" Pip shrugged dismissively. "You think it is wrong to eat dog meat, some people think it is okay. You think it is wrong to lie. Some people think it is okay. Your girlfriend has an opinion, that is all. And she is not a scientist. She does not have the head of a scientist, or the hunger of a scientist. She does not have that drive that you and I have, to explore, to unravel secrets, to find new truths. So her opinion is moot."

"But her intention is not. I wish there were some other way to capture one unharmed…"

"There is not, Marty. We have discussed this thoroughly. A merfolk has never been caught in a trawler's net the world over. You will not catch one in a net either, not even if you know precisely where to search. Do not lose your spine."

"I'm not losing anything, Pip—spine, nerve, or otherwise." He sighed. "I don't believe I ever asked you: why did you become a scientist in the first place?"

"No, you have not asked me that, *mon capitaine*, and we have known each other for a long time now. I wonder where your head is sometimes. No, I know where it is. Do not answer that." She paused. "Why did I become a scientist? Do you really want to know, or are you simply eating my brain?"

"Picking your brain. And I'd like nothing more than to know."

"After I graduated university, I flew to Spain to visit my sister. She was teaching French there. Her contract had finished, and we made plans to travel Europe."

"You stayed in hostels?"

"That is where poor backpackers stay, yes? We also took overnight trains and buses to save on that night's accommodation. One overnight train to Austria was full, so we ended up getting seats in different carriages. I woke in the middle of the night to find an old man rubbing my feet on his crotch. I kicked him in the stomach and got away and found a conductor. I brought him back to my seat, but the pervert was gone—and he took my shoes and handbag with him."

"Why would he do that?"

"Because he was a pervert, Marty. That is what perverts do. Anyway, he must have gotten off at the next stop because I could not find him anywhere on the train. I could not find my sister either. It turned out the train had split during the night. The end my sister was in continued to Austria, while my end was en route to Slovakia."

"With no money or shoes…"

"And no phone."

"What did you do?"

"Walked barefoot through Bratislava until I found an internet café and begged the owner to let me send an email to my sister."

"This is interesting, Pip, but what does it have to do with you becoming a scientist?"

"I was setting the scene, Marty. But I see that I am boring you, so I will give you the annotated version. Eventually my sister and I ended up in Israel. This was right when a mermaid craze swept the country. You know what I am talking about, yes?"

Marty nodded. In 2009 dozens of eyewitnesses reported seeing a mermaid in the Mediterranean Sea near Haifa. The local legend became an international phenomenon, and tourists began flocking to the beach where it was spotted to catch a glimpse of the creature, which supposedly looked like a cross between a little girl and a dolphin.

"Mermaids were all anybody talked about for weeks," Pip continued. "The town's tourism board offered an award of one million dollars to anyone who caught one on film. No one ever did."

"Because it wasn't real, Pip."

"No, it was not," she agreed. "But the power of suggestion and imagination is very strong. I became caught up in the craze too. I convinced my sister to stay in a hostel near the beach so I could look for the mermaid myself. Eventually I came to the conclusion the sightings were innocent mistakes that were exploited for tourism. But that experience did not stop me from believing in mermaids in general. I was as convinced then as I am now that they exist, and I realized I had found my calling. I would dedicate my life to proving they are real. When I returned to France, I completed a master's degree in marine science. I became involved in a small community of sirentologists. I even traveled to London to attend a lecture of yours at the University of Cambridge."

"You never told me that!"

"I went to many of your lectures, if you want the truth."

Marty had a revelation. "Did you follow me to Sri Lanka, Pip?" he asked, stunned.

"When I saw in the news that you were hiding in Sri Lanka—"

"I wasn't *hiding*. I came here to—"

"I would hide too, *mon capitaine*, if I had been in your position. The things people were saying about you were not very nice. But did I follow you? I do not know if I would say that. One of my sirentologist friends is from Calcutta. She was returning home for a few weeks and asked if I wanted to join her. I had not been traveling since the Europe trip with my sister, so I agreed. That is where we were—Calcutta—when we heard the news that you were in Sri Lanka. It was so close, we decided to go looking for you."

"Whatever the bloody hell for?"

"Because you were the biggest sirentologist on the planet, and we were nerdy groupies. You seem to be getting upset, Marty. Should I finish my story?"

"Please do, Pip," he said sternly.

"We went to the *Daily Mirror* and spoke to Jacky, who had just written the story about you—"

"Jacky!"

"She said you lived on a big boat in Galle Port. We couldn't find it and figured you must be out at sea. My friend went back to India, but I stayed behind to wait for you. When you returned, and I saw that the 'boat' you lived on was a research vessel, and I realized you were not just hiding here but searching for merfolk, I decided you might need an assistant. And look! Now we are living happy and everlasting."

"Happily ever after?"

"That is what I said."

Marty was staring at Pip, gobsmacked. He'd had no idea about any of this. Admittedly he hadn't asked many questions when he'd initially hired her. She'd told him she was impressed by his ship, she was a marine biologist, and she was looking for work. Some preliminary questions confirmed she was familiar with the operation and analysis of sonar, and that had been good enough for him. After all, he'd never thought she would be anything more than a temporary assistant, sticking around for a few weeks at tops. It had been months before he'd confessed to her that he was searching for merfolk—something it was now clear she had known the entire time!

"There, on the horizon," Pip said, pointing through the pilot-house's inclined windshield. "You can see the island now."

CHAPTER 17

MARTY

Marty snagged a pair of binoculars hanging on a wall hook and pressed them to his eyes. The island was covered with verdant vegetation, an emerald dot suspended in a world of blue.

"We'll continue this talk later, Pip," he said. "Deploy the sonar winches and keep an eye out for the best locations to place the hydrophones. I'll go get them ready."

Marty left the pilothouse and transferred fourteen hydrophones from the ship's workshop to the aft deck. They were cylindrical, made from ceramic so as to not interfere with the reception of audio input, and mounted on stainless steel cones to keep them from touching the seabed. Chunky waterproof battery packs allowed them to record the first two minutes of acoustic data every ten minutes for up to three months. Over the next few hours, he used the A-frame boom to deploy four of them in a vertical line array at a depth of 150 meters.

At five o'clock he called it a day and went below deck to shower and change into evening clothes. When he returned to the main deck, he found everybody gathered and talking excitedly. It took him a moment to realize what all the fuss was about: a curlicue of smoke rising from the center of Demon Island into the darkening twilight.

Brow furrowed, he said, "I thought the island was unpopulated."

Elsa nodded. "It's a designated wildlife sanctuary."

"That's what I read. So who's that over there? A ranger?"

"Or a castaway," said Rad. "That could be an SOS smoke signal."

"At nighttime?"

"I'm with Marty," Jacky said. "It's simply some ranger cooking his dinner."

"Looks like a lot of smoke for a cooking fire," said Rad.

"You know, that island used to be used as a prison of sorts?" Marty said, deciding to have some fun with Rad, knowing she was superstitious to her core. "At the beginning of the eighteenth century a Dutch soldier was convicted of sodomy while stationed in what was then Ceylon. He was marooned on Demon Island as punishment. Perhaps his ghost still haunts it?"

"Ghosts don't make fires."

"Perhaps it uses the smoke to lure unsuspecting sailors to the island?"

Rad folded her arms across her chest. "You're not scaring me, Marty. You're being condescending."

Grinning, Marty lit his pipe, stuck the stem in the corner of his mouth, and puffed. "I'm going to make myself a much-deserved drink," he announced. "Would anyone care to join me?"

ΔΔΔ

Earlier in the day Marty had caught several bony fish on trolling lines. He baked two of them—a mullet and snapper—for dinner, which everybody ate on the foredeck. Afterward they sat around beneath the stars for a nightcap. Jacky and Rad chatted with Pip, while Marty and Elsa had an erudite discussion on the acidification of the oceans. Nobody seemed in the mood to talk about merfolk, Marty included, and at seven thirty they retired to their cabins for an early night.

Marty dreamed he was lost on Demon Island, pursued by creatures he couldn't identify. He woke before dawn, sheathed in sweat. He showered, shaved, dressed, then went to the dry lab to check on the preliminary data from the hydrophones.

An hour later, he went to the kitchen to make a coffee and was surprised to find Elsa there, scrambling eggs in a skillet on the stove.

"Good morning, Elsa," he said. "Smells good."

"Good morning, Marty. I hope you don't mind that I raided your cupboards. I'm making enough for everyone." She removed a tray filled with crispy bacon from the oven and set it on the counter."

"Is that coffee freshly brewed?"

"Indeed." She filled two mugs from the coffee pot. "Milk? Sugar?"

"Black for me, thank you."

She handed him a mug and took the other for herself. "You're up early."

"I can say the same about you. But, yes, I've been in the dry lab for about an hour already. We have a curious pod of dolphins hanging around the ship. I suppose they don't get many people out this way."

To the east, the sun crept above the horizon, orange and yellow rays of light fanning out against the waking sky. Marty and Elsa watched the sunrise in silence for several long moments.

"It's beautiful," Elsa said finally.

"Do you get out on the ocean often?"

"I used to. Not so much anymore."

"What made you and your husband relocate to Sri Lanka, if I may ask? Or did you meet him here?"

"Excuse me? Oh." She glanced down at the diamond on her ring finger. "My husband isn't with us anymore."

"I'm terribly sorry. I had no idea—"

"No idea about what?" Rad asked, entering the kitchen dressed in a pair of blue silk pajamas.

Elsa cleared her throat. "Coffee, Miss Fernandez?"

"Yes, please." She accepted a mug of coffee and filled it to the rim with milk. "Have you guys eaten?"

"Not yet," said Marty, "but help yourself."

"I believe I will." Rad retrieved a stack of plates from a cupboard and filled one with two scoops of scrambled eggs and three pieces of bacon. "Have to fill up for my big day."

"Lounging in the sun sure does burn a lot of calories."

"Actually, Jacky and I are going to explore the island."

Marty blinked. "What are you talking about?"

"Just what I said. We planned everything last night."

Believing it would have been inappropriate for Rad to sleep in the master stateroom with him while there were other guests onboard, Marty had suggested she sleep in the second bed in Jacky's cabin.

Apparently they'd done more than sleep.

"It's a wildlife sanctuary," he reminded her. "Tourists aren't permitted."

"Do you see any cops around, Marty?"

"There's a ranger on the island."

"*You* say it's a ranger. We think it's a castaway. We're going to try to find him."

He chuffed. "Oh, no, you're not."

"Why not?"

"You have no idea who it might be."

"You just said it's a ranger. If it is, we'll tell him we saw the smoke and were concerned, that's all. No harm, no foul."

"It's *likely* a ranger, Rad. But there's a chance it's not. It could be a criminal hiding out from the law. I'm sorry. You two aren't going to the island."

"I'm a grown woman, Marty! You can't tell me what to—"

"And I'm the captain of this ship. I make the calls."

"Have you forgotten that I've explored some extremely remote locations—"

"With an entire TV crew. That's a little different than striking off with just Jacky—"

"We can more than handle ourselves. Stop being such a male chauvinist. Besides, who knows? We might even find some more evidence of your mermaids. Dr. Montero, would you like to join us?"

"Me? Oh no." She shook her head. "My…exploration days…are behind me. I think I'll be fine staying right here on the ship."

CHAPTER 18

ELSA

Elsa took her coffee to the foredeck to let Marty and Radhika continue their argument in private. The sun was higher above the horizon now, revealing a dreary morning sky scuffed with gray clouds. Demon Island was off starboard, a green and lonely chunk of land, untouched by man. Admittedly her first reaction to Radhika's invitation to explore the island had been curiosity and interest. Exploration was in her blood. It was why cave diving had become an irresistible pastime of hers. Of course, she was no longer the person she used to be. Her selfish desire for exploration had not only gotten her husband killed but had also killed that very desire in the same fell swoop. She didn't need to go traipsing around an uncharted island in the hopes of solving a silly mystery. She was in her forties now. She was a still-grieving widow.

Dr. Murdoch and Radhika started shouting at one another. Elsa glanced through the window to the kitchen in time to see Marty storm off into the salon.

A moment later Radhika emerged on the foredeck with her coffee.

"He can be such a man-baby sometimes," she said, stopping next to Elsa at the railing and staring out to sea.

"He certainly seems protective of you."

"He has a big heart, even if he's not very good at showing it. I mean, I know he's concerned for me. But I'm not a little girl. I can make my own decisions."

"You're still going to the island?"

"As soon as Jacky's up."

"And Marty's okay with that?"

"Of course not." She sipped her coffee. "Which, I guess, is why he's decided to come with us."

CHAPTER 19

MARTY

After his argument with Rad, Marty went to the davit on the starboard main deck. Stowed against the crane-like structure was a 4.8-meter rigid inflatable boat (RIB), which was essentially a pair of synthetic rubber pontoons connected to a laminate hull. He went about checking the davit's tracks for debris, then removed the boat's cover. He was in the process of detaching the grips that held the inflatable boat in place when Rad and Jacky joined him. They wore their new bikinis under shorts and singlets, as well as big straw hats. Once again, they reminded him of twins.

"Tweedle Dee and Tweedle Dum," he muttered. When it had become clear that Rad wasn't going to back down from her plan to search the island for her castaway, he reluctantly told her he'd take them over in the RIB as long as they were all back on the *Oannes* by noon. It meant his morning would be wasted, but at least he'd have the afternoon to get another hydrophone array in the water.

"Sticks and stones, Marty," Rad said, adjusting the beach bag slung over her shoulder.

His mouth twisted. "Your dog better not be in that bag."

"Just some supplies."

"We're not going on a bloody picnic."

"Sunscreen, for starters. Have you put on any yet?"

"I don't wear sunscreen."

"You really should, Marty," Jacky said. "The sun's bad for your skin. It ages you prematurely."

"Think it's a bit late to be telling him that," said Rad.

"Will you two get on the boat so we can get this show on the road?"

Marty followed them onto the inflatable boat, then used a remote control to activate the crane's wire pulleys, which lowered the boat to the water. With a push of a button, the clamps released their magnetic moorings on the prow and stern. They hit the water with a flat splash. He untied the painter line and got behind the wheel at the center console. He turned the key and shifted into forward, letting the boat idle.

When the engine was primed, he throttled up and accelerated away from the *Oannes*. Piloting a small boat through violent swells was dangerous, but Marty knew the principles of severe weather seamanship well. Even so, the sea was rougher than it had appeared, and he shot down the crest of a large wave too quickly, submerging the bow beneath the subsequent wave. Jacky and Rad, seated up front, shrieked as water drenched them. Marty, amidship, received only a light spray.

"Hold onto your hats!" he told them, tasting salt on his lips.

They stuck their hats between their knees. Rad shouted something back at him, but he couldn't make it out above the roar of the wind and the growl of the motor.

For the next few minutes, Marty steered the boat through the roiling waves at angles so the boat rose and fell on its long axis, avoiding, for the most part, further soakings. When they reached the aquamarine coral reef surrounding Demon Island, the rougher seas subsided, and he trimmed the speed as they approached the beach.

"You're the worst driver ever, Marty!" Rad said, looking green and releasing her death grip on the gunwale handle.

"I got us here without capsizing, didn't I?"

He switched off the engine, hopped into the waist-high water, and dragged the boat up onto the sand. Unlike the well-maintained tourist beaches along Sri Lanka's southern coast, this one was littered with clumps of seaweed, broken seashells, and deadwood. Behind grassy dunes fifty meters inland, a snarl of jungle climbed a steep, rocky hill, creating a nearly vertical wall of green that towered high above them.

There was no way in hell they were forging a path through that. Rad and Jacky were frowning at the impassable vegetation; they clearly had the same thought.

He glanced at his wristwatch. It was eight thirty a.m.

"Three hours and counting to find your castaway," he told them. "Where do you want to start looking?"

△△△

They went west along the beach, Jacky and Rad walking abreast and chatting gaily, Marty bringing up the rear. He'd taken off his boat shoes and was enjoying the feel of the sand beneath his bare feet and between his toes. However, his mind was on the work back at the *Oannes* this afternoon. Hopefully he and Pip would get another four hydrophones in the water. That would leave them seven more to deploy the next day which, if there were no more distractions, would be doable.

Then the waiting game would begin.

How long until they recorded a merfolk's vocalization was anyone's guess, but he was confident it would happen. Yes, the merfolk eaten by the great white could have been an outlier. It could have been on its own, lost or migrating or an outcast from society. There might not be another of the creatures within a thousand kilometers of Demon Island. Yet he didn't believe that was so.

They were here. He felt it in his bones.

Gut feelings aside, logic also told him they were here. Most eyewitness reports of merfolk occurred in island coastal waters. This made sense if merfolk, like most marine mammals, occasionally hauled themselves out of the water onto terrestrial habitats. Lying about on the rocky shores or the mudflats of a remote, isolated island would be much safer than doing so on continental land where, historically, there were more danger-ous predators—namely, the genus Homo. When Homo mastered fire, they were able to forge more complex and deadly weapons, becoming formidable hunters that hunted Australopithecus to extinction; they would have likely had no qualms doing the same to their distant, defenseless aquatic cousins.

Rad and Jacky had stopped up ahead. They were speaking excitedly.

"What is it?" Marty asked them when he caught up.

Jacky pointed to the jungle. "Can't you see it?" she said. "That's a trail right there."

$$\triangle\triangle\triangle$$

They stomped up the stoss side of a dune to investigate, grab-bing handfuls of the long grass for purchase. At the top Marty saw that Jacky was right. There was a clearly demarcated foot-path leading into the dense growth of jungle.

"I knew we'd find our castaway!" said Rad.

"Don't get ahead of yourself," said Marty. "The path is too es-tablished to have been made by a single ranger—or castaway. It was likely made by boar, deer, and other wildlife."

"That's a total guess, Marty. I say we follow it. Some shade will be nice for a change."

"Sounds good to me," Jacky said.

Marty glanced at his watch and said, "We've been walking for an hour, which means we've an hour walk back to the boat. That only leaves us with one more hour. Half an hour down the path, half an hour back out."

"What's your point?" asked Rad.

"It's not much time, that's my point. We'll get a little way in and then have to turn around. There's no way we'll get anywhere near the middle of the island, which was where the smoke ap-peared to originate."

"It's still worth a look," Jacky said. "And like Rad said, it beats walking in the sun."

"What I'm saying," Marty said, "is why don't we just give up the wild goose chase and turn back now."

"You can go back, Marty," Rad said dismissively. "We'll meet you at the dinghy. Jacky and I are going to check out the jungle."

With that, they descended the lee side of the dune, disappearing into the thick vegetation.

Exhaling heavily, Marty followed.

△△△

Tropical rainforests are often incorrectly referred to as jungles. The actual 'jungle'—tangles of overgrown, impassable vegetation—exists only at the margins of the rainforest, where the woodland has been knocked down by natural events (such as hurricanes or typhoons) and replaced with dense, ground-level flora. This was true of the rainforest on Demon Island, and the jungle fringe would have been impassable had it not been for the dirt path Marty, Jacky, and Rad were following.

Nevertheless, it wasn't too long before the belly of the rainforest opened up, a consequence of the canopy depriving sunlight from reaching the forest floor. Small shrubs, ferns, and palms managed to thrive in the shadowy world, as did the moss, herbs, and fungi that coated the spongy ground and decomposing deadfall in shades of green. Higher in the dark understory, flowering plants such as orchids and bromeliads, as well as edible fruits, flourished. Vines and leafy creepers snaked their way up giant buttress roots and ancient tree trunks, searching for a way out of the gloomy dungeon in which they'd sprouted. Woody lianas, some hundreds of meters in length and as thick as telephone poles, coiled in gravity-defying loops from tree branches, linking them together to create a canopy superhighway for arboreal animals.

On first glance, the dusky emerald forest seemed tranquil and harmonious. In reality, a ruthless, invisible war was taking place, only at a pace too slow to see with the naked eye. Some species of trees regularly dropped their fronds and branches in an attempt to rid themselves from the freeloading, light-stealing lianas; other species swayed out of phase from their neighbors to snap the smothering vines and creepers; and still others had evolved peeling bark to shed cumbersome epiphytes, or produced toxins to ward off infestation by pests. Yet perhaps nothing illustrated the dog-eat-dog world better than the giant, prehistoric-looking strangler figs, parasites whose aerial roots encased their host trees in a living mesh, squeezing and killing even the largest victims before growing over their corpses to become colossi themselves.

Marty called a break before one such strangler fig, its roots merged into stout pillars as thick as English oaks. He swatted at a wasp flying uncomfortably close to his head. The drone of its wings was especially loud in the still, hushed forest. The silence was unnatural and disturbing; it was the silence of being watched by unknown eyes, as if all the creatures of the forest had stopped whatever they were doing to take stock of the interlopers.

Rad and Jacky sank down on a mossy log.

"Do you want bug spray, Marty?" Rad asked, rooting through her bag.

"If you two haven't noticed," he said, "our path has disappeared, which means unless we start leaving a trail of breadcrumbs, we're going to have a heck of a time finding our way out again."

"You want to turn back already?"

"I'm saying we don't have a choice."

Uncertainty hung in the warm, wet air as Rad and Jacky weighed their options. Marty took the can of aerosol insect repellant that Rad had produced and sprayed himself in a cloud of chemicals.

Rad said, "We were hoping to find a waterhole to swim in."

Marty shook his head. "We have no path to follow. We can't see the sky. If we get turned around, we could become hopelessly lost."

Jacky said, "Maybe he's right…"

In the distance, a troop of macaques belted out a series of barking calls. The sound echoed throughout the canopy. Suddenly Marty felt small and vulnerable, a fish out of water in a primeval world that had existed relatively unchanged for millions of years before him and would exist for millions more to come.

We shouldn't be here, he thought. *We need to leave.*

Rad, appearing uneasy, said, "Okay, let's head back—"

Jacky screamed.

CHAPTER 20

MARTY

Jacky and Rad leapt to their feet. Marty looked to where Jacky was looking. He saw nothing at first but palm fronds and shrubbery and shadows...before making out a darker shape, solid and unmoving, what might have been a head, and shoulders. The full man came into focus, and Marty wasn't sure how he'd missed him in the first place. He had shoulder-length black hair and a long beard that reached the middle of his smooth, brown chest. He wore a necklace made of curved animal teeth and a loincloth suspended by a string around his waist. An axe was hooked over his shoulder, the wooden haft parallel to his right arm, within easy reach. He was staring unblinking at the group, his brow angry, his eyes intense.

From beside Marty, Rad gasped. She saw him too.

Unconsciously he moved his hand, found hers, and gripped it firmly.

Jacky was turning in a circle, her feet disturbing dead leaves, the only sound Marty heard aside from the blood pounding in his temples. She said something so softly he didn't catch what it was until Rad asked "Where?" and he realized Jacky had said there were more of them.

More of whom? Marty wondered, picking out the other men camouflaged in shadows and vegetation, all of them statue-still, wraith-like, watching...and holding weapons. Axes, bows, spears. They looked as though they had just stepped out of the Neolithic era.

"What should we do?" Rad asked in a stilted way that suggested she was trying not to move her lips.

"Don't do anything," Marty told her.

Jacky had stopped turning. "They're all around us."

"What do they want?" Rad demanded.

"Likely nothing," he said. "Stay calm. Maybe they'll go away."

The one with the axe hooked over his shoulder stepped forward. He was shorter than Marty, stocky yet muscular.

"It's okay," Marty said to him. "We're leaving." He pointed the way they'd come.

The man's dark eyes showed no sign of understanding. The frown lines between his eyebrows bunched tighter.

"Follow me," he said to Rad and Jacky.

He only took two steps when three of the tribesmen moved with the quiet stealth of hunters to stand shoulder to shoulder, blocking his path.

"Shit," he muttered.

"What do they *want*?" Jacky hissed.

The one with the axe spoke, a quick, short burst of words.

"Did either of you understand that?" Marty asked.

"No," said Rad.

"No," said Jacky.

The man, presumably the leader of the pack, turned and walked away from them. He looked back over his shoulder and issued that same burst of unintelligible words.

"I think he wants us to follow him," Marty said.

"I don't *want* to follow him," Jacky said.

"We don't have much of a choice, do we?"

△△△

They had been walking for at least half an hour, allowing Marty time to try to make sense of the situation. Judging by the indigenous tribe's primitive dress and weapons, they had lived on Demon Island for a very long time with little communication with the modern world. He doubted they had randomly crossed paths with Marty and the girls. The island was too large for such a coincidental encounter. It was more likely they had spotted the *Oannes* yesterday or today and had been watching it. Which meant they would have been aware of the inflatable boat coming to shore. Perhaps they had been shadowing the three of them from the forest the entire time. The question was, why? What did a few outsiders matter to them? Mere curiosity? Yet if that was so, why intercept them? Why march them like a chain gang to...where? To their village?

Did they, like other primitive tribes unaccustomed to Westerners, consider Marty with his lighter skin to be some sort of ghost person? An evil spirit? Were they going to find him guilty in a kangaroo court of witchcraft and punish him? Execute him? God forbid, *eat* him?

Holy hell, no. Surely the Sri Lankan government knew about these people. If they were indeed cannibals, they would have been reported in the news. The public would have been warned. This was the bloody twenty-first century, after all.

Marty cast a sidelong glance at Rad. She had her head down, watching the ground where she stepped. Sweat saturated the front of her singlet, creating a damp V. She must have felt his eyes on her because she looked up at him. Her face was drawn tight, etched with distress. He almost didn't recognize her.

He offered a reassuring smile; she smiled back, though it was thin and forced.

The terrain angled upward. The leader kept up a brisk pace, walking easily despite the moist heat. Marty, already tiring from the long trek, began breathing heavily. Sweat stung his eyes. His thighs burned. Rad and Jacky, he noted, were also struggling.

He called loudly for a break, consequences be damned.

The leader stopped and studied them. Marty, doubled over and panting, said, "We need to rest." He pointed at the ground. "Rest?"

The leader said nothing, which Marty took as acquiescence. He sat down on the ground with an aggrieved sigh. Jacky sat next to him, while Rad, still standing, rummaged through her beach bag.

One of the hunters surrounding them—there were eight in total—levelled his spear at her.

"Hey!" Marty said, pushing himself to his feet.

"It's water," Rad told the guy, producing a plastic bottle. "Just water."

The leader said something, and the hunter lowered the spear.

Rad twisted the cap, breaking the plastic seal, and took a gulp. When Marty and Jacky had their share, she dumped the bottle back in her bag.

Marty glanced up the hill, trying to determine how much higher it rose. All he saw were trees and trees and more trees.

The leader set off again.

Groaning, Jacky reluctantly got up. Rad glowered at the hunters prodding them to move. Marty cursed them under his breath.

Yet they all fell into line.

Some ten minutes later they reached the summit. Marty thought he might be sick from the exertion. Rad, who was in the best shape of the three of them, was calling him to come over and look. He joined her at a break in the vegetation. They stood, it turned out, not at the top of a hill but on the rim of a caldera. The bowl-shaped hollow was several kilometers across and rimmed with steep forested slopes and rocky scarps. At the bottom of the depression was a small aquamarine lake shrouded in mist. They were at the lowest section of the rim, likely where the molten lava had escaped the crater before the volcano collapsed in upon itself.

"Huh," Marty said, struck by the contrast between the lush calm of the caldera today and the extreme violence and chaos that would have accompanied its formation all those millennia ago. "Didn't expect this."

"Isn't it incredible?" Rad said.

"Oh, wow," Jacky said, appearing at Marty's shoulder. "We can finally see the sky."

Marty glanced at the tribesmen. They were a dozen feet away, conversing amongst themselves. "Do you think those guys just took us here to show us the view?"

Rad said, "I think they want to stick us in a pot of boiling water with carrots and potatoes."

Jacky said, "Not funny."

"They're not cannibals," Marty assured her.

"Then you tell me what they want from us," said Rad. "The only good we are to them is either forced labor or as a food source."

Jacky moaned and turned away.

"Jesus, Rad…"

"You tell me what their interest in us is then, Marty."

He squeezed Jacky's shoulder affectionately. "You okay?"

"I don't want to be here."

"We'll be back on the *Oannes* soon enough."

Shaking her head, she stepped away from him, and his hand fell limply to his side.

ΔΔΔ

The descent down the caldera's inner wall was tough on Marty's knees but easier than the grueling ascent up the outer wall. Even so, the path was uneven and steep, and at one point Jacky tripped on a partly concealed root, slamming into the back of Rad and nearly sending them both tumbling down the slope. Marty too had a close call when he lost his balance on a collection of igneous rocks and slid on his hands and butt for a couple of meters before coming to a jarring halt at the base of a tree fern.

When the ground leveled out again, Marty saw subtle signs of habitation: banana trees stripped of ripe fruit, an axe next to a felled tree, the ashes of a small fire, discarded coconut shells that had been cut open and the meat taken. A short time later they reached the shore of the volcanic lake, which they followed to a village populated with dozens of palm-thatched mud huts. The tribespeople dotted about the settlement stopped what they were doing (preparing food, weaving baskets, sorting flowers and berries) to watch the arrival of the foreigners. Unlike the hunters in their loincloths, they wore more modest sarongs knotted around their chests or waists. The clothing buoyed Marty's spirit, as it meant they had indeed made contact with industrialized society, which lessened the chances that he and Rad and Jacky were going to end up on the dinner table as the main course. Even so, the stoic reception was unnerving. You would think an isolated tribe would be excited, or at least curious, by the appearance of a trio of outsiders. The stolid looks and general indifference made Marty feel as though they were all in on some sinister secret.

The leader of the hunters stopped before one of the thatched huts and gestured for Marty to enter. Pushing aside a hanging reed matt, he was forced to duck, as the doorway was not made for someone of his height. The hut's interior was roomy enough that he could stand upright again. Jacky and Rad followed him in, and they huddled in the middle of the dark room, alone for now, frowning at each other.

"What the hell is this?" Rad said finally.

"At least they didn't lock us in," said Marty.

"They may as well have," Jacky said. "Where are we going to go? You wouldn't get anywhere before one of those hunters launched a spear into your back."

"Did you see the way they were looking at us?" Rad said.

"You mean, *not* looking at us," said Jacky. "It was like they didn't care about us one way or another."

"That's good," Marty said. "It means they've seen people like us before. They're used to seeing people like us—rangers, or surveyors, or government people of some sort. They certainly didn't make those sarongs they're wearing. That means they've made peaceful contact with the modern world."

"So if we're no big deal, why are they holding us captive?"

Marty didn't have an answer to that and said, "Are either of you two aware of any indigenous tribes living in Sri Lanka?"

Jacky nodded and said, "The Vedda."

"They used to be called 'Forest People,'" added Rad. "Because they lived deep in the country's forests before the Buddhists arrived, and the Dutch. Nobody knows how long they've been in Sri Lanka, only that it's been a really long time. Perhaps since the Stone Age."

"And they're around today?"

"A few remote tribes still practice hunting and gathering. But most of them have started adopting modern customs, turning their reservations into tourist traps, or integrating into Sinhalese and Tamil villages."

"So these villagers could be Vedda?"

"I don't know who else they'd be."

"Have Vedda ever been known to kidnap people before?"

"You think they're *kidnapping* us?" Jacky asked.

"We're certainly not here of our own free will."

"But they're going to let us go?"

"I'm sure of it," he told her. "In fact, I'm sure this is just some big misunderstanding."

△△△

Less than ten minutes later a hunter returned and brought them through the village to a larger hut. Inside it, a well-fed man sat on a woven mat atop an L-shaped mud bench. He had a full head of wild gray hair and a snow-white beard that clashed dramatically with his tawny skin. Incongruously, he wore a blue-and-yellow cricket jersey, black gym shorts, Adidas flip flops, and four wristwatches, two on each wrist. Behind him on the wall was a weather-worn oil self-portrait in which he wore a white sarong and held a bow and cocked arrow. At the end of the bench were an assortment of glass and plastic bottles filled with different colored liquids.

Marty exchanged looks with Rad and Jacky. The man could have been a street hawker touting his wares on a busy Colombo street. When the hunter bowed in respect, however, Marty realized the old guy was likely the chief of the village.

He stood and approached them. Surprisingly, he took Marty's right hand in both of his and offered a firm double handshake, keeping eye contact the entire time. He greeted Rad and Jacky in the same manner and then, smiling broadly, said, "Hello."

△△△

"Thank the Lord!" Rad blurted, laughing shrilly. "You speak English!"

The chief stared at her, still smiling.

"My name's Martin," Marty said. "What's your name?"

He looked at Marty and nodded.

"Um, this is Jacqueline, and this is Radhika."

He kept nodding.

"I don't think he speaks English, after all," Jacky said, speaking through a smile.

"Hello," Marty said.

"Hello!" the man said.

"Is that the only word you know?" Rad asked.

He smiled at her.

"*Vanakkam*," Jacky said, which is an approximation of "hello" in Tamil.

The chief pointed at her feet and said, "Shoes!"

"Shoes, that's right," she said, nodding agreeably.

He pointed at Rad's feet, then Marty's, then his own, saying, "Shoes! Shoes! Shoes!" Then he pointed at the hunter's bare feet and said, "No shoes!" This observation caused him to burst into croaky laughter.

Marty and the girls laughed hesitantly, and Marty tried introducing himself again. He pointed to his chest, saying, "Martin."

The chief pointed at Marty's chest. "Martin."

"Yes!"

"Yes!"

Marty pointed at the chief's chest. "Name?"

The chief touched his chest. "Name."

"So he knows 'shoes' but not 'name'?" said Rad. "Who taught him English?"

The chief held out his arms, showing off his wrist jewelry. Three of the watches were analogue and one was digital. None were working. He said, "Watch."

"They're very nice," Marty said, then raised his own wrist-watch. "Watch."

"Watch!" the man said, staring at it. He pointed at Rad's bare wrist, then at Jacky's, then at the hunter's, saying, "No watch!" each time. This once again cracked him up.

Marty found the old man's materialism amusing and laughed as well, this time genuinely.

The chief pointed at Marty's watch again and said, "No watch."

Marty frowned and said, "Watch."

"No watch."

"Watch."

"No watch!"

Rad said, "I think he wants *your* watch, Marty."

"The hell he does!"

"Where do you think he got his watches from? They're likely gifts from previous visitors. You better give yours to him as well."

"I'm not giving him my bloody watch, Rad. It's a Rolex."

"Give it to him, Marty," Jacky said. "Maybe then he'll let us go."

Cursing under his breath, Marty unclasped the Rolex and held it forth in offering, the eighteen-karat gold gleaming brightly. The chief accepted it with both hands. After a perfunctory examination of the gift, he slid it onto his left wrist next to a fifty-dollar Casio and said, "Friend."

ΔΔΔ

The chief showed his new "friends" around the village, at-tempting to communicate using random English words, facial gestures, and hand signs. He summoned one of the tribesmen to demonstrate how they made fire, and another to show them how to properly aim a bow and arrow. Eventually they ended up at a long table in a spacious communal hut, where an old woman served them areca nuts rolled in beta leaves, as well as coconut shells filled with a very potent moonshine. Marty didn't plan on taking a second sip of the horrible-tasting brew (and neither did Rad or Jacky judging by the distasteful expressions on their faces), but the chief prodded them to finish every last drop. The old woman returned at some point—Marty's head was spinning by then—with a platter of venison and honey. She topped up their coconuts with more moonshine. The food was good, and the hooch started going down easier. Marty knew Pip would be getting concerned that they hadn't yet returned to the *Oannes*, and he must have suggested a half dozen times that they wrap things up and head back. Nevertheless, Rad and Jacky weren't listening to him. They were clearly inebriated, and their attention had become fixated on the chief as they playfully teased him about his wristwatches and choice of clothing (knowing he couldn't understand what they were saying). They were also trying to teach him everything from new English words to elaborate handshakes and nursery-school clapping games. It was a ridiculous scene, especially considering they had once considered the tribe to be a bunch of bloodthirsty cannibals.

At a little past two o'clock (Marty glimpsed the time on his relinquished Rolex), a group of dancers performed a frenetic number for them, which involved rhythmic drums and leafy branches and fast, flat-footed hopping that made it appear as though their bodies were vibrating. Marty guessed it was a ritualistic performance, perhaps some communication with the elements, or a pagan god. Whatever the purpose, it was mesmerizing to watch, and he couldn't take his eyes off the spectacle.

Nearing the climax, a young female removed a skull from a plant-weaved basket, thrusting it high into the air as she quivered and juked in circles, headbanging, black hair screaming.

"Holy shit!" Rad exclaimed.

Marty was speechless.

The skull was merfolk.

CHAPTER 21

MARTY

When the performance ended, Marty hurried to the dancer with the skull. She held it aloft proudly, allowing him to study the sagittal crest, the pronounced brow ridge, the bulbous frontal bone. The mutations were all nearly identical to those of the skull in the dry lab on the *Oannes*, and it all but confirmed the merfolk in the belly of the great white wasn't an outlier. There were more of its kind nearby. They lived somewhere around this island.

You're close, Marty-boy! You're getting so damn close!

Jacky and Rad and the chief joined him, and the chief began talking incomprehensibly about the skull. Marty would have given anything to have been able to understand him.

"Where?" he demanded.

"Where?" the chief said.

"For the love of God," Marty griped. "How do we get through to him?"

Jacky pointed at the skull, then raised a hand in a salute over her eyes, pantomiming looking around.

"Where?" the chief repeated.

"Yes, *where*?" Marty snapped. "Where the bloody hell did you find it?"

"Easy, Marty," Rad said. "He doesn't understand."

"I know he doesn't. But it's a simple question, isn't it?"

She touched the chief's wrist to get his attention. She pointed at the skull, then shrugged in feigned bafflement, turning left and right, as if she were searching for something.

The chief spoke a word they had come to associate with the moonshine.

"We don't want anything more to drink!" Marty said. "We want to know where you found that!" He jabbed a finger at the skull.

The chief stared at him blankly.

Rad said, "Maybe you can come back with a Vedda translator, Marty?"

"Know any good ones?" he asked sardonically.

"They would have found it on the beach," said Jacky. "Where else would they have found it? It washed up, or maybe a complete merfolk washed up, and they only kept its skull? Either way, isn't that all that matters? That it washed up on the beach? Now you know merfolk are definitely in these waters."

Rad said, "She's right, Marty."

"I *know* she's right. It's just... Perhaps there are *more* somewhere, more remains. Perhaps the skull is from a graveyard of sorts. Something like that... A discovery like that..."

"Hey," Jacky said, "where are you going?"

The chief had started walking away from them and gestured for them to follow.

ΔΔΔ

He led them out of the village and through lush rainforest for about ten minutes before coming to a depression carved into the vegetation. At the bottom was the crumbling mouth of a cave, overarched by an eldritch, gnarled tree with beards of moss and lichen veiling the darkness beyond. Just inside the cavity was a stockpile of resources from the village. The chief quickly went to work creating a fire in a nearby stone-ringed pit. He retrieved a torch that lay next to the pit, smeared the cloth-wrapped end in what appeared to be animal fat, and lit it in the fire. Holding the brightly burning torch above his head, he gestured once again for them to follow.

"Where's he taking us?" Jacky asked. "There clearly won't be merfolk bones in a cave."

"I'll go," Marty said. "You two can wait here."

"Forget that!" said Rad. "I live for creepy crawly cave walks."

"I guess I'm coming along too then," Jacky said. "After you, Marty. And try not to trip and break your ankle, because Rad and I aren't strong enough to carry you back out."

They didn't have to worry about tripping on anything, as the floor of the cave was unnaturally smooth and free from typical rocky debris. Marty realized it was not a limestone cave but a volcanic lava tube. When the volcano in the center of Demon Island erupted however many thousands of years ago, the surface of the flowing lava would have inevitably cooled and crusted to form a roof above the still-flowing stream of molten rock, and when the last of the lava drained away, all that remained behind were empty, snaking tunnels.

And if I'm not mistaken, Marty thought excitedly, *some of the tunnels most certainly connect with the ocean, making the discovery of merfolk bones a distinct possibility after all.*

Soon the tunnel opened to a cavernous hall with twenty-foot ceilings. It appeared to be a dead end, but the chief went confidently to the left side, where there was a small fissure in the wall. The passage was so tight they were forced to duckwalk and shimmy through. They emerged in another large tunnel in which they could once again walk comfortably upright and abreast of one another. They knew they were still close to the surface because here and there tree roots broke through the tunnel roofs, dangling down like spidery appendages.

After progressing for several minutes with only the torchlight to see by, Marty suddenly made out a different light source in the distance, which turned out to be sun shining through a section of collapsed ceiling. Verdant jungle rimmed the edge of the hole, which was the size of a baseball diamond. Tangles of vines dripped to the cavity floor. The light filtering through the canopy far above them was much brighter than the torchlight, revealing the solidified drips and waves the lava had scoured into the tunnel walls, as well as the many different minerals coloring the igneous rock.

Jacky and Rad oohed and aahed at the sights and seemed ready to take a break, but the chief had other plans, climbing over the scree and continuing onward.

For the next five hundred meters the lava tube remained so straight and uniform it would have been easy to believe it had been manmade. The chief pointed out several large holes in the floor, deep shafts that would connect to lower-level tunnels, and they all steered clear of them. And then light appeared in the distance again. The source turned out to be another skylight, yet unlike the previous section of broken tunnel, here the ground disappeared beneath a perfectly still subterranean lake.

"I knew it!" Marty cried triumphantly, joining the chief at the water's edge. "The tunnel connects with the ocean! I bloody well knew it!"

The chief pointed at the water and said, "Where."

"Yes, yes, where!" he said, clapping the old fellow on the shoulder. "*Where* you found the merfolk skull. You're a linguistic genius, my good man!" He turned, intent on telling Jacky and Rad the good news—and his eyes widened in amazement.

CHAPTER 22

MARTY

They returned to the *Oannes* just past six o'clock in the evening, as the sun was dipping beneath the horizon. Pip and Elsa had been relieved to find them none the worse for wear, though Pip let loose on Marty for causing them to worry. Yet her anger quickly gave way to fascination as he described their time at the tribal village and the discovery in the lava tube.

"There were cave paintings on the walls?" Pip said.

Marty nodded. "Petroglyphs too, though not nearly as many. It was remarkable, Pip. There must have been over five hundred paintings. Geometric, zoomorphic, anthropomorphic. Some appeared to be symbolic—"

"For heaven's sake, speak English, Marty," said Rad. To Pip and Elsa, she added, "Most of them were silhouettes of people hunting and dancing and mating. A lot were of animals too. Deer, big birds, fish. And most notably..." She looked at Marty.

He grinned. "Merfolk."

"Merfolk!" Pip exclaimed. "Are you pulling my legs?"

"Pulling my leg, Pip. Singular. And, no, I am most certainly not."

Elsa was regarding him skeptically. "Are you sure the representations you saw were merfolk, Marty?"

"Upper body of a human, lower body of a fish? What would you classify that as?"

"I assume the paintings must have been old and degraded by

the elements?"

"Old, yes. I can't say how old, but some were created with bat excrement and were extremely simplistic. Bi-triangular females, T-shaped males, figures with raised and rounded arms. But degraded? Not at all. The cover of the dense vegetation and overhanging rock protected them well from nature's vagaries, it seems."

"And the merfolk, *mon capitaine*?" Pip pressed.

"They were often depicted standing side by side with the humans with no discernible connection to each other. However, in some scenes they were in swimming positions, facing away from the humans. Fleeing from hunters? Many prehistoric cave paintings depict animals in the running position for just that reason. Prehistoric hominin bragging, I suppose you might say. Then again, there appeared to be ritualistic scenes in which the humans were worshipping the merfolk. So did the people who created the paintings consider the merfolk spirits that needed to be appeased? Or prey? I can't answer that. I wish one of us had brought a phone to take pictures. But no matter. I'll be returning first thing tomorrow morning."

"Tomorrow?" Rad said, surprised. "You're going to hike all the way back there tomorrow?"

"Of course! A discovery such as this needs to be thoroughly documented."

"Good luck finding the entrance to that lava tube again," Jacky said.

"I paid particular attention to the path we took to the beach. I'm sure finding the cave again won't pose a problem. Of course, I wouldn't mind a volunteer to accompany me and lighten the load of my gear."

"How much does your camera weight?" Rad quipped.

"My scuba gear, Rad."

"You're going *diving* in that lake?"

"The majority of merfolk sightings throughout the ages have been of the creatures in terrestrial environs—tidal flats, sandbars, rocky shores, and so forth. Which means, unlike whales and dolphins, they don't spend one hundred percent of their lives in the water. They appear to be more akin to seals, which come ashore to mate or to escape predators or to simply rest and relax. And coming ashore on remote islands rather than continental land would have offered merfolk refuge from their more technologically advanced, and landlocked, hominin cousins. The first ocean-faring ships weren't invented by modern humans until five thousand years ago, which is yesterday in geological timescales. Which is to say, merfolk would have been able to exist and evolve in isolation and safety for nearly two million years. What am I getting at?" He lit the tobacco in the bowl of his corncob pipe. "It's always been a pet hypothesis of mine that merfolk don't only live in the waters around islands but—"

"In submerged caves *beneath* islands," Elsa finished, nodding thoughtfully.

"It would certainly explain why they've been so elusive over the centuries, wouldn't it?"

Rad said, "And you think there are merfolk in that lake?"

"In the flooded lava tubes, yes, I think it's a distinct possibility."

Jacky said, "It would be pitch-black down there."

"Which they could navigate perfectly fine with echolocation."

"It's an interesting premise, Marty," Elsa said. "Yet I must ask, why would a presumably intelligent species choose to live in such a bleak environment?"

"Because the ocean is the most dangerous place on this planet, Elsa. Sharks and killer whales make the fiercest land predators seem tame by comparison. Just as early humans retreated to terrestrial caves for protection against giant birds and jaguars and bears, merfolk likely sought out underwater caves for the same reason."

"Cave diving is not open water diving, *mon capitaine*," Pip said. "It is dangerous and requires different training and equipment."

"She's right, Marty," Rad said. "I don't think you've thought this through completely."

"I'm flattered by your concern, both of you. But rest assured,

I've been on my fair share of cave diving expeditions throughout the British Isles, and I have the necessary equipment on board the *Oannes* to safely explore the lava tubes beneath Demon Island."

"And what if you find merfolk, Marty?" Elsa said. "Or perhaps I should say, what if they find *you*? I can't imagine they'd be thrilled by a surface-dwelling trespasser in their submarine domain?"

"They might consider human flesh to be a delicacy," Rad said.

"I highly doubt that," Marty told her, puffing on his pipe. "The two merfolk skulls featured sagittal crests. You typically find these in animals with strong jaws and powerful bites because the ridge of bone serves as a point of attachment for the temporalis muscle, which is one of the main muscles used for chewing. Dogs and cats and numerous other carnivores have sagittal crests."

"So merfolk are carnivores? Great. Shouldn't that deter you from swimming into their home?"

"I didn't say they were carnivores, Rad. Primates are the exception to the rule. Many species of early humans had sagittal crests, and they weren't meat-eaters. Their diet consisted of leaves and grasses. Sagittal crests allowed for the prolonged chewing of tough and fibrous vegetation with less muscle fatigue. The crests only began to disappear during the time of Homo erectus, which was the earliest human relative to control fire. With fire, Homo erectus began to cook their food, allowing for a more varied diet and a higher consumption of meat. Merfolk, being aquatic creatures, clearly never mastered fire, which leads me to believe they've retained a plant-based diet similar to early, pre-fire hominins."

"You're saying you think merfolk are vegetarians?"

"I'm saying it's reasonable to assume their diet consists mostly of kelp and seaweed. In other words, they're not underwater savages that would find human flesh to be a delicacy." Marty shrugged, tiring of defending a decision that was preordained. "Look, everyone. Either merfolk live beneath Demon

Island or they don't. Either they're friendly or they're not. The only way to know for certain is to investigate. Is there a risk involved in that? Certainly. But in the words of a philosopher I respect, 'Never was anything great achieved without danger.' Now enough of this. My mind is made up. Tomorrow I'm going to explore the submerged sections of the lava tubes. If anyone would like to accompany me to the cavern with the paintings, you're more than welcome to do so."

CHAPTER 23

ELSA

After everyone else had retired to their cabins for the night, Elsa remained on the foredeck of the *Oannes*, content to sit beneath the star-lit night sky and be alone with her thoughts. She had been doing a lot of soul-searching for the last hour, and she had decided to accompany Dr. Murdoch on his dive beneath Demon Island. This had been an easier conclusion than she had anticipated. After Ron's death, she had vowed she was done with cave diving. Nevertheless, what she didn't know up until today—or at least didn't acknowledge—was that she had been living a lie these last few years, merely biding her time, waiting for an excuse, any excuse, to get back in the water. Dr. Murdoch had given her that excuse. The golden safety rule of scuba diving was to never dive alone—a rule that was even more important when diving beneath an overhead environment. If she allowed Marty to dive the lava tubes on his own, and he suffered a fatal accident, she would be as culpable as if she had dived with him...yet because the chances of something disastrous happening were significantly reduced when diving with a buddy, she had a moral obligation to accompany him.

It was sound—and agreeable—logic. And now that she had decided on her course of action (and her guilt at being unable to save Ron temporarily and conveniently assuaged), she could barely contain her excitement at the prospect of the dive. Much of this was for the simple thrill of once again exploring where few (if anybody) had been before. Yet she had to admit she was also cautiously enthralled about the possibility, however remote, of encountering merfolk. She would never have entertained such a thought twenty-four hours ago, but the evidence was proving to be quite persuasive—as was Dr. Murdoch himself. Reading about his merfolk theories in dry academic journals had always been interesting and amusing but little more than that. Listening to him argue them firsthand was something else altogether. His unwavering conviction that he was right and everyone else was wrong was admirable and attractive and infectious...so much so for the first time in Elsa's career as an oceanographer she found herself accepting, or at least considering, scientific claims on faith before completing the rigorous process of verifiability and falsifiability.

And it feels damn good to finally let down your hair, doesn't it? she thought. *When was the last time you felt so free, so alive—?*

"Hello there, Dr. Montero. I thought everyone had gone to bed."

Elsa looked away from the black expanse of sky to find Marty emerging from the salon. "Hello, Marty. I've just been enjoying some me-time."

"May I join you?"

"I would like that."

He settled into the seat next to her with a sigh.

"What's kept you up?" she asked.

"I've been analyzing the sonar data. The pod of dolphins has apparently lost interest in us and moved on, leaving this neck of the ocean oddly quiet. Ah, a full moon. My favorite lunar phase."

"It makes you feel small, doesn't it?"

"The moon? Sure. It's a large celestial body, after all."

"The moon, the stars, space..." They were silent for a few moments, and then Elsa added, "This might sound strange, but the moon is why I became an oceanographer in the first place."

"You do know there's no water up there, right?"

"Did you believe your mother when she told you there was a Man in the Moon?"

"I don't imagine she ever told me such a thing. She is a rather sensible woman."

"My mother told me there was a Man in the Moon, and I

believed her. I used to think he could see everything that I did. When I said my prayers, I often included him in them, telling him I was sorry for doing this or that. Even when I grew older, and learned the image of the human face was just various lunar maria, the moon retained a special place in my heart. In fact, as a teenager I wanted to become an astronaut. That dream fizzled out in university when I learned that qualified applicants had less than a half-percent chance of being selected by NASA."

"Astronomical odds."

"Funny, but yes. I didn't have a realistic hope in hell. So to scratch my itch for exploration, I turned my attention to the oceans. And here I am some twenty years later—cataloguing whale shit. Can you see those black dots on the moon?"

"The craters?"

"No, the much smaller pockmarks. They're the skylights of collapsed lava tubes."

"Must be damn big lava tubes."

"Some are more than a mile in diameter and twenty times that in length."

"Why are they so much bigger than the lava tubes on earth?"

"The lower gravity affects volcanism differently there. It also keeps the lava tubes in remarkably good shape. Scientists are talking about how future astronauts could use them as shelter from the harsh environment, fluctuating temperatures, and radiation. It's interesting—prehistoric humans started out in caves on earth, and when we establish permanent settlements on the moon, we'll be starting out in caves all over again. I wanted to ask you something, Marty. Would you consider putting off your dive beneath Demon Island for another day or so?"

He frowned. "Whatever for?"

"I would like to accompany you."

"Accompany me?" He shook his head. "I'm sure you're an accomplished scuba diver, Elsa. But as Pip mentioned earlier, cave diving is not your typical recreational dive."

"I'm well aware of the dangers, Marty," she said firmly. "I've logged hundreds of dives and thousands of hours in underwater caves throughout the Americas."

He blinked in surprise. "Is that so?"

"I was researching cave animals specifically adapted to light-less, food-poor environments. Unfortunately, pollution and habitat destruction are causing many of them to go extinct."

"I never knew this."

"Biodiversity conservation often fails to take cave species into account. Because nobody knows much about species like eyeless crustaceans, nobody seems to care about them."

"I meant, I never knew you were an experienced cave diver."

"Why would you?"

"I wouldn't. And...well, this changes everything, doesn't it?" He grinned at her. "I would be honored for you to join me on the dive. However, why do we need to postpone it a day?"

"We need to return to the mainland so I could collect my gear."

"No, that shouldn't be necessary." He sized her up. "You're nearly my height. One of my wetsuits should fit you fine. And I have more than enough equipment to kit us both out."

Elsa always used her own scuba gear as so many things could go wrong during a cave dive. However, Dr. Murdoch wasn't a shady expat running a dive shop targeting tourists; his equipment was likely top-of-the-line and properly maintained.

"All right then," she told him. "We dive tomorrow."

CHAPTER 24

Merfolk: From the Deep. The making-of the original Netflix documentary.

"Rolling," Gus the cameraman said.

Jamie, clad head-to-toe in black for the third consecutive day, clapped the slate.

Fat Mike, stretching a New York Rangers jersey to the seams, in his director's chair said, "Whenever you're ready, Double M. You can pick up from where you left off yesterday."

Beneath the spotlights in the West London studio, Marty nodded. "Thanks to the numerous eyewitness accounts throughout the ages," he began, regurgitating what he'd rehearsed the night before, "we have a pretty good idea about what merfolk look like. It seems they bear a strong resemblance to us, which isn't surprising given we likely share a common ancestor. But what about merfolk behavior? Do they *act* like us? Are they like Disney's Ariel, all peaches and cream? Or are they like Homer's sirens, predators that lure men to their watery graves? Some eyewitness accounts suggest the former, and some suggest the latter. Yet we must remember that, historically, the majority of merfolk sightings were by sailors long at sea. They would undoubtedly have had active imaginations, and it would be understandable if they interwove hearsay with superstition and lust and fear, ultimately creating a merfolk antithetical to the real thing. The truth, unfortunately, is that we simply don't know, and can't know, anything about the general behavior of merfolk without sustained scientific observation.

"Nevertheless, I believe we can make some relatively safe logical deductions. Everybody seems to agree that merfolk have two mammary glands, which means the females bear one, or occasionally two, offspring at a time. Given their anatomical base of arms and hands, they likely carry their young as well, as do all land-dwelling primates. Yet due to their relatively small size in comparison to sharks and squid and other threats, merfolk, especially the young, would be vulnerable to predation. Thus it is my opinion that they are social mammals that live together in large numbers for protection. It is improbable they would have a complex language to communicate with one another as do humans, as we only began talking in a unique and complex form some 100,000 years ago. But I would argue they have a rudimentary one. Great apes, for example, can comprehend symbols; they understand that *this* stands for *that* even though *this* has no resemblance to *that*. They can learn American Sign Language, computer language, and spoken language. They only have trouble with syntax and stringing symbols together into meaningful sentences. So, yes, merfolk likely possess a language, but one at the linguistic stage of early hominins rather than the articulatory capabilities of modern humans. Does this mean they would possess theory of mind? That is, the ability to attribute thoughts, desires, and intentions to others; to predict or explain their actions; and to posit their intentions? Human children develop theory of mind at three or four years of age. Prior to that time, they do not realize that they or others may have incomplete information. Whether merfolk have this ability or not is anyone's guess.

"In considering the technological achievements of merfolk, I believe they would be rather unremarkable. Assuming merfolk have a brain size on par with Australopithecus, and a similar level of manual dexterity, they would have the cognitive complexity and physical ability to use simple tools for acquiring and processing animal and plant food. Cracking mollusks, butchering carcasses, disarticulation, marrow extraction, cutting stalks. Nevertheless, the marine realm offers no fibers suitable for basketry or weaving clothing, and the lack of fire would make pottery and metallurgy impossible. These two facts alone would hamper any sort of cultural and technological innovation, preventing merfolk from evolving contemporaneously with the genus Homo beyond an early Paleolithic lifestyle. Sorry, folks, there's no shining Atlantis down on the seabed somewhere.

"You may be wondering where do merfolk live then? Given their lack of advanced weaponry, I propose they are forager-scavengers that move from location to location, subsisting on sea grasses and shellfish, carcasses leftover by larger predators, and small fish they hunt opportunistically. However, it's also possible they group in particular areas for periods of time for central place foraging activities. A home base, if you will. Underwater island caves come to mind as a particularly likely location. These would offer shelter from their landlocked cousins—which would include modern humans—as well as dangerous marine predators, including invertebrates such as poisonous jellyfish.

"So what happened to merfolk populations? Why are the creatures so rare and elusive? One hypothesis is that they've gone extinct. When modern humans set out on the Age of Discovery in the fifteenth century, and began to explore remote islands, we may have hunted merfolk to extinction just as we hunted Steller's sea cows to extinction less than thirty years after first discovering the species. Indeed, the number of recorded merfolk sightings declined significantly in the following centuries, falling to nearly zero today. However, the broad scale hunting necessary to wipe out a species would not have gone undocumented, and unlike with sea cows, no records speak of this happening to merfolk.

"The more likely scenario, if you ask me, is that there hasn't been a decline in merfolk populations; there's only been a decline in sightings or, more accurately, *reported* sightings. In the Age of Enlightenment in the 17th and 18th centuries, there was a new bias in observation and reporting. Science had become the new faith. Pragmatic people no longer spoke of creatures from folklore for fear of being ridiculed, and the editors of scholarly journals refused to publish any references to them. This trend accelerated with industrialization in the 19th and 20th centuries and continues into the present.

"So I ask again: What happened to merfolk populations? Where did the creatures go? I posit they haven't gone anywhere. They're where they've always been. We've just stopped looking for them."

$$\triangle\triangle\triangle$$

Marty woke at 5:30 a.m., pleasantly surprised that he had slept through the night without waking. Sitting up, he recalled dreaming about the Netflix documentary, and his lips twisted in a scowl. "Correction, Fat Mike," he muttered as he swung his legs out of bed and got up, anxious for the day to begin, "*I* never stopped looking."

CHAPTER 25

PIP

At 6:30 a.m. Pip stood on the starboard side of the *Oannes'* main deck, watching Marty pilot the RIB through the rolling swell toward Demon Island. Dr. Montero, Radhika Fernandez, and Jacqueline DeSilva were also on the small boat, the latter two having decided over breakfast that a hike to the lava tubes would be more interesting than lounging about on the *Oannes*.

Pip raised her hand in goodbye, unbeknownst to her that she would never see any of them ever again.

PART 4
The Dive

"Aye, tough mermaids are, the lot of them."
—Blackbeard

CHAPTER 26

MARTY

In the flooded cavern, Marty and Elsa performed a predive safety check of their equipment, went over their dive plan for the final time, changed into neoprene wetsuits, and geared up.

Marty called to Rad and Jacky, who were filming the cave art with their phones.

"We have three hours of air in our tanks," he told them. "We'll use one-third of that for exploring the lava tubes, and another third getting back here, meaning you should expect us in about two hours."

"What about the last third?" Rad asked.

"That's in case we get into any sort of trouble," Elsa said.

"What kind of trouble?"

"Nothing will happen to us, Rad," Marty told her. "Diving with extra air is a standard safety redundancy, that's all."

"Are you sure you want to do this, Marty?" Concern showed in her eyes. "I mean, what if there really *are* merfolk down there...?"

"I'm counting on it," he replied, offering her a reassuring smile. He hiked the twin one hundred-cubic-foot steel tanks onto his back, then tossed a black ripstop nylon bag over his shoulder. He picked up the small diver propulsion vehicle (DPV) and fin-walked into the perfectly still water.

△△△

The boulder-strewn cavern slid away as he sank beneath the surface of the subterranean pool. Rad's and Jacky's chatter ("See you guys soon!" "Be careful!" "Don't get eaten!") faded. Marty clipped one end of the double-braided nylon guide reel to his buoyancy control device (BCD). The other end was attached to an anchor point in the cave so they could find their way out of the pitch-black lava tubes again.

He switched on the diver propulsion vehicle, which was basically a bullet-shaped electric engine that powered a propellor. Since the range they could travel underwater was limited by the amount of breathing gas they could carry, the DPV would allow them to achieve a greater penetration distance in the time they had.

Back on the *Oannes*, he had devised a tow rope with a large D-ring on one end for Elsa to hold onto. He passed this to her now. She gave him a thumbs up, and he clicked the DPV's throttle on the stern handlebars. They began moving swiftly forward, the propellor wash parallel to and below them.

With the dive underway, Marty's nerves were on edge, and he realized he was incredibly grateful that Elsa had decided to accompany him. Cave diving solo, even for an experienced diver such as himself, was a dangerous activity. A dive buddy considerably lessened the chances of something going wrong. And Elsa wasn't any run-of-the-mill dive buddy. Curious about her credentials, he had looked her up on the internet the night before and had been more than impressed with her accomplished career as an internationally acclaimed cave biologist. He had been saddened to learn about the death of her husband on what appeared to be her final dive. There wasn't much information available on the exact circumstances of the tragedy, only that the man became tangled in their guideline and panicked and drowned. For something like that to happen to your spouse would be heartbreaking; for it to happen right before your eyes would be devastatingly traumatic. Marty thought he now understood why Elsa was living abroad in Sri Lanka. Presumably she'd wanted to reboot a life that had gone off the rails.

She and he were not so different after all, it seemed.

Pushing the tangential thoughts aside, Marty concentrated on the dive. The water was magnificently clear, offering twice the visibility one would expect in the open ocean on a perfect day. Horizontal layers of flow lines and ledges carved into the mineral-colored igneous rock walls marked the successively shallower depths at which the lava had flowed through the tube. The floor, created when the surface of the final stream of lava solidified, was flat and covered with a layer of muck washed down through the skylight from the rainforest above.

At the far end of the pool, where the lava tube's roof sank below the water, they entered a tunnel about the size of those in the London Underground. The high-intensity LED lights strapped to the back of their hands cut cones of white light through the blackness. In places the terrain was silky and rounded, and in others it was rough and jagged and festooned with psychedelic lavacicles. Some were broad and tapering to points resembling giant shark teeth, while others were irregularly shaped like stretched taffy. Similar formations in limestone caves took thousands of years to develop; these would have been forged in a few anarchic hours.

Marty recalled Elsa mentioning the lava tubes on the moon, and he could very easily imagine he was not on Earth but some alien, primordial celestial body, millions of kilometers from home.

When the tunnel tightened to a narrow, elliptical restriction with a shallow roof, he slowed the scooter so he could navigate the space without knocking their heads or tanks on the rocky surroundings. The lava tube opened up substantially again on the other side, and it was there they spotted their first cavedweller: a three-centimeter remipede lacking both eyes and pigmentation. The exotic encounters became more abundant the farther they went: an albino squat lobster; a snowball sea slug; numerous small shrimp-like crustaceans and segmented worms; a school of paeony bulleye fish, their bright red color reminiscent of the molten lava which had carved out their underwater refuge so long ago.

Eventually they arrived at a gallery that was so large their lights barely reached the distant walls. At the farthest end it split into an upper and lower passage. Marty chose the upper one for the simple reason that it was the larger of the two. At the front of a lava flow, the lava behaves much like a river delta, branching off from the original flow to create smaller distributaries, and he knew that keeping to the main channel would yield the best chance of reaching the ocean.

Thirty meters down the passage, they surfaced in an air pocket trapped above the water table. The concave chamber offered a bubble of headspace, the size of which would likely vary based on the rise and fall of the tides.

Marty plucked his respirator from his mouth and said, "Having fun yet?"

Elsa removed her respirator also. "Wouldn't want to be anywhere else."

He checked his pressure gauge. His stage cylinder was nearly two-thirds empty, and he suggested it was a good time to switch to their back-mounted tanks. They detached the pony bottles from their harnesses, tied them off on the guideline, and resumed the dive breathing from their main tanks.

The morphology of the tunnels continued much the same as they had before, alternating between smooth and jagged surfaces that were ornamented with crystal formations and lavacicles and the occasional lava pillar. One cathedral-like cavern featured rippled walls that looked stolen from Antoni Gaudi's gothic Sagrada Familia. Another smaller room had a sandy island in the middle of it. This reminded Marty of a tragic tale of a diver who had perished in the Sterkfontein Caves in South Africa. The young man had left the safety of his guideline and got lost in a maze of tunnels. With his air running dangerously low, he got lucky finding a small island at the end of one tunnel—or so he thought. Rescuers found his skeleton six weeks later. Marty could only imagine the terror and loneliness of sitting in the unrelenting black for days on end, starving, understanding no one was ever going to come for you. The young man clearly realized this was his sad fate, because beside his corpse, scrawled into the sand, was a message telling his wife and mother that he loved them.

They came to their second restriction twenty-five minutes into the dive. He couldn't see how far the narrow shaft went before opening up again, and he didn't want to get stuck in the middle of it with the scooter, so he tied it off on the guideline. He gave Elsa an okay hand signal, she okayed back, and he entered the restriction using what was known as the bent-knee kick. Propulsion was limited, but the technique worked well in cramped areas. Most importantly, it minimized the disruption of silt on the cave floor, which could turn gin-clear water into a soupy brown mess, the last thing a diver wanted when there was no direct access to the surface.

The initial twenty feet into the restriction went smoothly, but then the shaft flattened to a horizonal wedge, forcing Marty to wiggle through, scraping his chest and tanks on the rock and stirring up the fine silt that had gathered there over the years. His visibility deteriorated to two meters. As he fumbled deeper along the squeeze, it dropped to zero. He couldn't see his hands when he held them before his face, forcing him to feel his way forward.

Quiet panic nibbled at his insides, and he told himself to remain calm. Panic led to fear, and fear shut down rational thought.

After another twenty or twenty-five feet of slow progress through the blackout, the passage corkscrewed, becoming more vertical than horizontal. Marty twisted his body to compensate —and at some point realized he no longer knew up from down.

The panic returned, louder and hungrier. Marty's breathing became more rapid. Thoughts of hypoxia and carbon dioxide poisoning snowballed the panic, causing the mildly stressful situation to spiral into full-blown anxiety. He began kicking faster and clawing at the rock to escape the claustrophobic space. His throat felt clogged with coppery pennies, and his hand went to his respirator, instinct shouting at him to yank it free. He nearly followed the fatal advice, but some higher-level cognitive process stopped him.

Stop—think—breathe.

He forced himself to stop flailing.

Stop—think—breathe.

He forced himself to take deep, even breaths.

Stop...think...breathe...

His heartbeat slowed. The heaviness in his chest subsided. The sense of impending doom faded.

And before he knew it, he could see his light again, and his elbows and knees were no longer slapping against rock.

He was out!

The relief was immeasurable, yet he remained completely disoriented. Only when he noted which direction his bubbles were traveling did he once again know up from down. He quickly finned back the way he had come, concerned that Elsa might have panicked too. He was steeling himself to swim back into the cloud of silt when she emerged from it. Behind her mask, her eyes were intense yet calm.

He gave her the okay sign; she okayed back.

Jesus H. Christ, he thought, realizing just how close he had come to killing them both.

△△△

Over the next half an hour, they were faced with numerous forks in the tunnels and nearly as many dead ends. This disheartened Marty, as he began to resign himself to the fact they would never make it to the mouth of the cave, which would be the most likely location for the merfolk to reside.

Now they were floating in proper trim in a passage about three meters wide and five high. Ahead of them it shrank into yet another restriction...from which he could feel a slight current. This buoyed his spirits, as he believed the current meant it likely connected back to the main conduit from which they had deviated at some point. Even so, proceeding would be chancy. The two previous restrictions would be classified as "minor" in diving terminology. This one would be classified as "major," meaning they would need to unbuckle their tanks to get through.

Marty checked his dive computer: they had ten minutes before they had to turn back.

Was the major restriction worth exploring given how little time they had left and the high risk involved? Or should they play it safe, cut their losses, and call it a day?

Marty knew the answer right away, but he wasn't going to endanger Elsa again.

He signaled for her to wait where she was, then removed his tanks from his back. She tapped him on the shoulder and shook her head. He thought she was telling him not to proceed, but then she signed that she was coming with him.

There was no time to debate the matter, or even a way to do so, and he simply nodded.

Pushing his tanks ahead of him, he entered the shaft first.

△△△

He had to swim sideways to fit through the tight space. After a short distance the passage doglegged. He twisted his body to swim upward, his tanks scraping the rock the entire way. Thankfully there was little silt due to the current, and his visibility remained good. Then the tunnel leveled out again, but it was so shallow that even with perfect buoyancy he was dragging his belly on the ground and hitting his head on the ceiling at the same time. There wasn't room to look behind him to see how

Elsa was doing.

He tried not to think about what they would do if the squeeze tightened to a point that they couldn't pass through.

And then it did just that.

He hesitated a moment, then shoved his tanks through the basalt sphincter. They became wedged.

Cursing to himself, he shoved again.

They popped through.

Marty exhaled to make his chest smaller, sucked in his belly, and bullied his way through too.

ΔΔΔ

Finally the exit passage swelled to a comfortable size. When Elsa joined him, they swam side-by-side against the current, following an upward gradient. The tunnel became larger and larger, the current stronger and stronger. On the other side of a duck-under, they came to a cavernous area about the size of a small house.

Marty checked his dive computer. They were ten minutes past the time they had agreed to turn back. He checked his pressure gauge. He had started with 2800psi in the double steel tanks, and he had already used 1100psi, dipping into his safety reserves.

Even so, they had to be close to where the channel emptied into the ocean. They could push on, surface in the sea, and swim to shore—

No. That wasn't the plan. They could still get lost, never find the exit, and then they wouldn't have enough air to return the way they had come.

There was a saying amongst divers that watching your air pressure go down to zero is no way to spend the rest of your life, and he wholeheartedly agreed.

I'll come back tomorrow, he consoled himself, *and the day after that, if need be. I don't care if it takes weeks or years, I'll come back every bloody day until I find the creatures.*

He twirled his pointer finger in tight circles, indicating to Elsa they were ending the dive. She nodded.

As they were turning around, something large and fast darted past them before disappearing back into the inky abyss.

CHAPTER 27

ELSA

Elsa knew they were pushing their luck. They had already added an extra twenty minutes to their maximum bottom time. That meant twenty minutes less reserve air, leaving them a forty-minute safety window. Still plenty of time, but you never knew what emergencies could happen, and even a few minutes of extra air could mean the difference between life and death.

Plan your dive; dive your plan.

It was that simple.

She was about to signal to Marty that they needed to head back when he signaled this to her first. She nodded and was performing a helicopter turn, pivoting on a horizontal axis, when she saw a flash of blue bioluminescent light and a wash of white flesh.

She swung her LED light, trying to track the lightning-quick movement—and saw a powerful, finned tail.

Then it was gone.

Marty began swimming after the creature. Elsa remained frozen in shock.

Was that what she thought it was?

Could it really be…?

She wanted to scream at Marty to come back. Tell him they had to stay together. *There was a merfolk in the water with them.* But of course she couldn't do any of that with a respirator in her mouth.

CHAPTER 28

MARTY

Marty felt as though every neuron was firing inside his brain at once, a fireworks of amazement, horror, elation, and surprise. Danger and caution and prudence—none of that mattered right then. All he could think was: *It's there, it's right there, don't let it get away!*

It had been darting in and out of his LED light, leading him, almost playing with him—and suddenly it disappeared altogether.

Marty assumed an upright, treading-water orientation. He spun left and right, his light arcing through the black water at frantic angles.

There! A dozen feet away! It was directly in front of him and holding itself in a position mirroring his own.

To avoid blinding the merfolk, he lowered the light to its abdomen and stared in wonder. The creature was both everything and nothing he had imagined it would be. A mane of blue, bioluminescent hair flowed away from its head like a halo. Its face was a mashup of simian and human and Klingon (the latter due to its oversized forehead). Its streamlined upper body was bone-white and hairless, though its flesh darkened to a mottled gray along the tops of its shoulders and the length of its arms. A pair of taut, small breasts, a narrow waist, and a delicate bone structure suggested it was a female.

It had no legs.

From its pelvis down was a smooth, powerful tail that tapered into a symmetrical caudal fin remarkably similar to that of a cetacean.

With a sudden up and down undulation of the tail, the mer-folk propelled itself easily through the water, stopping a few feet before him to reveal its grotesque majesty in all its glory. The glowing blue hair and liquid-black eyes—flecked with blue and clearly intelligent—captivated Marty with their alien beauty. Yet the rest of the merfolk's features were so sleekly eroded he almost felt as though he were looking at a burn victim that had received a too-tight face transplant. The nose was little more than a bump with vertical slits for nostrils. There were no external ears to speak of, only cavities in the sides of its skull. And the mouth, which extended nearly the width of the jaw, featured unnaturally swollen lips that curled upward at the edges to form a surgically butchered smile.

Then it blinked—translucent eyelids moving horizontally across each eyeball.

Speechless, Marty raised both his hands, palms outward, in a gesture of amity.

After a moment the merfolk did the same. Its hands were much larger than his and webbed with thin membranes connecting the elongated fingers to one another up to the third knuckle joints.

Spontaneously Marty extended his right arm, wanting nothing more than to touch the fairytale creature before him.

The merfolk extended its own arm, and for one absurdly comical moment he thought it was going to shake his hand. Instead it gripped his forearm, its long fingers wrapping around him with ease. This was painful and instantly menacing.

Marty stared in confusion at the merfolk. It blinked again, and its puffy lips parted, revealing rows of sharp teeth.

Alarmed, he tried tugging his hand free. The creature's grip was like a vice.

He tried again, pulling with all his strength and kicking with his flippers.

With its other hand, the merfolk yanked the respirator from his mouth.

CHAPTER 29

ELSA

It was the most astonishing sight Elsa had ever seen: a human being floating face-to-face, palms-to-palms, with a living and breathing mermaid.

She couldn't fathom what Marty must be thinking, having made first contact with a creature he had been chasing most of his adult life, an endeavor that had cost him his career and reputation. Equally, she couldn't fathom what the *merfolk* must be thinking. Did it see any of itself in Marty, who shared more anatomical similarities with it than anything else in the oceans? Did it recognize in him a distant, land-dwelling cousin? Did its kind have a collective unconsciousness, and did humans have a place in it? Then again, the mermaid was a primitive animal with no comprehension of modern manufacturing. Clad in his black neoprene wetsuit and twinset tanks and all the hoses and tubes and other scuba accoutrements, Marty was possibly as alien to it as a human a million years in the future would be to her.

Marty extended his hand, as if wanting to touch the mermaid, perhaps wanting to convince himself it was real.

The mermaid gripped his forearm.

Elsa's awe turned to apprehension when Marty began struggling, a conga line of bubbles streaming upwards from his respirator...then to terror when the creature plucked the respirator from his mouth.

She could hardly believe her eyes. What had been a peaceful, glorious meeting of kindred species transformed into one of horror and bedlam in a matter of seconds. And all she could think was:

It knows. It knows he needs the respirator to breathe. It's trying to kill him.

Acting on instinct, Elsa removed the titanium knife from the sheath attached to the left shoulder strap of her BCD and swam toward the creature. It turned its head in her direction. For the first time she saw into its eyes. They were watchful and knowing like an owl's, sending a shot of icy fear down her spine.

Elsa would have plunged the serrated blade into the mermaid's chest if she had the chance, but it seemed to recognize the threat she posed and vanished into the black water.

She snagged the regulator and handed it to Marty, who stuck it back in his mouth. She flashed him a thumbs-up, meaning they should surface immediately, and they ascended quickly. They broke through the surface of the water into a domed area roughly twice the size of the first air pocket in which they had surfaced an hour earlier.

They removed the regulators from their mouths and gasped the stale air. Elsa's heart was pounding far too fast for her liking, and she said, "It knew what it was doing! It tried to drown you!"

Marty said, "It couldn't possibly know—"

"It did! And we need to get out of the water right now." She aimed her light around the dome and discovered a flow ledge carved into one wall. "There!"

"Shite! My bag! I dropped my bag!"

"To hell with your bag! That thing might be right below us!"

Without waiting for a reply, she swam toward the ledge.

CHAPTER 30

MARTY

K nowing there was nothing he could do about his bag right then, Marty followed Elsa, reaching the rocky rampart a few moments after her. The edge of the rock was a little distance above the water table, and he needed all of his might to haul himself up and onto it. He suddenly felt as heavy as an elephant without the buoyancy of the water to lighten the load of his scuba gear. Elsa, he noticed, was also struggling to get herself out of the water. As he reached for her hands, her eyes went wide and her body shuddered, as if something had tugged at her.

In the next instant she was dragged beneath the surface of the black pool.

"Elsa!" Marty cried, shining his light into the water where she had vanished. He couldn't see anything but a flurry of bubbles, and he was contemplating jumping in after her (*suicidal likely, but you can't just stand there doing nothing, can you?*), when she crashed through the surface, panting for air, her face a mask of terror, her dive knife gripped in her right hand. He snatched her wrists and lugged her up onto the ledge with so much force he stumbled backward and landed hard on the steel tanks still strapped to his back. His skull whip-cracked against the rock, the sharp pain lasting only a split-second before he blacked out.

CHAPTER 31

RAD

Rad and Jacky were sitting on boulders that had once been part of the cavern's roof. Legs crossed, right foot tapping anxiously, Rad glanced at her wristwatch again. The butterfly wings in her stomach beat a little faster. "They should have been back ten minutes ago."

"Relax," Jacky said. She was scrolling through the pictures that she'd taken of the cave art. "They'll be back any minute."

"I can't stop thinking about them swimming through pitch-black tunnels with no way to surface if something happened. Who would ever want to do that?"

"People a lot braver than us, I'll tell you that much. Did you know Marty was a cave diver?"

"I knew he was a good open-water diver. He's taken me diving to a few coral reefs. But, no, he never mentioned cave diving."

"I guess it comes with the territory."

"What do you mean?"

"If you dedicate your life to finding mermaids," Jacky explained, "and you think they live in underwater tunnels beneath islands, you're probably going to want to explore those tunnels at some point."

Rad shook her head. "I've tried almost every extreme sport there is on land, but there's no way I'd go squeezing through a tight little tunnel underwater. I'd completely freak out."

"What extreme sports have you done?"

"Name something."

"Rock climbing?"

"Yup. Been ice climbing in Switzerland too."

"Paragliding?"

"Of course."

"Skateboarding?"

"Skateboarding? That's not exactly an extreme sport, is it?"

"I mean, downhill skateboarding. When they close off a stretch of highway. I've seen it on TV."

"You got me beat there."

"White water rafting?"

"Yup! I love it."

"Parkour?"

"Park what?"

"It's an urban sport. Have you seen those nuts who scale the sides of buildings and leap from rooftops over alleyways and stuff?"

"I'm not Spider-Man, Jacks."

Jacky tucked her phone away. "I wrote a story in the *Daily Mirror* a couple of years ago when parkour was starting to take off in Colombo. It's based on those obstacle courses in military training. My Lord, it's cringeworthy to watch. One wrong move or calculation and you're likely to find a bone protruding from a limb or your skull smashed open. While researching the sport— if you really want to call it a sport—I followed a teenager around Colombo for a day. He was one of the best traceurs—that's what they call themselves—in the city. His last trick was running up the wall of a building to a second-floor balcony, and then doing a back flip off it to the ground. I looked away at the last minute because I knew he wasn't going to land properly. When I looked back, he was lying flat on his stomach, not moving. The doctors at the hospital told me he had compression injuries to his C5 and C6 vertebrae and had no movement below his shoulders."

Rad felt queasy. "He became a quadriplegic?"

Jacky shrugged. "I never found out. The doctor told me the swelling around his spinal cord and neck could take months to go down before they could determine the severity of the injury.

I visited him every couple of weeks to check on his progress. Somehow he kept his humor, but I think he was just putting on a brave face for me. The last time I went to the hospital he wasn't there. His family had checked him out, and nobody seemed to know where he lived." She appeared introspective. "I hope he recovered. He was a really nice kid."

They fell silent for a bit, and Rad's queasiness refused to subside, as the tale had hit a little too close to home for her liking. She knew the risks involved in extreme sports, of course; they were what attracted her to them in the first place. However, she was under the mindset that the horrible accidents you heard about only ever happened to other people. They wouldn't happen to her. They couldn't. She was always well prepared, properly trained, and surrounded by experts.

It was naïve, she knew, because nothing in life was ever certain, nothing was ever guaranteed.

She glanced at her wristwatch again and said, "They're fifteen minutes late now."

Jacky said, "Which means they still have forty-five minutes of safety air. Let's not get too worried yet."

Rad nodded reluctantly. "How's your story coming along?" she asked to change the topic.

"It's coming. I'm going to have to sit down with Marty at some point to pick his brain about all the scientific mumbo jumbo he's been spewing these last couple of days."

"Will your editor publish it without video evidence of merfolk?"

"I can't see why not. There's the skull and the DNA results, the spear tips, and now all these cave paintings. I think that's plenty of evidence for a compelling story. I guess the big question is whether Marty will let me reference him by name if he doesn't find his irrefutable proof that merfolk exist. He's so damn paranoid about negative media attention, isn't he?"

"He thinks everyone is casting aspersions on him. And when I say everyone, I mean the *world*. What he wants more than anything is to prove all the doubters wrong. At the same time what he fears more than anything is being mocked in the media again. It's a tough spot to be in."

"So you're saying you don't think he's going to let me use his name?"

"If he doesn't return with video footage of a merfolk on his GoPro, no, I don't think there's a chance in hell."

Jacky sighed. "Still, even without—" She stopped mid-sentence, a puzzled expression on her face.

Rad turned...and saw what appeared to be a glowing blue head poking out of the still pool.

Jacky rose slowly to her feet. "What the...?"

Rad got up as well. "Oh my god..."

Jacky fumbled in her pocket for her phone, but by the time she had it in her hands the mermaid had disappeared beneath the surface of the water, leaving only a ring of ripples where its head had been.

Rad and Jacky stared at each other in wide-eyed amazement.

"Did we really see that...?" Rad asked, dumbfounded.

"It had blue hair," Jacky said.

"It looked like a person. Its face... It looked..."

"It had blue hair."

"Oh my god," Rad said. "Oh my god."

CHAPTER 32

ELSA

Still panting heavily from her narrow escape, Elsa checked on Marty. His face was pale and slack, sunken in the harsh white beam of her LED light. His breathing sounded shallow but steady. She tilted his head to the side and gingerly felt the bump on the back of his skull. It was the size of a golf ball and slimy with blood. The ledge they were on was perhaps ten feet deep, so she dragged his body away from the water until it was snug up against the wall. She sat next to him and rested his head on her thigh. Her pulse continued to race, and she forced herself to calm down and think rationally.

Turn off the light. You need to save the battery. If it goes, you're never leaving this place alive.

Reluctantly, Elsa turned it off. The blackness was absolute. The only sound in the empty silence was their breathing.

She played over what had happened in the water. The mermaid had clearly tried to kill them, first Marty by removing his respirator from his mouth, then herself by dragging her beneath the surface of the water. It only released its powerful grip on her ankles when she slashed it with her knife.

So it wanted them dead. The million-dollar question was, Why?

Did it consider them a threat? Interlopers? Food?

Elsa didn't know, and she wasn't going to dwell on hypotheticals. She needed to focus on finding a way out of the subterranean tomb. Yet this quickly proved to be just as nerve-wracking because the only exit was through the water, and that thing was there, and it was stronger and more agile than them. They didn't stand a chance getting past it if it didn't want them to.

They were trapped.

It knew that. It was likely biding its time, waiting in ambuscade, until they ventured back into the water, where it would kill them and feast on their flesh—

Stop it! she thought shrilly. *Stop thinking like that! You need to stay positive.*

Stay positive. Right. She was trying to. God, she was trying to. But how did you stay positive when you were being hunted by a creature that should only exist in nightmares?

$$\triangle\triangle\triangle$$

Rescue.

That was how they would escape.

They would simply stay put and wait to be rescued.

When she and Marty didn't return to the cavern as scheduled, Jacky and Rad would know something had gone wrong. They would head back to the *Oannes*. Pip would radio for help.

Elsa's fragile hope shattered.

Who *could* help? Cave diving was a niche activity. There were perhaps a few thousand certified cave divers in the world. The number of active divers was much less—and the number of *rescue* divers would number in the hundreds. So finding volunteers who could help them would be difficult, and even if a group was assembled, it would take days (if not weeks) before they would be organized enough to undertake the rescue.

And by that time it would no longer be a search and rescue; it would be a recovery operation.

When someone is trapped in an enclosed space, they're exhaling carbon dioxide with each breath, and it's that increase in CO_2, not a lack of oxygen, which ultimately kills them.

The air pocket Elsa and Marty were in was the size of a large garage and probably contained about fifty cubic meters of air. Humans required ten cubic meters of air per day. Double that because there were two of them, and they likely only had two and a half days of air.

Two and a half days.

Elsa heard water move, a small splash. She snapped on the light and scanned the ominous pool. Ripples the size of tractor-tires shimmered on the surface, but whatever had made them was gone.

Can merfolk see in the dark?

Has it been watching me?

Elsa turned off the light to save its battery and sat perfectly still in the overwhelming blackness.

Two and a half days.

CHAPTER 33

RAD

The mermaid reappeared a few seconds later. This time it was swimming toward Rad and Jacky, small wavelets trailing behind its neck and grayish shoulders.

"Jesus, Jesus, Jesus," Jacky said, almost dropping her phone in her haste to open the video app. "Got it! I'm filming it. Oh my God, I'm filming it. *I'm filming it.*"

Rad didn't share Jacky's enthusiasm.

Everything was happening too fast.

Everything felt wrong, very wrong.

She took a step back from the water's edge and told Jacky to do the same. Instead, Jacky lowered herself to a crouch to capture a better angle of the approaching creature.

"Jacks," Rad warned again, her voice tight, "get away from the water."

"Shush!" she hissed. "You're going to scare it away!"

The mermaid kept coming. Rad made out a fish-like body beneath the water's surface, undulating, abhorrent. Human-like arms were pressed against its sides. In one hand appeared to be—

"Jacks!" she cried. "It has a spear in its hand!"

"Oh my God, it does!" she said in awe, clearly not appreciating the impending danger. "Marty was right! They use tools!"

Marty, Rad thought frenziedly. Where was Marty? He and Dr. Montero should have been back long before now. There could be a myriad of reasons for their delay, some innocent (they lost track of the time), some more worrisome (they experienced an equipment malfunction), and some positively horrific (they were murdered by a bad-tempered mermaid).

The latter seemed all too possible. After all, the mermaid was here, and they weren't. It would have likely passed them on its way. If they saw it, they would have followed it. They would be back here too.

But they weren't.

"Jacks!" Rad shrieked. "For Christ's sake, get away from the water!"

The hysteria in Rad's voice finally cut through the dreamy spell that Jacky had been under. She looked at Rad, dazed, as if wondering where she was. Then she looked back at the mermaid just as it sprang out of the water, exposing its slug-white chest and the wooden spear clutched in its hand.

Jacky gasped, backed away.

It was too late.

With a powerful thrust of its sinewy arm, the mermaid skewered her on the spear, the tip punching through the back of her white singlet, spraying it red. In the next instant the tip disappeared with a sludgy slurp as the mermaid tugged the spear free.

Jacky tottered like a marionette whose strings had been cut. The momentum of the retracted spear would have pulled her forward into the water and the waiting arms of the mermaid had Rad not lunged forward and grabbed her arm, yanking her backward. She made it two steps before Jacky tumbled flat on her back, becoming a fifty-kilogram deadweight.

Fueled with adrenaline, Rad barely noticed and dragged her across the ground, two meters, four, six, before finally collapsing, breathless from fear and exertion.

Jacky's eyes were closed, her singlet saturated with crimson blood.

She's dead.

Rad glanced at the pool, expecting to see the mermaid slithering onto land to finish her off too.

It was gone.

CHAPTER 34

ELSA

They had been trapped for two hours, and Elsa now knew that passing out and dying from carbon dioxide poisoning in two and a half days' time wasn't her most pressing concern.

It was trying not to go crazy before then.

Two hours and she already felt like she was losing her mind. She could deal with the perpetual darkness, as unnerving as it was. She could deal with being trapped beneath immovable tons of rock. What she *couldn't* deal with was the fact there was a mythical monster that wanted her dead circling in the water below her...and knowing that eventually, inexorably, she was going to have to get in that water if she had any hope of escaping this nightmare.

So the new million-dollar question was, When?

The sooner, the better.

Before she lost her nerve.

Before she lost her mind.

Before the carbon dioxide buildup started affecting her judgement, because she would need all her wits about her if she had any hope in hell of fighting off the merfolk and getting out of the cave system alive.

The problem was Marty. Elsa had no idea when he was going to regain consciousness. What if he didn't?

She would have to leave him.

Could she do that?

If he didn't wake up soon, his death was all but guaranteed, and if she stayed with him, hers was too.

Did she really have a choice?

She wanted to shake him until he opened his eyes, but she didn't because...

Because you need him to remain unconscious, need him to offer you an excuse to remain where you are. Because you're scared to get in the water.

You're scared of what's in the water—

"Marty," she said, her voice sounding double its usual volume in the stagnant dark. "You need to wake up so we can get out of here. We can do it together. We both have knives. It's scared of knives. I've already scared it away twice. Maybe it's even gone? You need to wake up so we can get out of here."

She listened for a response. Nothing. In fact, she couldn't even hear his ragged breathing anymore.

"Marty?" She punched on her light. "Marty!"

His head still rested on her thigh. His mouth was slightly parted.

She pressed her fingers against his throat, positive she wasn't going to find a pulse.

It was there, strong and regular.

"I wasn't going to leave you," she said softly. "I wasn't going to leave you. I *won't* leave you. Either we both get out of here together, or neither of us do. So please wake up, Marty. I need you."

He didn't wake up, and she reluctantly turned off the light.

"Oh God," she whispered. She didn't like how the words sounded in the dark—small, lost, wretched—and so she said nothing more.

ΔΔΔ

Time ticked on. She had no idea how much; she had stopped keeping track. She simply sat in the same place with her back to the wall and stared into the blackness. With nothing to see, her thoughts and memories assumed an outsized focus and clarity, almost as if they were playing on a screen before her.

Elsa saw herself when she was no older than five or six, sitting at the head of a table with about ten of her classmates from kindergarten, torn wrapping paper from the presents she had opened, paper plates loaded with chocolate cake and vanilla ice cream, paper cups filled with Coca-Cola or cream soda. Eating her slice of cake and reacting in surprise when she bit down on a quarter wrapped in waxed paper. Standing in the hallway and waving goodbye to her friends as their moms showed up to take them home. Filling her sticker book with the scratch 'n' sniff stickers from her loot bag, scratching a root beer sticker, her favorite one, over and over until the scent began to fade. Her dad returning from work and carrying a firetruck-red tricycle, a purple bow stuck to the white banana seat. Riding the trike up and down the driveway, the tinsel streamers on the ends of the handlebars fluttering in the wind, and when she built up the nerve, taking it for a test drive around the block. Years later, sitting on a beach in front of a bonfire, some of the older kids she was with smoking cigarettes and drinking beers. Talking to a chubby boy her age who she didn't like romantically but who liked her. Going for a walk down the beach with him, eventually holding hands when they were far enough away that nobody could see them, stopping and kissing, *French* kissing. Disliking the tongue-touching but going with it because some of her friends were doing it. Thinking about the boy when she went to sleep that night, wondering if she was going to marry him, never telling anyone what she had done...and never seeing the boy again, as it turned out he was visiting from a different state. Dressed in a black graduation gown and mortarboard hat, being called up onto the stage, shaking the chancellor's hand and receiving her degree certificate. Participating in a photograph outside with her entire class, everyone throwing their hats in the air, the future big and bright. Hooking her first great white in the waters of Southern California when she was twenty-four, guiding it onto the research vessel's lift, throwing a wet towel over its eyes and removing the hook from its jaws, pumping water over its gills with a large hose, screwing a satellite tag onto its dorsal fin with a power drill. Collecting measurements, blood, and tissue samples before letting it go again in the water. Clinking beers with the rest of the crew for a job well done and never feeling so alive. Performing her first overhead environment dive that same year in Florida's Devil's Spring cave system, exploring the mystical passageways with a colleague and marveling at the limestone formations and intricately decorated caverns and knowing this was the beginning of what would become a lifelong passion.

Fifteen years and nearly a thousand dives later, arriving at the Sistema Huautla cave system in Mexico with Ron, rappelling down canyon walls through crashing waterfalls, sleeping underground for days on end, mapping some of the most remote tunnels on earth...Ron getting tangled in the guideline in a narrow horizontal traverse. Working to free him. Ron panicking, his eyes widening behind his mask. Opening his mouth in a silent scream. Swallowing water. Dying in front of her.

Elsa had never felt as lost and lonely as she had during the days after her husband's death. Not only was Ron stolen from her and gone forever, but she didn't even have the small comfort of putting his body to rest. After diving to the site of the accident, the Mexican police had decided Ron's corpse could not be freed without risk to the rescue divers and called off the recovery efforts.

Leaving Ron's body in the cave system, however, was not an option for Elsa—it would be like leaving the victim of a car crash on the side of the road—and over the next two weeks she planned her own recovery effort in secret, organizing a group of twenty divers from the US and Mexico to assist her. The police were right; recovering Ron's corpse from the way he'd entered the traverse was not possible. That meant they would have to enter the cave system from an alternate entrance and approach his body from the other side. After nearly a month of exploring a warren of unmapped tunnels, they found the one that led to him. The first step in what would be a three-day operation was to lug more than half a ton of gear to the new cave entrance, which was at the top of a large hill. On the second day they got everything into position, leaving twenty cylinders of gas along the route to Ron's corpse. And on the third day they began the recovery itself, a team of support divers waiting in the shallower level of the traverse while Elsa and a former Navy SEAL named Tom Jarrett dived to the deep section to extricate Ron's body. Elsa's nerves had been tense, but by then—six weeks since Ron's death—she'd had time to process her emotions, and she was laser-focused on the task at hand. When they reached Ron's corpse, they cut away his equipment. She tried not to look at his exposed hands and lower face, which had been chewed to the skeleton by shrimp, crabs, and other scavengers. Finally they freed his body, but while they were trying to manipulate it into a body bag (which they would tow behind them out of the tunnel), his head snapped free from his neck and sank to the floor. Horrified, Elsa began breathing more quickly, her rebreather struggling to filter out the excess carbon dioxide. Knowing she was doomed if she didn't get her breathing back under control, she calmed herself, collected Ron's skull, and returned to the surface with his body to raucous applause from the gathered team. The second she removed the rebreather from her mouth she doubled over and vomited...

An awful, echoing sound, shrill and discordant, assaulted her ears.

Elsa thought she was hallucinating, but it was real, coming from the water ahead of her—where she could see two pale faces bobbing above the surface and illuminated by blue bioluminescent hair.

They were looking at her with their black eyes.

Their mouths were open.

They were laughing at her.

CHAPTER 35

RAD

Jacky wasn't dead, after all—her chest was rising and falling ever so slightly—but she wasn't in very good shape. When Rad pushed up Jacky's singlet to examine the spear wound, she nearly gagged. The jagged hole to the left of her belly button was bleeding freely and bloated with exposed grayish-purple intestines that appeared ready to slip free.

Rad took off her own singlet and used it to apply pressure to the gash to help stop the bleeding. When Jacky began spasming, however, Rad immediately removed it. Not knowing what else to do, she rested Jacky's head on her lap and whispered to her reassuringly, telling her everything was going to be fine.

All the while her eyes probed the deadly pool of water ahead of her, watching for the slightest ripple on the surface. They were six meters from the water's edge. Rad would have liked to have been much farther away, but there was nothing she could do about that. She wasn't strong enough to carry Jacky, and she wasn't going to drag her for fear of exacerbating any of her injuries.

What am I going to do? What the hell am I going to do?

She couldn't leave Jacky to go get help because, unconscious, Jacky would be at the mercy of the mermaid. She needed Marty and Dr. Montero to return. Then one of them could go to the *Oannes* while the other two stayed behind to watch over Jacky.

But Marty and Dr. Montero weren't going to return, were they? There was a mermaid in the water—a killer mermaid—and it had already gotten them. That was why they were an hour late.

They were dead.

This seemed impossible. Marty was too smart to be dead. He knew too much about mermaids to be *killed* by one. Dead? No. Impossible.

But he is, she thought blackly. *He's dead. Dr. Montero's dead. And Jacky's going to be dead soon too.*

Rad felt like crying. She brushed her fingertips across Jacky's cheek. They had so much in common, the two of them. Even though she had only known Jacky for a couple of days, she felt like a sister to her.

"Pip's going to find us," she said confidently. "When we don't return to the boat, she'll come looking for us. She'll find the village. The chief will bring her here. Everything's going to be okay. You just have to hold on, okay?"

Jacky's eyelids fluttered, or at least Rad thought they did.

"Jacks?"

Nothing.

"Jacks?"

Nothing.

Still, Rad thought maybe Jacky could hear her, even if she couldn't respond, in the same way people in comas can hear loved ones speaking to them.

"Want to hear a weird story?" she said. "Once, in the Philippines, I was filming an episode for my show in one of the western provinces. There's this underground river there that's really famous. It's about eight kilometers long and just amazing. It puts these tunnels to shame. We filmed it for the show, and we were walking back to where we were staying along this off-the-beaten path. It was really steep in parts, going up through overgrown forest and limestone cliffs. We came to a spot with an amazing view out over the ocean, and we decided to camp there for the night. Well, here's where the story gets weird. I woke up in the middle of the night to my crew calling my name from really far away, and I realized I was in a remote part of the forest. I was in my sleeping bag, just lying there on the ground, but it wasn't where I went to sleep. When my crew found me, I was about a kilometer from where we made camp. I have no idea in the world how I got there. So—weird, huh?"

Jacky didn't reply—didn't show any signs that she'd heard a word of the story—but Rad continued talking regardless.

"Maybe I'm cursed or something because freaky stuff just seems to happen to me. There was another time, my crew and I were in Japan doing an episode on Suicide Forest. You know, that place people go to kill themselves? Well, we decided to camp overnight in the forest. I woke up in the middle of the night again because I heard a strange noise outside my tent. I unzipped the door to investigate and saw this horrifying old woman crawling toward me on all fours—torn clothes, unkempt hair in front of her face, you know, like the ghosts in movies. Well, I screamed and woke up—it was just a dream, okay? But the scream was real and my crew heard it. When I told them about the dream, they got scared. I figured it was because of where we were. The forest is hugely creepy. Anyway, we went back to sleep, and it wasn't until the next day, when we were in the van heading back to Tokyo, that they told me they all dreamed of the creepy woman too—only in each of their dreams, she was crawling into my tent."

Rad shivered at the memory and fell silent. She looked at Jacky's face. Still alabaster, still serene, still…dead-looking. She felt her forehead. No fever; her skin was cool and clammy.

What Rad wouldn't give to be back on the *Oannes*, everything like it had been the previous night.

To hell with mermaids. She wished they didn't exist. She wished…

Well, she wished Marty and Dr. Montero would emerge from the water right now. She would throw her arms around Marty's neck and smother him with kisses and tell him that she loved him.

That was something she'd never told him before, even though she'd felt it for some time now. She'd been too scared he wouldn't feel the same way, too scared he thought she was just some crazy girl with a fetish for being strangled, fun to be around maybe, but someone he'd bring home to meet his parents? Someone with whom he saw a future? Someone more important to him than a sex buddy he called up every now and then?

"My neighbor used to abuse me," Rad said quietly, speaking more to Marty than to Jacky, even though he wasn't there. "He would invite me into his house when my parents were out. He would give me chocolates. He would also make me play sick little games. I didn't know they were sick then. I was too young. It wasn't until I was twelve or thirteen that I realized them for what they were. I was disgusted and scared and never went to his house again. I still see him when I go back to visit my parents. He's an old man now. He sits on his porch and watches me when I walk up the path to my parents' front door. I want to yell at him, call him out...but I can't even make eye contact. He scares me that much, even though I'm an adult now. It's like I've developed a phobia of him or something. I'm just not myself. It's so frustrating and infuriating because I'm not a weak person. But when I see him...I'm that little kid again, and there's nothing I can do about it. I can't even tell anyone what he did. I can't tell anyone because it's Sri Lanka and women always cop the blame and people are going to say, 'You didn't say no, so it wasn't really abuse, was it?' But that's bullshit. Because I didn't know what sex was then or that what we were doing was sexual. And, well...it really fucked me up. But probably not in the way that you'd think. You'd think I'd hate men or something, but I don't. It's the opposite. I can't be without a man, because when I am I feel restless and lonely and vulnerable. I understand women don't need men to be safe. I understand women are stronger emotionally than men, and that dependence on men for security is so patriarchal. But, again, I can't help it. Being around men is the only way I feel safe now. But you never wanted me around, did you, Marty? Or at least all the time. You wanted your space. And so I spent a lot of time with other men. Not to spite you. Not because I didn't want to be with you. But because I *needed* to. I needed to feel safe. And this is something else you wouldn't have known.

The strangling, the submission and domination...I still don't understand it exactly, but it lets me tap into the part of myself that needs to be healed, the part of myself that was abused. It's cathartic because I'm allowing you to do it, I'm trusting you with my life. I trust you that much, Marty, and that makes me feel safe. Does that make sense?" She smiled affectionately. "I understand it makes you uncomfortable. You're a sweetheart, an old-school sweetheart. And I know the strangling is what's been holding back our relationship. I always wanted to tell you all this. But I just felt that it would be easier letting you believe I was some kinky freak with death fetishes rather than telling you I was abused..." She wiped a tear from her eye. "And now I *can't* tell you the truth, can I? I'll never be able to explain."

More tears came, hot, stinging, blurring her vision.

Marty was gone.

Dr. Montero, gone.

Jacky...

Rad glanced at her wristwatch. It was half past four in the afternoon.

Two hours until dark.

CHAPTER 36

ELSA

"Go away!" Elsa screamed at the merfolk. "I hate you! Go away, you bastards!"

Their eerily human laughter continued.

"Leave me alone!"

"LEAVE ME ALONE."

Elsa stiffened. That had been her voice. It was dissonant and reverberating—almost electronically tinged—yet it had clearly been her voice. Only it hadn't come from her.

It came from the two merfolk.

It's the carbon dioxide, she thought. *The buildup is making me hallucinate. Merfolk can't speak, you goose.*

The merfolk were still there, in the pool, their glowing blue heads visible in the dark.

They were silent.

See! It's all in my head. Thank God.

Thank God? Carbon dioxide poisoning isn't anything to thank God for, El. Sooner or later it's going to lead to unconsciousness and then death.

Maybe that wouldn't be such a bad thing. It would be peaceful. I'll simply...fade away. That's certainly a better death than drowning, or worse, being eaten alive...

So is that it? Is that your decision? You're giving up? Whatever happened to not going gentle into the good night? To raging against the dying of the light? You're not a quitter. You've never been one. Yet now you're simply going to throw in the towel?

No. No, I'm not. Of course I'm not. I'm going to get into that water. And when the merfolk come for me, I'm going to fight tooth and nail, and I'm going to take at least one of the ghastly things to the grave with me.

Then do it, now. No more putting it off.

I can't leave Marty...

He's not waking up! He's as good as dead already! Stop making excuses!

Elsa clicked on her light and zigzagged it across the still pool. The merfolk had disappeared below the surface.

Or were they ever there? Had she imagined them just as she'd imagined the voice?

She aimed the light at the rock next to Marty's head, indirectly illuminating his face.

"I need to go," she told him. "I'll bring back help. I won't be long. You'll be okay—"

He moaned.

"Marty!"

His brow furrowed and his eyes moved beneath his eyelids a moment before he opened them. His pupils were dilated, and he seemed confused. He pushed himself onto his elbows. Blinking, he frowned at his wetsuit. He finally noticed her. "What...?" He cleared his throat. "Are we...?"

"We're in the lava tubes beneath Demon Island," she explained quickly. It felt as though a year had passed since she'd spoken to him last. "Do you remember what happened?"

Grimacing, he raised a hand to the back of his head.

"You hit it on the rock."

His eyes widened. "The merfolk!"

"It tried to kill you."

"It reached for my respirator..."

"It was trying to kill you, Marty. Then it tried to kill me. You pulled me out of the water. You saved my life—"

"I remember." He looked around the small air pocket, assessing their dire predicament. "How long have we been here for?"

"I don't know. A couple of hours, at least."

"The air is still breathable."

"I figure we might have two days' worth." She exhaled heavily. "You don't know how relieved I am that you're awake, Marty. I didn't know what I was going to do. What *are* we going to do?" She bit her lip in frustration. Marty regaining consciousness might be a comforting development, but it hadn't changed anything: they were still trapped and in peril.

Marty clenched his jaw. "I'm such a fool," he muttered.

Elsa frowned. "What are you talking about?"

"I should have known. It was right there in front of my eyes. I refused to see it."

"What the hell are you talking about, Marty?"

"I told you and everyone else that merfolk were likely mostly herbivorous." He shook his head. "Did you see the merfolk's teeth when it opened its mouth? They weren't for gnawing down kelp and seaweed."

"You couldn't have known that. Both merfolk skulls were missing their teeth—"

"But I *should* have known. The sagittal crests meant they had powerful jaws—powerful jaws that were either needed to break down tough vegetation or to tear flesh from bone. I decided on the former explanation because it's what I wanted to believe, because it reinforced my hypotheses that merfolk subsided on a largely plant-based diet similar to that of Great Apes and pre-fire hominins. But the evidence was pointing to the latter."

"What evidence?"

"Both merfolk skulls that we've observed have been roughly the same size as a modern human's."

"Why's that significant?"

"Because the size of an organism's brain directly correlates with the amount and quality of energy it consumes. The human brain consumes twenty-five percent of our daily caloric intake. It wouldn't have been possible for us to have evolved such a metabolically expensive organ eating a low-calorie, plant-based diet. Australopithecus had a cranial capacity roughly the size of a gorilla or chimpanzee. It was only when Homo erectus came onto the scene that brain sizes began increasing rapidly due to their mastery of fire and the advent of cooking."

"Better nutrition, more calories, bigger brains..."

He nodded. "The fact the merfolk skulls have a braincase roughly the size of a modern human's means they too have converted to a meat-rich diet." He scowled. "So you see, it's my fault we're trapped here. If I hadn't been so eager for the reality of merfolk to conform to my paradigm of them, if I hadn't leapt to ad hoc conclusions—"

"Stop it, Marty," Elsa said sternly. "It was my decision to accompany you on this dive, my choice. And I probably would have made the same decision had you told me merfolk were man-eating monsters because, to be honest, I don't think I ever bought into the idea that we would encounter one. So stop blaming yourself. It's a waste of oxygen, something of which we have precious little. We need to figure a way out of the mess we're in—"

"LEAVE ME ALONE. LEAVE ME ALONE. LEAVE ME ALONE."

Elsa snapped her head toward the pool. She saw no merfolk at first. But then her light washed over two heads floating side by side. They had somehow turned off their bioluminescence, yet their mouths were once again open.

"LEAVE ME ALONE. LEAVE ME ALONE. LEAVE ME ALONE."

One of the heads sank beneath the surface, followed by the second a moment later.

Elsa looked at Marty, bewildered. "Tell me you heard that? Tell me I didn't imagine that?"

"They're mimics," he replied, grinning zealously. "Bloody hell, *they're mimics.*"

CHAPTER 37

MARTY

"**M**imics?" Elsa repeated.

"Absolutely remarkable," Marty told her, trying to absorb the revelation, while at the same time berating himself for never advancing the hypothesis himself. "But it makes perfect sense, doesn't it?"

"Perfect sense?" She shook her head. "No. No, it doesn't, Marty. Not to me. So please explain why merfolk speaking in my voice makes perfect sense to you."

Mimicry, Marty knew, is widespread in nature and crucial to the survival of many species. Often it's an antipredator adaptation in which a harmless animal shares characteristics with a dangerous or aposematic one, deterring potential predators or competitors. Viceroy butterflies evolved to look like noxious and thus unpalatable monarch butterflies. Stick insects resemble the leaves and twigs on which they live. Nonvenomous snakes adopt the colors and patterns of venomous ones.

Aggressive mimicry, on the other hand, takes a wolf-in-sheep's-clothing approach in which the opposite occurs: a dangerous animal shares characteristics with a harmless one in order to fool unsuspecting prey. Zone-tailed hawks look a lot like turkey vultures and soar amongst groups of the scavengers to sneak up on doves and lizards and other small animals undetected. Alligator snapping turtles wiggle their worm-like tongues to lure and catch fish. The European cuckoo lays its eggs in the nests of other species of birds to deceive the host parents into incubating the similar-looking eggs and rearing cuckoo chicks alongside their own.

While visual mimicry is covered extensively in the literature of evolutionary biology, in recent years, acoustic mimicry has been gaining a lot of interest. Lyrebirds and mockingbirds can copy almost any sound they hear to both deter predators and attract prey. Margays imitate the call of infant monkeys to attract and ambush the curious adult primates. And most domestic cat owners likely don't know their little fluffball is playing them as a dupe, having evolved a meow at the same frequency as an infant's cry, which pulls at the heart strings and often gets them whatever they want.

Using aquatic examples to appeal to Elsa's sensibilities, he said, "The oceans are filled with copycat species that use mimicry to their advantage. I'm sure you're familiar with the mimic octopus. To avoid predators, it impersonates the appearance and behaviors of a wide range of venomous or bad-tasting sea creatures. Contrary, to attract prey, the anglerfish uses its spiny protrusion and bioluminescent growth to lure and devour other small fish."

"And merfolk?" she replied dubiously. "They mimic other creatures to...?"

Marty shrugged. "I don't know if they would use some sort of defensive mimicry to fool larger predators in the oceans, but after hearing what we did, the way they imitated your voice, I'm quite positive they use aggressive mimicry for predation."

"You're saying those two merfolk were imitating my voice in the hopes of luring me to the water's edge?"

"Or close enough to the water so they could strike with a spear. It sounds fantastical, doesn't it? But there's a historical precedence of merfolk-like creatures luring humans to their deaths. Look no further than Homer's *Odyssey*. The sirens he writes about lured Odysseus' sailors to their graves with seductive songs. Was that merely Greek folklore? Or was it based on some semblance of truth? Were the sirens in fact merfolk using not their songs—which would involve a comprehension and appreciation of music, which seems to be a uniquely human trait—but *our* songs, which they heard and stole from us?"

Elsa began shaking her head, but Marty plowed on: "Look, this is all speculation. I haven't thought it through. But damned if it's not *possible*. And here's something else: the ability to mimic prey would solve the riddle of how merfolk secured a meat-rich diet to evolve and sustain their large brains. They lack dorsal fins and flippers like dolphins and other marine mammals, which means they're almost certainly not fast or agile swimmers. But if they could lure fish, squid, octopi, and other prey to them via acoustic mimicry...well, there you go! A constant, easy supply of protein."

Elsa was shaking her head again and said, "No, Marty. You might be right that merfolk use mimicry to lure prey to them. But I don't think those two in the pool were trying to lure me to the water. I don't think that was their intention." She held his gaze. "They were laughing at me earlier—mimicking human laughter, I suppose, but laughing nonetheless. So I think...I think they're intelligent, they know we're trapped...and I think they were mocking us."

CHAPTER 38

RAD

The sun had set and the cavern was filled with inky black shadows. Little moonlight filtered through the rainforest canopy and skylight, and Rad could barely see a few meters in front of her. Thankfully she'd had the presence of mind earlier to scavenge about a dozen potato-sized rocks, which now sat in a pile next to her within easy reach. If the mermaid returned, its glowing blue head would serve as a warning and give her something to aim at. If it slithered up onto land to come after her, it would be slow and cumbersome, making pelting a stone in its face all the easier.

Yet as reassuring as the projectiles were, they hardly guaranteed her safety, as the mermaid had a spear, which it could launch at *her*. What if she nodded off at some point during the night? She would likely wake up to a wood shaft protruding from her chest. Even if she remained vigilant until morning, what then? She would have to sleep at some point. Which brought her thinking back to Pip. The French woman was still the only hope for Jacky. But where was she? On the *Oannes*, waiting for them to return? That seemed unlikely. They were several hours overdue. Pip would know something had gone wrong. Was she scouring the island for them then? Had she discovered the village? Was the chief leading her to the cavern right now?

Rad pressed two fingers gently against Jacky's neck, felt the faint pulse of her carotid artery, and was assaulted with more questions. Was it getting weaker? Was her body shutting down?

How much time did she have until her shallow breathing ceased altogether? How would Rad even know if that happened other than by checking her pulse every few seconds? Jacky could fade away right before her without her knowledge. She would be dead and—

And you could finally leave this hellhole. You could return to the ship. You could be back in Colombo by tomorrow...

Rad banished the selfish thoughts, feeling small and ashamed of herself for entertaining them. Jacky would be watching over her if their positions were reversed. She wouldn't be wishing her dead so she could high-tail it out of there.

"I'm sorry," she whispered, brushing a finger along Jacky's jawline. Her skin was cold and clammy, almost rubbery. "I'm not going anywhere—"

With a yelp, Rad leapt into a crouch and stumbled backward in the dark. Something cool had touched her ankles. A moment later she realized what it was.

Water.

Impossible, she thought. *The edge of the pool is—*

The tide.

It came in, or went out, or did whatever the hell it does.

And if the water level rose enough to touch my ankles, then Jacky must be practically submerged—

Jacky cried out, a twisted, anguished screech. Rad saw, or thought she saw, a shifting of shadows. It was impossible to see anything for certain in the blackness.

But if the mermaid had returned, why can't I see its head? Why isn't its hair glowing like it did before?

There was no time to contemplate those questions. Jacky was screaming now, in what sounded like either unbearable pain or unadulterated fear.

"Stop it!" Rad shouted hysterically. "Let her go!" She felt frantically around on the ground for the pile of rocks she had gathered. She couldn't find them...and decided it didn't matter. She had no target to aim at. If she threw them blindly, she'd have just as much chance striking Jacky as she would the mermaid.

Jacky's screams turned muffled and watery. A second later there was a splash and a breathless retch—what sounded uncannily like a final gasp for air—then silence.

"Jacky!" Rad charged into the water up to her knees. "Jacks!"

Nothing. Only Rad's rapid breathing and her frantic thoughts: *It got her. It pulled her under. She's gone.*

"Jacks!"

No reply.

"Jacks!" Rad wailed, sounding more animal than human. She was close to hyperventilating, a hard lump in her throat making it difficult to swallow or catch her breath. "Jacks...?" she managed, the single word little more than a strangled gasp.

She heard a new sound then, pitiful and mewling, and she realized she was crying.

CHAPTER 39

JACKY

T *his is the worst way to die. My God, I'm being eaten. I'm being EATEN.*

In her mind, Jacky had been in a safe place—the gymnasium of her elementary school. It was a weekday morning. She was in grade two, and her class had been paraded down to the gym to participate in the Western-inspired Halloween-themed bake sale. Numerous adults Jacky didn't recognize—and some she did like Neja's mom and Brittany's mom and her own mom —stood behind small tables loaded with baked goods: witchhat cookies, brownie spiders, boneyard cupcakes, Frankenstein marshmallows, gingerbread mummies, pumpkin Rice Krispy squares, and so many more. Jacky had three hundred rupees to spend, and she was going happily from one table to the next, filing her brown paper bag with the goodies when a terrible pain erupted inside her tummy. She screamed, but none of the adults seemed to notice. And then some part of her mind told her she wasn't in her school's gymnasium; she was in a dark and dangerous place.

Cold water was washing over her. She realized someone was holding onto her ankles.

Her head became submerged. Water clogged her mouth, cutting off her scream. Flooded with sheer panic, she thrashed her arms and legs and broke back through the surface only long enough to expel the water she was choking on and to wheeze back the smallest amount of air.

Then she was dragged under once again, the hands pulling her deeper and deeper.

The mermaid's *hands*, she thought, suddenly remembering exactly where she was and what had happened to her. *It stabbed me in the stomach, and now it's trying to drown me.*

Terror coursing through her like an electrical current, Jacky continued to thrash to free herself, but the mermaid's grip was unrelenting. Soon she no longer knew which direction the surface was, her bulging eyes seeing only perfect blackness. Spasmodic breaths drew more and more water into her mouth and down her windpipe, causing it to lock up and divert the water into her stomach. Her oxygen-starved lungs felt as though they were filled with fire and ready to explode.

Despite all of this, Jacky was aware that the hands were no longer holding her ankles; they were tearing her clothes from her body, which was floating with her torso arched forward, her limbs flowing backward. She couldn't fathom what was happening, why the mermaid was stripping her, and she found she no longer cared. The pain had ceased and the struggle had left her. Half-conscious and enfeebled by oxygen depletion, she felt tranquil. Nothing mattered except—

Except it wants to eat me. It's stripping me to eat my flesh.

This understanding was so repellent it jumpstarted her brain, kicking her from the pleasant stupor that had washed over her. Yet she discovered she couldn't move, couldn't fight back; she could only think again and again with abhorrent clarity that she was going to be eaten alive.

Please don't do this, she begged. *Please let me go…*

And then fresh pain, sharp, hot, in her belly, yet somehow distant, fading quickly, leaving behind only a ticklish sensation, and she was glad she couldn't see in the blackness, because she knew that ticklish sensation was her organs floating free of her body into the bloodied water.

This is the worst way to die. My God, I'm being eaten. I'm being EATEN.

As her energy continued to fade, she was no longer begging to be let go.

She was begging to die quickly.

CHAPTER 40

MARTY

"**M**ocking you?" Marty said, surprised.

"Their laughter…I would swear it was…contemptuous." She shook her head. "I suppose I'm being foolish, aren't I? It's this cave, being trapped here. It's driving me loopy."

"I can't tell you if the merfolk were mocking you or not, Elsa. I will only say that we must be careful not to anthropomorphize other animal behavior, despite how similar they appear to us. Having said that, it *is* a fascinating idea, and I would love nothing more than to spend an evening debating the matter with you. To do that, though, we need to find a way out of this bloody tomb. Any ideas that don't involve us getting eaten alive?"

"I was hoping you might have one."

He was silent for a long moment before saying, "The bag I dropped. We need to retrieve it."

She blinked. "I forgot about that bag. I meant to ask you what was in it when we surfaced in the first air pocket…?"

"An assault rifle," he said matter-of-factly.

"An *assault rifle*?"

"An amphibious one, yes, designed specifically to be fired both on land and in water."

Elsa laughed, a braying cackle. "You've got to be kidding me! No—please tell me you're *not* kidding me."

He wasn't. The United States and the Soviet Union became interested in underwater firearms when the two countries began deploying underwater saboteurs during World War II. The problem they faced was that water was bulletproof. Traditional bullets lost their trajectory and penetration ability almost immediately because drag at high speeds was much greater in water than in air. During the early Seventies, the US Navy introduced the first underwater assault rifle that fired dart-like bullets. Around the same time, the Soviets created a more sophisticated assault rifle that used the phenomenon of supercavitation, in which a blunt-nosed projectile created a bubble around itself to reduce drag. The weapon was used by Soviet and Russian Navy special forces for more than forty years until it was recently replaced by the ADS amphibious rifle—which was what was in the black ripstop bag on the floor of the lava tube.

"I'm not kidding you, Elsa," Marty told her. "The weapon went into mass production last year in Russia. When it became available for export several months ago, I was able to get my hands on one."

She wore a bemused expression. "So you could hunt merfolk?"

"I've always believed—or hoped—it would only be a matter of time before Pip and I located merfolk. When we did, I wasn't going to take a picture of one. Even a high-definition video wouldn't convince skeptics, not after the Netflix debacle. I would need a specimen, dead or alive. Preferably alive, but how the hell was I supposed to accomplish that? Which meant I would have to kill one, and I didn't think a speargun would do the trick."

"You were planning on murdering a merfolk on this dive?"

"Murder? No, I wouldn't call it that. Merfolk might share an ancient ancestor with us, but they're not human. Now, I've already gotten an earful about the ethics of all of this from Rad, and this is neither the time nor the place to get into it with you—not to mention that my decision to bring that gun might just get us out of here alive."

"I'm not arguing, Marty. I'm just…surprised, is all." She took a deep breath. "Okay. Let's go get the damn thing."

△△△

They stood at the water's perimeter. It had risen nearly to the lip of the rocky rampart.

"High tide," Elsa said somberly. "Jesus, that completely slipped my mind. It might get high enough to flood the entire air pocket."

"Good thing we're not sticking around then." Marty criss-crossed his light over the black water. "Where are you guys?"

"I don't see them anywhere."

"That doesn't mean they're not down there."

"They're bioluminescent. We should be able to see them—" She stiffened. "They turned it off. Earlier, their hair wasn't glowing…"

He nodded. "Animals can control when they luminesce depending on their immediate needs, whether that's to find a meal or a mate, or to scare off a predator. In hindsight, I'm guessing the merfolk we first encountered was lit up as a warning to us. We startled it. Now, having realized we're not threats but potential prey, however many of them down there have likely turned off their lights to lie in ambush."

Elsa swallowed. "Thanks, Marty. You're full of good news."

"We have to be prepared for the worst. This isn't going to be a walk in the park."

"No, it's not. So how are we going to go about this?"

"Very carefully," he told her. "And hopefully with a lot of luck."

△△△

They strapped their air cylinders to their chests to act as steel vests of sorts, then slipped into the water as quietly as possible, lights on, dive knives out. With their backs to the wall of the cavern, they exhaled into their respirators and began their descent.

CHAPTER 41

RAD

J*acky's gone, she isn't coming back, and if you remain standing there in the knee-deep water, you're going to be pulled under next.*

Splashing up onto solid land, Rad ran through the grave-black lava tube back the way they had all come. Once she was a safe distance from the pool she should have slowed and proceeded more cautiously, since the merfolk could no longer catch her. Yet logic didn't matter to her right then. She could have been free from the tunnels completely and careening through the jungle, and she wouldn't have slowed down. The reptile part of her mind had wrestled control from her higher-level brain functions, it was telling her to run, and so she ran, no questions asked. She bounced off the walls, stumbled several times, and once fell hard to her knees but sprang up immediately, running, running, running.

And then the ground disappeared beneath her. She had fallen through one of the shafts they had circumvented on the way in, a shaft that connected with lower, parallel lava tubes.

She plunged through the unending dark in total silence. The impact with the ground shattered both of her legs an instant before she kissed stone, swallowed half her teeth, and lost consciousness.

CHAPTER 42

ELSA

The only sounds were her timed exhalations and her tanks clanking against one another. Perspiration beaded her forehead. One drop trickled down her left temple into her eye, stinging it. When she reached the point where she could no longer control her descent with her lungs, she allowed a tiny amount of air into her BCD to compensate for the negative buoyancy. As she sank farther and farther down the water column, she swung the light strapped to her wrist as if she were blessing herself: left, right, up, down, left, right, up, down—

She spotted a merfolk—sans luminescence—during the last downward gesture. It darted through the white beam with amazing speed, there one moment, gone the next.

Stung with fear, she tried tracking where it had gone but couldn't find it.

Where the hell did it go? Where are the others?

How many are there?

This was suicidal, Elsa knew with certainty. The merfolk were at home in the submarine environment, swift and dexterous, while she and Marty were slow and ponderous. The merfolk were stronger and had mouthfuls of razor-sharp teeth, while all she and Marty had for defense were dive knives with short blades. They were sitting ducks.

But what other choice did they have but to attempt to reach the assault rifle?

None. If they had stayed put, they would have either run out of air or been swallowed by the tide. Descending through the merfolk-infested water was a do-or-die moment—desperate, extreme, yet inescapable. In all of her years of cave diving, Elsa had never experienced anything so harrowing, not even during the deep dive to retrieve Ron's body. That had been a dangerous undertaking, but she had spent weeks planning it and had been ready for any contingency. Conversely, what she was doing now had been conceived on a whim and felt about as reckless as swimming with sharks while smeared in chum.

You didn't have a choice! So shut up and keep your eyes open! You'll reach the bag, you'll get the gun, and you'll get out of there—

Suddenly there was a swirl and boil of water, a flash of a tail. Elsa felt as though she'd been punched in the chest and realized the merfolk had thrust a spear at her. She swung her light back and forth, probing the black water. She raised her knife, readying to slash the creature if it returned.

It didn't.

Marty was aiming his light at her chest. She glanced down, expecting to see blood leaking out of a gaping wound. There was none. The stingray barb attached to the tip of the spear had deflected off, or shattered against, one of the steel cylinders. She was uninjured.

Slowing her rapid breathing, Elsa made an okay sign.

Marty did the same.

They continued the descent.

CHAPTER 43

MARTY

When Marty's light illuminated the black ripstop bag sitting on the cavern floor, his chest tightened. It was only a few meters below them and an equal distance from the wall. He halted his descent, touched Elsa's shoulder, and pointed with his light. She saw it too and nodded.

As they'd discussed, they promptly moved their twin tanks to the proper positions on their backs. They had reasoned that, being this deep, any attack would now likely come from above and not below. When they were ready, they finned quickly toward the black bag. Almost immediately Marty sensed movement swooping toward them from above and felt a sharp prick in his shoulder. Guessing the merfolk had misjudged the distance to him, hence the ineffectual jab, he rolled over in anticipation of a second and more violent attack.

The merfolk—or perhaps it was a different one—appeared from nowhere and thrust its spear at his torso. He tried twisting out of the way but was too slow. The stingray barb impaled his side. This time the pain was hot and fierce.

As the merfolk yanked the spear free, Marty grabbed the shaft and tugged it—and the merfolk gripping it—toward him. Simultaneously he drove his dive knife in an overhead hammer strike, plunging it into the side of the creature's neck.

It spasmed wildly, tearing the lodged knife from his hand and disappearing into the blackness. Marty was already rolling into a prone position and finning toward the bag. Elsa, he saw in his light, was already at it. She produced the assault rifle and pushed off the bottom, raising clouds of silt. When she was a meter from him she jerked suddenly and released the weapon.

He finned past her without stopping, knowing if he didn't retrieve the assault rifle they were both dead.

It disappeared into the silt. Cursing to himself, he went in after it, feeling around blindly, fully aware that just because he couldn't see anything didn't mean the merfolk couldn't see him. With echolocation, they would know exactly where he was.

Patting the ground, he felt only stone and began to despair. He wasn't going to find it in time—

One of his hands brushed metal. In the next instant he had the assault rifle in both hands and was pushing off the bottom. When he emerged from the turbid water, he saw Elsa brandishing her knife, fending off two merfolk that floated before her, spears in their hands.

His confusion as to why they weren't attacking her lasted only a fraction of a second, because in the next instant he realized they were acting as a distraction.

A third merfolk was soaring toward her, spear extended, from behind.

Marty aimed the assault rifle at it and squeezed the trigger. The weapon had a firing rate of seven hundred rounds per minute with an effective underwater range of about fifteen to twenty meters at this depth. The merfolk was only three meters from him, and the onslaught of bullets shredded its body, killing it instantly. He swung the weapon toward the other two creatures, ready to unleash a thunderstorm of lead on them, but they had retreated out of sight.

CHAPTER 44

PIP

Standing in the pilot house behind the softly glowing control panel, Pip was steering the *Oannes* around the perimeter of Demon Island yet one more time, the ship's spotlight sweeping over the shoreline seventy meters away.

When Marty and the others didn't return on time, she wasn't immediately concerned. They would be a little late, she told herself, just as they had been a little late the day before.

When an hour passed, she became worried.

When two hours passed, she became very worried.

When three hours passed, she made the decision to circle Demon Island, not knowing what else she could do but unwilling and unable to do nothing.

This was now her seventh circuit and she had all but lost hope of spotting them.

Where they were completely eluded her. If something had happened to Marty and Dr. Montero on the dive, why hadn't Radhika and Jacqueline returned to the *Oannes*? Surely they wouldn't still be waiting around in the painted cavern they'd described? Surely they'd know that if Marty and Dr. Montero hadn't yet returned, they wouldn't be returning? At least not via the water. It was possible they had discovered where the lava tube emptied into the ocean. If the dive had been more difficult than they'd anticipated and they'd run low on air, it was possible they had decided not to backtrack through the tube but to do so on land. They might then have become lost in the rainforest.

This was what Pip hoped for, but it didn't explain Radhika's and Jacqueline's absence. Had they arrived at the same conclusion as Pip? Had they gone looking for Marty and the doctor? Had they become lost themselves? Had the villagers turned hostile and come after them? Were they holding them against their will?

If you are drinking moonshine right now at some jungle orgy party, Marty, I will never forgive you. I will—

Starting in surprise, Pip squinted through the pilothouse's windshield before jamming the binoculars hanging around her neck to her eye sockets. She eased the barrels slightly apart, and when the circular field of view focused, she couldn't believe what she was seeing.

A merfolk was lying motionless on the beach.

△△△

Pip ran helter-skelter to the aft deck workshop. Under one bench were two charcoal hard-shell tactical cases. She yanked them both out, ignored the lighter one, and opened the lid of the other. She removed the assault rifle cushioned within high-density foam, as well as the magazine, which she knew was loaded with 5.45mm underwater cartridges. Slinging the weapon over her shoulder, she skipped down the ladder to the aft hydraulic loading platform. She unclamped the tender that was strapped to it, shoved the inflatable boat into the water, and hopped aboard. It was equipped with an outboard motor, but right then she preferred stealth over speed and opted for the oars. When she reached the beach a hundred feet from the mermaid (the *Oannes'* momentum had kept the ship moving even after she'd throttled down the engines), she pulled the tender up onto the sand, then ran barefoot toward the creature.

Washed in silvery moonlight, the merfolk was the most hideous yet beautiful thing Pip had ever witnessed, a human-like hybrid being that could have been one of Dr. Moreau's Beast Folk stitched together via vivisection. Its bone-white neck and torso were smeared with bright blood. Eyes closed, it very well might have been dead.

Pip glanced back at the tender. She had to bring it closer so she could lug the merfolk's body into it. Yet what if the thing was still alive? What if it dragged itself into the ocean before she returned?

She would have to make sure it was dead. It would be a shame to kill it. But even if it was alive, it wouldn't be for long, not bleeding out like it was. And if she allowed it to escape, she would never forgive herself. Marty would never forgive her.

Marty.

Did Marty do this to the creature? It seemed too coincidental that the day he went hunting for merfolk, one turned up injured on the beach.

So perhaps he's safe and sound, after all, she thought. *Perhaps he's captured a merfolk and is waiting for dawn before attempting to transport it back to the* Oannes. *Perhaps everything is going to be all right…*

Pip raised the assault rifle, pressing the backplate snug against her shoulder. She had fired the weapon underwater on several occasions under Marty's supervision, using small bony fish such as mullets and herrings as target practice. She had never fired it on land, however, and she recalled Marty telling her the cartridges used underwater and on land were different. Nevertheless, she didn't think it would matter if the magazine was filled with aquatic rather than conventional bullets. She wasn't sniping from four hundred meters away; she was firing point-blank.

The only real question, she decided, was where to shoot the merfolk? She didn't want to destroy its brain or other important organs that would shed scientific light on its biology. Perhaps a burst of bullets to the throat would be best…?

"*Je suis désolé,*" Pip muttered under her breath as she aimed the gun. She was about to squeeze the trigger when ice-cold pain erupted inside her chest. Dumbfounded, she looked down at herself to find a bloody stingray barb protruding from between her breasts. She experienced no pain, only confusion, as she fell to her knees.

The coldness in her chest seemed to encase her entire body, freezing it, so she could no longer move or feel her extremities... and this was likely a good thing. Because the merfolk that had launched the spear through her back was slithering across the sand toward her, mouth agape, jagged teeth bared, black eyes shining with hatred and hunger.

CHAPTER 45

MARTY

Marty and Elsa continued in the direction they had been heading when they'd encountered the first merfolk. They had planned this course of action before diving for the assault rifle. Their reasoning had been that it would take them nearly thirty minutes to return the way they had come; that was a hell of a long time to be in the water, even with the protection of the firearm. Moreover, they would be all but helpless when passing through the tight restrictions, unable to turn around and fight back.

Continuing forward, on the other hand, was a gamble. They could encounter dead ends, become lost, or run out of air before finding their way to the open ocean. Yet given the alternative of being skewered with a spear, it was a gamble they were willing to take. Chances were good, they'd reasoned, that they were close to the exit. The distance they had already traveled and the strong currents they had experienced suggested it—not to mention the presence of the merfolk. Early humans holed up in the mouths of terrestrial caves rather than deep within the systems to be close to their hunting grounds, and Marty had assumed the same likely held for merfolk as well.

Elsa was in the lead, with Marty close behind her. The pain in his side had subsided, and he believed the wound was not as bad as he'd initially imagined. Every ten or twenty seconds he would glance behind them and expect to see any number of merfolk following in pursuit. There were never any there. The assault rifle had apparently scared them away for good. This was not surprising, as it had decimated one of their kind before their eyes. While white sharks and orcas and other pinnacle predators had formidable jaws that could tear them apart, those jaws had to catch them first. Marty simply had to point a strange device at them, and they were dead. The risk-reward trade-off was simply not worth it.

Elsa was looking back at him and pointing to the floor of the lava tube.

Parts of it were covered with scattered pockets of sand.

Marty experienced a wave of overwhelming relief, but he wasn't going to celebrate until they were out of the water and on dry, solid land.

Rather quickly they began to see coral and urchins growing on the solidified lava, as well as small fish swimming in schools. Then there were no longer walls to either side of them, and the midnight-black water lightened to something slightly less opaque.

They surfaced at the same time. Marty shoved his mask up his forehead and removed his respirator from his mouth. The star-filled night sky had never been so big or beautiful.

Elsa removed her respirator and blurted, "We made it!"

"Let's not celebrate until—" The rest of the sentence died in his throat. Some distance down the beach, the *Oannes* floated a little way out to sea. "It's Pip! She must have come looking for us."

They swam toward shore. When it became shallow enough to stand, they tugged off their flippers and ran side-by-side up onto the beach. Elsa stumbled to her knees, then fell on her chest in the sand, laughing in a way that sounded like she might be crying too.

Marty knelt next to her and offered his hand. "There will be time for that later. Let's get to the ship. Pip and the others will be worried sick about us."

Wiping tears from her eyes, Elsa took his hand and they hurried at a brisk walk toward the hulking research vessel. Yet after only a few meters she squeezed his hand tightly and came to an abrupt halt.

He was about to ask what was wrong when he saw what had startled her. Ahead of them, huddled together on the sand, were the silhouettes of what appeared to be two or three merfolk.

Marty's initial zap of fright was promptly pushed aside by reason and calculation.

They were on land. They no longer posed a serious threat.

This is your chance to kill one, he thought. *Your chance to finally prove to everyone that you were right all along. Hurry! Before they get away.*

"Stay here," he told Elsa quietly, and then hurried toward the merfolk.

One was lying off on its own, unmoving. Another was sitting up, its pale back to him, bent over and...feasting on something? Marty had a bad feeling in his gut even before he made out the "something's" head and frozen, terror-stricken expression.

Oh Lord, Pip, no.

A mournful sound had unwittingly escaped his lips, causing the merfolk to whirl around in alarm, its bloodied mouth dripping with torn flesh, its black eyes unafraid.

Aiming down the assault rifle's iron sight at the center of the creature's swollen forehead, Marty felt only cool rage as he squeezed the trigger and ended the blasphemous thing's life.

EPILOGUE

25 YEARS LATER

RBC Place London, London, England

Jointly hosted by the Society for Marine Mammalogy and the European Cetacean Society, the World Mammal Conference was a biennial event that drew interdisciplinary scientists from every continent. This year it was a jam-packed six days filled with academic presentations, panel discussions, round tables, poster sessions, and workshops. Capping off the final evening was a sold-out closing banquet. The cocktail dinner was followed by a live performance of a band playing soul, funk, R&B, and pop. Presently the waitstaff were bustling about the auditorium, topping up empty champagne flutes in anticipation for the evening's main event: the presentation of the lifetime achievement award to Martin Murdoch, emeritus professor of marine biology at Oxford University.

Dressed in a tuxedo and polished wingtips, Marty sat at the table of honor near the front of the large room. To his right was Radhika, ravishing in a ruby-red, off-shoulder gown. She had aged gracefully over the years, her brown eyes remaining bright with humor. At some point she'd developed a white streak through her glossy black hair à la Elsa Lanchester in *Bride of Frankenstein*. She had been self-conscious of it at first, but he repeatedly told her it lent her a certain sophistication, and now she wore it with undyed pride. Also seated at the table were their three children. Sara, the eldest, had Rad's eyes, sense of humor, and thin physique. She was in her final year at Bangor University in Wales, completing a degree in marine biotechnology. The other two kids had fallen farther from the tree and showed no interest in following in their father's footsteps. Joe, fifteen, had his sights set on becoming an AI psychologist, and Freddie, eleven, had been talking nonstop about becoming a space tour guide after returning from his first family trip to the moon the year before.

Directly to Marty's left was a conspicuously vacant seat that had been reserved for Dr. Elsa Montero. By the time the world had learned of the existence of merfolk, she had quietly gone off the radar. Marty had tried to get in touch with her over the years but had zero luck. The first he'd heard from her was when she'd rung him the week before to offer her congratulations on his lifetime achievement award. He invited her to the event, she demurred, he persisted, and she ended the call by telling him she would think it over.

As it turned out, she had decided not to come, and Marty was more disappointed than he would have anticipated; he had been looking forward to seeing her again.

To Rad he said, "Too much bubbly. Be back soon."

"Don't be long," she replied, pecking him on the cheek. "They'll be starting any minute."

Marty made his way to the restroom, returning the smiles and nods of the people he passed. He relieved himself, rinsed his hands, and exhaled deeply—something he seemed to do more and more the older he became—as he stood in front of a mirror, studying his reflection. At seventy, he looked to himself as he always had, only with more wrinkles and gray in his sideburns.

Twenty-five years, he thought, reminding himself of the time that had passed since the events of Demon Island. Nevertheless, what happened then, and in the weeks and months that followed, still felt like yesterday.

When the Sri Lankan Coast Guard arrived at the island in response to the distress call Marty had made from the *Oannes*, they established a crime scene around the bodies of Pip and the two merfolk, and then whisked Marty and Elsa into custody aboard their two-hundred-plus-foot cutter. Senior officers interrogated them for an hour before they were flown by helicopter to a navy base in Tangalla, a large town on the southern coast of the country. They were held in separate rooms and grilled once again by a slew of high-ranking military officials. This continued throughout the night, causing Marty to object that the circumstances of the detainment felt more like a de facto arrest, and if they were going to charge him with a crime, charge him. When they didn't do so by noon the following day, he refused to cooperate any further without an attorney present. An hour later they released both he and Elsa on the provision that they hand over their passports to the police when they returned to Colombo, and that they would not attempt to leave the country for the foreseeable future.

Marty spent the next two days organizing to have the *Oannes* piloted back to Colombo, while also trying to find out where Rad and Jacky were being held, as neither of them were answering their phones. Frustratingly, all the people he spoke with insisted they didn't know anything about their whereabouts. Then he received a call from a nurse at a Colombo hospital who informed him that Rad had been admitted into the ER with significant orthopedic injuries. When he arrived at the hospital, he wasn't permitted to see her, as she was undergoing emergency surgery. Twelve hours later the head surgeon explained to him where and how she had been discovered on Demon Island, he'd inserted rods into both her tibias, as well as a combination of screws and pins in the bones of her feet and ankles...and he wasn't sure whether she would walk again.

Marty visited her in the ICU the next morning. She was awake but barely responsive due to whatever concoction of drugs she was being fed through the IV drip. Aside from the injuries to her legs, which were bandaged and stabilized in splints, she was missing most of her visible teeth. He had her transferred to a private room on an upper floor, and he spent every day at her side while she recovered.

During that time, Navy divers retrieved Jacky's remains—what were left of them—from the bottom of the flooded cavern. After Rad detailed to military investigators how a merfolk had attacked and drowned Jacky, she and Marty were pressured to sign non-disclosure agreements preventing them from disclosing what happened on Demon Island to any other party, private or public. The same day the chief of police of Galle, the district in the Southern Province which had jurisdiction over Demon Island, stated during a televised press conference that "*Daily Mirror* reporter, Jacqueline DeSilva, and French national, Pip Jobert, were attacked and killed off Peytivu by a rogue shark that had since been captured and killed."

Pip's funeral was held in her hometown in France. Marty wasn't invited, and even had he been, he wouldn't have been able to attend as he was still prohibited from leaving Sri Lanka. Yet he called her parents the day after it to offer his condolences. They seemed grateful for this and told him something about Pip that he never knew: her birth name was Brigitte. "Pip" was a nickname she'd been given in high school, short for Pipsqueak. In typical Pip fashion, rather than let it bother her, she'd embraced it to the point it became her preferred name.

Jacky's funeral was a week later in Colombo. While it was covered extensively in the Sri Lankan media, it was a small, family-only affair. Marty attempted to contact her parents, but he was told by the help who answered the phone that they had no interest in speaking with him.

When Rad was released from the hospital, and returned to her house in Cinnamon Gardens, Marty arranged for a top dentist to replace her missing teeth with implants. When the swelling in her gums receded, it was as though she had never lost any of her teeth in the first place. He then hired a live-in physical therapist to get her back on her feet. Rad approached the locomotor training aggressively, spending hours each day performing task-specific, high-repetition movements. With the help of a weight-supporting treadmill, parallel bars, and crutches, she eventually regained enough balance, strength, and muscle memory in her legs to walk unassisted.

Marty visited her each day, stayed the night more and more often, and eventually checked out of the hotel down the road and moved in with her. Their relationship became one of mutual respect and friendship, far surpassing the transactional bond they had enjoyed before Demon Island, and he proposed to her six months after leaving the hospital.

While honeymooning in the north of the country, photographs and videos of the two dead merfolk were leaked to the public (as Marty always knew at some point they would be). A day later further leaks revealed that Jacky and Pip had not been killed by a rogue shark but rather man-eating merfolk, and that the infamous Dr. Martin Murdoch was at the center of this latest merfolk controversy. International news outlets jumped on the wild story, and Marty once again became an overnight sensation and punching-bag, inspiring wall-to-wall media coverage, viral memes, and fierce debates on message boards between skeptics and conspiracy heads.

When he and Rad returned early from their honeymoon, dozens of journalists and reporters were camped out on her front lawn and in the park across the street. Marty drove past them, lost the mob who scrambled to follow, and spent the next several days with Rad cooped up anonymously in a hotel room.

Public interest in the story grew exponentially, making the hullaballoo surrounding the Netflix hoax seem like a footnote in comparison. Marty made the decision to jump into the fray, screw the NDA, and screw the backlash and ridicule he knew he would attract without any hard proof to support his claims. This time the truth was on his side, and he was ready for the fight.

He organized a tell-all interview with the BBC, sat down with their biggest anchor in what would become the network's most-watched broadcast ever, and recounted everything that had happened, from the night Jacky showed up at the *Oannes* to tell him about the merfolk skull that had been discovered in the belly of the great white, to killing the merfolk that had been in the process of devouring his dear friend on the beach of Demon Island.

And the most amazing thing happened: public opinion swayed in his favor. People *believed* him. The swelling of support from around the globe, as well as anger that the Sri Lankan government was participating in a Roswellian-like cover-up, forced the country's Ministry of Defense to release a statement that they had in their possession the bodies of two mammals from an indeterminate species. Furthermore, they would donate one body to Oxford University, which had agreed to assemble a team of world-class scientists to study the specimen.

Three weeks later the scientists published their findings, stating unanimously and unequivocally that the specimen was both authentic and a mammal previously unknown to the fossil record. They exhaustively defined its anatomical and genetic features—especially those it shared with primates—and designated it the holotype for a new species they named Siren Sirena.

The world went nuts.

Mermaids and mermen existed.

A race by individuals and corporations to capture a live one commenced.

Sadly, to this day, not a single merfolk had been discovered, dead or alive.

Little was ever learned about the fate of the merfolk body under lock and key in Sri Lanka, but the holotype at Oxford University was transferred to the National History Museum in London, where it was put on display under the appropriate conditions to ensure it would be preserved for posterity.

As for Marty, there were those, of course, who remained outraged that he'd killed what they believed had been "defenseless" and "innocent" merfolk. Yet most people sympathized with his plight—the creatures had been trying to eat him, after all, and the one he'd killed point-blank had been halfway through eating his assistant—and they held no antipathy to his actions. Instead, he was largely celebrated, and his aquatic-ape theory became mainstream science. He was quickly flooded with offers for book deals and television appearances, and he was even approached by executives at Netflix to star in a new merfolk documentary. He turned all of the overtures down, opting to lead a quiet life in the English countryside with Rad, who had just become pregnant with Sara. After a restless year, however, he decided he was not a homebody. With Rad fully recovered from her fall (with the exception of an almost imperceptible limp), he returned to teaching at the University of Cambridge. His lectures remained the most popular on campus year after year until he retired five years ago. Now he spent his days painting, gardening, and raising his two boys—and he was more content than he had ever been at any other point in his life.

All right, old man, he thought. *Enough reminiscing. Better get back out there before Rad comes looking for you and gives you an earful.*

When he returned to the table, a tall woman in a black dress was seated in the previously empty chair. She was speaking to Rad, her shoulder-length blonde hair masking her profile.

Marty's pulse quickened, and he said, "Elsa…?"

The woman looked at him and smiled. "Marty!" She stood and they embraced warmly.

Stepping apart, he said, "My God! It's wonderful to see you. I didn't think you would come."

"Do you blame me? Look what happened the last time I accepted an invitation from you."

Marty chuckled. "Your decision to accept then was just as last minute, if I remember correctly." He studied her strong, attractive features, realizing that he had all but forgotten what she looked like until this moment. "You look fantastic. Like you haven't aged a day."

"Please, Marty. I'm nearly seventy. But thank you for the kind words."

They both sat, and Rad said, "Elsa and I were just talking about where she's been all these years. You'll never guess, Marty."

"Mirissa?" he said.

"I returned to Hartford shortly after the Sri Lankan police relinquished my passport."

He was surprised. "You've been there all this time?"

"And you'll never believe what she's been doing, Marty," said Rad.

"Cataloguing whale shit?"

They all laughed.

"She's been cave diving," said Rad.

"You're kidding me!" he said. "After everything that happened...?"

Elsa shrugged. "It's what I was meant to do, I suppose. And I'm remarried now. My husband, Bart, is also a diver. It's what makes us happy."

"Congratulations on finding love again. And you should have brought the lucky gentleman because...this award I'm receiving tonight, it really should be for the both of us. You were right there with me the entire time—"

"Nonsense, Marty. I was a tag-along on that trip. That's all I ever was. No—let me finish. I was a tag-along, and I simply happened to be with you when you made a discovery that your whole life had been building toward. And since then—well, I've kept tabs on you. You've single-handedly legitimized the scientific discipline of sirentology. So please don't utter anything so foolish again, or I might just get up and leave."

"A toast," Rad said, raising her champagne flute.

Elsa and Marty raised their glasses also.

"To?" Elsa said.

"To old friends," Marty said, and they all clinked to that.

Rad added, "And perhaps another cave dive, for old time's sake?"

Marty shook his head. "No bloody way."

The lights in the auditorium dimmed. They turned their attention to the stage. A young British comedian, who had likely been in diapers when Marty and Elsa had been trapped beneath Demon Island, strut out onto the stage. He had spiky red hair and skintight white clothing that clung to his beanpole figure.

Microphone in hand, he said, "Welcome, ladies and gents, to the 118th Academy Awards— Wait, no, what? Where am I? Don't tell me I'm having that dream again of MCing the World Mammal Conference. Blimey O'Reilly, I am! Just look at this crowd. There've never been so many nerds sitting together since Bill Gates' funeral. Where's Dr. Murdoch? Oi, there you are. Welcome to the preview of your own funeral, mate." Slightly uncomfortable laughter from the audience. "No, no, let's not get dark. We're here to celebrate your life and achievements. So let me start off with an oldy but a goody. Why did the merfolk cross the road?" A pause. "Because The Merdoc was stalking it with an assault rifle." More laughter, this time relaxed and genial. "I ain't kidding. Scientists are supposed to be nerdy, like all of you folks, and here you have a bloke that makes Rambo seem like a boy scout. No joke. Rambo took on a bunch of hick cops in the woods. Dr. Murdoch took on an underwater hive of bloodthirsty mermaids. Stabs one in the neck, shreds another with enough lead to make a...I don't fuckin' know. Shoots a third between the eyes. I'm surprised he didn't choke one with his bare hands."

Rad leaned close to Marty and whispered, "Oh, I wish."

He grinned and said, "I do have practice..."

"All right, enough with the jokes," the comedian said. "I've got somewhere else I've gotta be, and it's probably past most of your bedtimes. So without further ado, put your hands together for one of the most influential scientists of our time—The Merdoc, The Merminator, the one and only, Dr. Martin Murdoch!"

Marty stood to raucous applause and uplifting music playing over the loudspeakers. He kissed Rad on the lips, kissed Elsa on the cheek, high-fived his children, then ascended the steps to the stage to address his peers.